P9-EEM-949

A Wealth

of

Deception

A Wealth

of

Deception

A SCANDAL MOUNTAIN ANTIQUES MYSTERY

Trish Esden

CROOKED
LANE

NEW YORK

Published in the United States by Crooked Lane Books, an imprint of The Quick Brown Fox & Company LLC.

Crooked Lane Books and its logo are trademarks of The Quick Brown Fox & Company LLC.

Library of Congress Catalog-in-Publication data available upon request.

ISBN (hardcover): 978-1-63910-254-9
ISBN (ebook): 978-1-63910-255-6

Cover design by Alan Ayers

Printed in the United States.

www.crookedlanebooks.com

Crooked Lane Books
34 West 27th St., 10th Floor
New York, NY 10001

First Edition: April 2023

10 9 8 7 6 5 4 3 2 1

To collectors of antiques and art,
books and stones, ugly sweaters,
international stamps . . . whatever it is
that gives you joy, keep up the hunt.
Life's too short not to pursue your
passions.

"When I was seventeen, my grandparents died in a plane crash. A single-engine plane. Within sight of our house. The therapist suggested I create a memory box dedicated to them. I didn't tell her I'd already declared the field where they went down a living memorial, at least in my mind. Instead of opening my heart, I bristled and did as she asked, gluing photographs, newspaper articles, and other odds and ends into the craft store box she provided. Then I closed the box's lid and scrawled orange and red flames on the outside, crayons snapping under the ferocity of my grip.

Satisfied, the therapist smiled.

That afternoon, I buried the box in the field. It felt like a hollow tribute compared to my living memorial. Still, the act of creating had left its mark. A few years later, when I was working on my degrees and interning at auction houses, I found my chest tightening when I saw or handled certain pieces, outsider art most often. Art created from pure intentions, emotion without the hindrance that can come with formal training. Sure, the neurons at the back of my brain

1

always went crazy when I crossed paths with any genuine, quality piece of art or antique. But outsider art hit me the hardest.

Love and loss. Pain and secrets. Emotions made manifest."

—Edie Brown

Chapter One

"Whoa, check this out!"

It was late afternoon on June twenty-fifth. Kala and I were sitting in the shade of the front porch, sipping citrus vodka on the rocks while we sorted through a mountain of vintage jewelry, pricing what was sellable and setting the rest aside.

I looked up in time to see her pluck a glittering monkey-shaped brooch out of the pile. I studied the creature, hands raised to cover its eyes. "Is that one of the three wise monkeys?"

"See No Evil. Isn't he wonderful?" She pinned the brooch onto the bandana that held back her curly afro. "Take him off my paycheck. He's mine—and I claim the other two monkeys if they surface."

I laughed. "You can have them all. Call it a bonus for cruel and unusual punishment." I slid plastic pearls off a broken necklace string, letting them dribble between my fingers and patter into a shoebox already half full of odds and ends. "I swear if I look at another piece of junk, I'm going to scream."

"You're nuts, Edie. This is the best job ever." Kala nudged the vodka bottle my way.

I took it but only poured a finger of liquid into my glass. "I just wish there were a few nicer pieces mixed in, like some Victorian mourning jewelry."

She gave me a sidelong glance. "The stuff made of human hair?"

"Exactly. Those are real antiques—folk art."

"You mean they're worth more money," she said.

"Well, that too."

As Kala resituated the brooch, I thought back to the first time I'd seen her. About a month ago, I'd come home to help with the family antique business after my mom went to prison for art forgery. I was supposed to meet up with my uncle Tuck at an *Antiques Roadshow* sort of event and do some appraisals with him. But when I arrived, I found our table staffed by an unfamiliar black woman in her early twenties—aka: Kala. She was a good six years younger than me, and a fair amount shorter. She'd had on overalls and a sleeveless purple T-shirt and was valuing vintage trolls.

The whole situation had taken me aback. I mean, I'm all for comfy clothing, but an appraisal event calls for a certain level of professionalism. And trolls? Our family business—Scandal Mountain Fine Arts and Antiques—had a reputation for dealing in upper-end pieces, not collectables, though that had somewhat fallen by the wayside thanks to my mom's lack of business acumen. Frankly, the largest surprise was that Mom had taken on an employee when she was headed to prison and the business was all but bankrupt. But I'd been wrong to criticize her decision. Kala was fabulous. She worked for room and board, and commission on the stuff she sold. She also came with an intriguing, though rather dubious, set of skills, including lockpicking and a familiarity with the darknet—not to mention that a bartender at the Jumping Café recently declared her ID a fake.

The buzz of my phone pulled me from my thoughts. I glanced at the caller ID.

Fisher's Auction House

"That's weird," I said to Kala. "It's Fisher's. I wasn't expecting to hear from them for another couple of weeks, after the Fourth of July at the earliest." A knot of apprehension tightened in my stomach. Fisher's was a local auction house with a reputation for bringing in top-notch buyers and record-breaking prices. I'd arranged for them to sell a valuable collection of Québécois decoys for a client. As acting intermediary agent, we'd earn a significant commission, money we desperately needed to cover overdue bills and upcoming property taxes, and to buy fresh inventory.

"Hello." I tried to sound casual rather than concerned.

"Hey, Edie." It was Albert Fisher's voice, owner of the auction house. "I've run into an issue we need to discuss."

"What is it?" I took a quick sip of vodka to moisten my mouth.

"I know we'd set the auction date for the end of September, but I was just made aware of a conflict. Winston & Windsor are having their annual decoy sale that weekend. I'm sorry. I should have checked more thoroughly before we chose the date."

"Damn it," I muttered. I'd interned at several auction houses, including the renowned Christie's in New York City. The timing of an auction was vital. The prices realized could plummet if similar specialty auctions happened too close together. And Winston & Windsor were known for their decoys sales.

"What are you proposing?" I asked, almost afraid to hear. As it was, September wasn't going to come any too soon as far as our dwindling bank accounts were concerned.

"I have an open weekend mid-November. It's primetime for a sale like this, right before the holidays. Honestly, September was cutting it close as far as cataloguing and building a buzz. This will be better for all of us."

A headache pulsed at the back of my skull. I squeezed my eyes shut. "Sounds perfect. I'll tell my client." At least I was certain he wouldn't have a problem with the change. My client, Jean-Claude Bouchard, had also been concerned that September was too soon.

I tucked my phone into my pocket, then glanced at Kala. "Bad news?" she asked.

"The decoy auction's not happening until November."

"That stinks."

"You can say that again."

The crunch of tires against gravel came from the driveway behind me. I looked over my shoulder as an unfamiliar hatchback sped into view. It winged past the gardens and house, then parked in front of the carriage barn that housed our shop and my mom's art studio. My uncle Tuck was watching the store. He'd moved back to our family home three years ago to help out after I left home. I got to my feet. "I'll be right back. I need to tell Tuck about the auction delay—and I'm curious to see who's here."

"Anything to get out of sorting jewelry, huh?" Kala teased.

I grinned. "It'll give you time to search for the other monkeys." I was grateful that Kala had gone back to teasing me about the jewelry rather than dwelling on the bad news. I had no doubt that it bothered her as well, but it helped to have someone remain upbeat.

* * *

As she dug back into the jewelry, I tied my free-flying hair into a respectable ponytail and hurried down the porch steps. I wound my way through the gardens, overflowing with daylilies and hollyhocks, bright orange and deep pinks melding in with dark green ferns still damp from last night's rain.

When I got closer to the carriage barn, I saw the hatchback had a Vermont license plate. In-state plates could mean almost anything—someone looking for advice or selling or, better yet, buying.

I opened the shop door. Immediately, a foul rotten-egg and ammonia odor invaded my nose, instead of the normal old wood and leather-bound book aroma. What was it? Not car exhaust or skunk.

My gaze went to where Tuck stood beside a harvest table with a dust cloth in his hand. Despite the rag, he looked as debonair as always, gray beard neatly trimmed, cheerful yellow polo shirt over broad, bear-like shoulders. Had the stench come from the polish he was using?

Whatever, the older woman in a turquoise shirtdress talking to him didn't seem aware of it. Her arms waved like a whirligig in a high wind. "I'm so fed up with Graham. He's such an idiot."

I knew who she was in an instant: Janet from Golden Stag Antiques & Gallery. Our local Miss Marple look-alike and one of Tuck's Garden Club lady friends.

Her powder-pink lips puckered into a smile as she swiveled to greet me. "Edie, how wonderful. I was about to tell Tuck about a friend of mine. She's in a horrible pickle, and Graham absolutely refuses to help her."

"What's wrong?" I walked over.

"It's Anna Gorin. I'm not sure if you know her. She moved to Scandal Mountain from Shelburne six, maybe seven years ago, and lives in Maple Farm Estates. One of those newer salt-box-style homes. It's such a pretty neighborhood. Her mother lived with her. She was a sweet old woman . . ."

As she began to ramble, I headed her off. She'd referred to the woman's mother in the past tense, and the fact that Graham was in the antique business and did appraisals like us clued me in. "I'm guessing Anna's mom passed away?"

Janet bobbed her head. She had worked for Felix Graham at the Golden Stag for quite a few years, and when Graham disrespected her or others, she tended to retaliate by sharing personal gossip or business tidbits Graham no doubt expected to remain secret. Dissing people wasn't uncommon for Graham—the slippery, self-satisfied, ladder-climbing snob. He wasn't one of my favorite people, and not just because I suspected he'd played a role in my mom's art forgery charge.

Janet sucked in a breath, then began again, "Her mom passed last winter. All she wanted was for Graham to stop by and tell her if any of her mother's belongings were too valuable to go in a yard sale." She rolled her eyes. "If Anna were cute and thirty-something, or married to someone in the Chamber of Commerce, Graham would've jumped at the chance. But she's close to fifty, widowed years ago."

"Don't worry," Tuck said. "We'd be happy to help."

I nodded in agreement, though I would have preferred to check the woman out myself before going along. Even more than an influx of cash, we desperately needed to restore our family's and business's reputations. It was vital to avoid people who might be easily offended and bad-mouth us. Not that this woman sounded like that sort, but sometimes treasured family belongings were worthless, and some people got angry and refused to believe the truth.

"Thank you, so much," Janet said. "Anna's going to be so relieved." She touched a finger to her lip. "She did mention something about her mom having lots of costume jewelry."

My eyes might have bugged out a little as I swallowed the urge to groan. Of all things. More junk jewelry to sort through.

"She also mentioned a Russian samovar," Janet said. "Or maybe it was a samovar lamp. I had to answer the shop phone, so I didn't hear the entire conversation."

I glanced at Tuck. He shrugged. Samovars—and especially when made into lamps—weren't all that valuable. However, a samovar did suggest her mother's taste leaned toward the quirky, which upped the chance of us finding more unusual pieces. With luck, this Anna Gorin might even be willing to let us buy a few goodies while we were there. After all, we would be giving her free advice.

I licked my lips. It certainly would be sweet to buy something unique and valuable from a woman Graham had brushed off.

* * *

After a bit more chitchat, Janet left. As she drove away, I glanced to where Tuck had set the dusting rag. "What are you using for polish? It stinks."

He pressed his lips into a grimace. "It's not the polish—and it's not good news. Remember the septic tank issue we had last fall?"

Puzzled, I thought for a moment. I hadn't been living at home then, but Mom had called me and gone on at length about some guy she'd met on the internet. She paid him in cash to pump the sludge out of the septic tank, something my grandparents previously had done almost every year. The guy took Mom's cash, promised to do it the next day, then vanished.

I eyed Tuck, wrinkled my nose. "The smell's from the septic tank?"

"You got it. The rain last night made it overflow."

Tuck led the way past the front counter and the stairs that went up to a balcony-like space and our book loft area. As we neared the closed door to my mom's art studio, the sulfur stench grew stronger.

"I don't know how long it's been doing this." He opened the door. "Until this morning, I hadn't been out here for weeks."

I stepped inside the studio. It was a large, open space with various wooden easels, paintings, and cupboards for Mom's art supplies. Sunlight filtered down through skylights. Atrium doors offered a view of her so-called secret garden. The place was surrounded by a lilac hedge and filled with ferns and flowering perennials.

Tuck pointed through the doors' glistening glass. Smack-dab in the middle of the gardens was an oily black puddle the size of a kiddie pool. "I'd open a door so you could get a closer look, but that's how I let the stink in this morning. It's nasty out there."

"More like disgusting," I said. "We have to get it pumped before the septic system totally fails."

"Edie, it's already failed. That's why the rain made it overflow. We have to get it replaced."

I gaped at him. "We can't afford that. You're talking major dollars."

"I can phone Martin's Septic, explain we're short on cash but will have the money after the decoy auction. I bet they'd be willing to do the job and wait until the end of September for payment. They're related to the Fishers. They can talk to Albert if they want."

The back of my throat clenched, strangling my voice. "I just got off the phone with Albert. The auction's not happening until November."

"You're kidding."

"I wish I were." I looked down at the floor, shook my head. "November's hunting season. The Martins will be away at camp. Then there's Thanksgiving. After that, it'll be freezing cold, and no one's going to do it earlier and wait five months for payment."

Tuck's tone gentled. "We could wholesale out some of your grandfather's books. They'd sell fast."

"We're not doing that," I snapped. "We can have it pumped for now. That's something we can afford."

"Putting it off isn't going to make the problem go away."

"But it'll buy us time. What we need is fresh merchandise for the store, trendy antiques or art, stuff that'll sell fast for a good profit. We can reinvest the money in more easy-sell items, build up enough cash that way."

"Your grandfather wouldn't mind if we sold the books. He intended them as an investment."

I ignored that. My grandpa was Tuck's and my mom's father. His book collection contained irreplaceable signed first editions and early volumes. After he and my grandma died, Mom had threatened to sell them along with the rest of our family's personal collections whenever she got conned by some guy or overspent on something foolish. But I wasn't her. I could take care of our property and bring the business back to its former glory without selling family treasures. I just had to work harder and play it smart.

I met Tuck's eyes. "While they're here pumping the septic tank, we can ask them for an estimate on a new system."

He raised his hands in surrender. "Alright, we'll do it your way. I'll phone Martin's right away and ask them to come out ASAP."

"Thank you. I have to call Jean-Claude Bouchard and tell him the auction's been rescheduled."

I turned away from Tuck, staring once more out at the puddle of sludge. Damn it. Just when things were starting to look up. A delayed auction. A failed septic system. When it rains, it pours—an unnervingly appropriate idiom in this case.

Chapter Two

The next day, Martin's arrived first thing in the morning to pump the septic tank. They confirmed Tuck's belief that the system had failed—the tank, the leach field—the whole enchilada was shot. The cost of replacing it made me sick to my stomach, not to mention that doing it was bound to destroy Mom's secret garden, including the lilac hedge. Worst of all, Martin's wouldn't accept delayed payment. No question about it, we had to come up with a pile of extra cash, and soon.

Feeling down in the dumps, Tuck and I left Kala in charge of the shop and headed out to see Anna Gorin. Three years ago, when I'd last lived at home, Maple Farm Estates had consisted of a dozen or so mid-century ranch houses. Now the development sprawled from the edge of Scandal Mountain village, all the way down past The Drunken Turkey Inn, to the river and McGrath's sugar woods.

Anna Gorin's saltbox was the third house on the right, partially hidden from the road by clumps of birch trees, each one circled by red bark mulch. Window boxes filled with geraniums hung under each window, blooms perfect despite the heat and humidity.

As I turned into her driveway, I glanced toward where Tuck sat in the passenger seat. "I bet there isn't a speck out of place inside the house."

"What makes you so sure?" A mischievous twinkle brightened his eyes, and it lightened my mood. "Her mom could've been addicted to buying storage lockers. The place might be packed to the beams with mysterious cardboard boxes and—"

Smiling, I finished the sentence for him. "Garbage bags full of Beanie Babies?"

"For sure." He laughed. I couldn't count the number of times I'd run into people who thought their run-of-the-mill Beanie Baby collections were worth a bundle, when in truth they were unsellable. Still, my grumpiness was driven off by the possibility of the sellable treasures we might find inside.

I tapped the car's brakes, slowing and parking in front of the garage. I was driving our family's Volvo, a classic wagon and previously my grandfather's pride and joy, mine to use since I'd totaled my van.

Tuck and I got out of the car. As we went up the walkway, Anna emerged from the front door. She was petite, with high cheekbones and dyed black hair. A bright scarf draped around her neck. Stylish amber earrings hung from her ears. A diamond adorned her ring finger, despite her husband having passed away.

"Come in, come in," she greeted us as we reached the stoop. "I'm so glad you were willing to stop by."

"Happy to help," I said. I smiled. "I'm Edie Brown, and this is my uncle, Angus Tuckerman. We decided it was better if we both came, since we have different areas of expertise."

"Thank you so much. I truly appreciate it." She gestured for us to go inside first. I filed past her, with Tuck on my heels, over the threshold, into the dimly lit front hall. The air was cool and scented with a hint of pine cleanser.

Tuck nodded at an assortment of silk slippers on a plastic mat. "Would you like us to take our shoes off?"

"If you don't mind."

As Tuck struggled with his loafers, I toed off my heels and placed them on the mat next to a pair of men's slip-on dress shoes, black and as glossy and spotless as the floor.

Anna cleared her throat. "There's no one else here. Those belong to my brother. He comes over quite often for dinner, prefers them over slippers."

"Oh, okay," I said, unsure why she felt the need to explain.

Tuck and I wedged our feet into slippers, then padded across the hallway and into the living room, a sunny space with floral drapes and newer furnishings. Family photos spanned a white mantel. Wall-to-wall carpeting covered the floor. A pink ceramic lamp sat on a modern marble-topped table. Nothing of interest to us.

Anna walked toward a pair of curtained French doors that hid what lay beyond them. "My mother couldn't do stairs, so I set up a suite for her back here. I'm hoping to clear it out in the next few weeks. A friend of mine is moving in."

As she opened the French doors, an aroma reminiscent of wild violets and dried roses reached my nose. Perhaps even a hint of orange peel and cigar smoke. An elegant, old-world fragrance. I breathed in the scent, and my instinct for quality antiques and art jumped to life, the neurons in the back of my brain snapping and prickling like crazy.

One time, when I'd been maybe ten years old, my grandparents brought me along to Manhattan to buy some items from a grand duchess's estate. Her apartment had smelled exactly like this. In retrospect, I wasn't certain the so-called duchess had really been royalty—more likely, my grandmother had said that to put me on my best behavior. But whether the duchess was real or not, my grandparents purchased several early oil paintings and some smaller items that day, including a silver and enamel box that contained dried rose petals and orange peel, a scent evocative of times gone by.

I smiled at the memories, and my heart squeezed at the thought of my grandmother's timeless nuggets of advice. *"Make sure your hair is brushed,"* she would've said today. *"Stand up straight. First impressions are the foundation of a good reputation."*

I stepped off the wall-to-wall carpeting and onto the silky plushness of a Persian rug, a noteworthy jewel-toned piece. The room itself was medium size and crowded with glass-fronted cabinets overflowing with family photos and tchotchkes: porcelain ballerinas, tea sets, blue elephants, Russian nesting dolls . . . high-quality collectables, perhaps vintage, but unlikely to be antique or particularly valuable, judging by a glance. They certainly weren't the trendy, quick-sell items we needed to buy.

A white recliner and loveseat were arranged into a sitting area. The infamous samovar lamp sat on a demilune table. Off to one side, an old treadle sewing machine and worktable occupied an alcove. A modern TV sat beside a window. Beyond the window, blue jays flew to and from a nearly empty feeder.

Tuck headed straight for a slender bookcase filled with mostly leatherbound volumes. "Do you mind if I start by going through these?" His specialty was appraising books and prints, especially anything relating to his hobby business, namely, outdoor gardening as well as hybridizing African violets and other gesneriads.

I studied the bookcase. It was antique, with beautiful stained-glass panels at the top of each door. I scrutinized it again and discovered I'd been mistaken. The stained-glass panels weren't high quality. They were poorly executed replacements, killing the piece's salability and value.

A sinking feeling gathered in the pit of my stomach. Perhaps the suite's old-world fragrance and my memories had steered my instinct wrong. The carpet was undeniably nice, but so far there appeared to be little else worth buying.

"Look at anything you wish," Anna said. "The only things I can't sell are the carpet and the samovar lamp. My uncle offered to buy those. He's picking them up later this week."

I forced a smile. "Family should always come first," I said. In truth, I felt let down about the carpet. I'd have dearly loved to make an offer on it. Still, she'd officially raised the subject of us buying, and that was good. "So, you're open to offers, then?"

"By all means. The less I have to run through a sale, the better." She glanced toward where Tuck was opening the bookcase, then pressed a finger to her lips. "I almost forgot. The books aren't spoken for, but my uncle wants that bookcase too."

I nodded. "I don't blame him. It's a nice piece." It didn't hurt to lie, especially when I had zero interest in the bookcase. However, I couldn't help wondering about Anna's uncle. I'd been involved with enough estates to know that vultures often came out when people died, snapping up what they could for next to nothing or free. I couldn't say for sure, but it sounded like he perhaps fell in that category—a category of people also likely to bad-mouth antique dealers rather than let them purchase anything.

Putting my fear of circling vultures aside, I followed Anna into her mom's bedroom while Tuck stayed behind with the books. The bedroom was dark. Heavy drapes were tightly drawn, blocking out any trace of illumination. Anna switched on the overhead light, revealing costume jewelry and collectable doo-dads glimmering on every available flat surface, including the double bed.

"I thought I'd lay everything out for you," she said. "To save time."

"Thank you, that does help." A sour taste flavored the back of my throat. Fake pearls. Newer rhinestones . . . *Arrrggghh*.

Fortunately, thanks to Anna's skillful organizing, it didn't take me long to sort through all the low-end stuff, recommending prices she should sell things for and adding tips on how to run a successful yard sale. I suspected she'd culled the best jewelry pieces for herself. There wasn't a trace of anything expensive or currently popular to be found.

I did, however, uncover a nice antique perfume atomizer in a box of scarves—crystal and sterling, with a Russian hallmark. I also found several vintage shawls and babushka-type headscarves mixed in with a stack of polyester nightgowns. I set them aside to offer on as a lot.

On the wall by the bathroom door, I spotted a diminutive Madonna and Child oil painting. Gold trim. Deep colors. Jesus resembled a tiny man rather than a child, a common trait in medieval depictions, such as Russian icons. But my instinct insisted this icon was on the modern side, a fact confirmed on a closer look by the style of earrings and necklace she wore, not to mention the gloss of peach polish on her neatly manicured fingernails. Still, the painting was attractive and sellable.

As I took it down from the wall, I looked at Anna, even more curious than before about her mother's heritage. "Was your mother from Russia?"

"She moved here as a child with her parents. A few of the things in here are family pieces—most my father brought back from his travels. He was in the import business." She angled her head, studying the painting. "I'm not sure where that came from."

I set the painting down with my other items. "Would you sell it?"

"I suppose. I'm terribly grateful for your help."

I made a good strong offer on the painting and the other items I'd set aside, enough that the vultures wouldn't have reason to bad-mouth us, while still leaving room for profit.

Anna smiled and accepted, then we headed back into the main room. As her attention went to Tuck and some ornithology books he'd set aside to purchase, my instinct once more nagged at me. Maybe the suite's fragrance had steered me off course, but I couldn't bring myself to explain the feeling away this time. I was overlooking something good. I was certain of it.

I tapped a finger against my leg. If I were Anna's mother, where would I put my most precious keepsake? Something better than vintage tchotchkes and smaller than a Persian carpet. Perhaps where I could enjoy it while I relaxed in my favorite chair?

Biting down on a smile, I made for the white recliner, well-worn and with a lavender and pink afghan draped over its back. The TV remote lay on a stand beside the recliner. I opened the drawers in the stand. All empty.

19

The prickle of instinct at the back of my skull grew stronger. I lowered myself onto the chair. Straight ahead was the TV. To the right of it was the window with the view of the bird-feeder, to the left the alcove with the treadle sewing machine—

My breath caught in my throat. I blinked. I couldn't be seeing right. How could I have missed something so large?

An enormous painting covered the entire wall above the sewing machine, easily three times as large as the nearby TV screen. It was very textured and lacked a frame. Perhaps my eye had registered it before as rough plaster or textured wallpaper. The alcove was darker than the rest of the room.

I got to my feet, legs shaking as I let the painting's power reel me toward it. A contemporary landscape. Not gilded or Russian in style, like the Madonna and Child painting. In truth, its style and forbidding tones were very much at odds with everything else in the place.

As I stepped closer, the details clarified. Not a landscape. It was a townscape, as bleak as a noir film, splattered with primary colors.

It depicted a main street in a small city or large town, like many we had in Vermont. Shoppers emerged from a store. Lovers kissed inside a car. A woman slumped against a storefront, shooting up. In an alleyway, a man stood near a puddle of blood, back turned to the viewer as he relieved himself. A woman screamed in horror from a second-story window . . . Dozens of lives, beautiful, brutal, chaotic, and messy, frozen in time.

I tilted my head, examining the piece, still from a distance. There was something familiar about the work. Very familiar.

For a heartbeat, my thoughts rushed back to gluing mementoes into a craft store memory box while my therapist watched from her desk. Newspaper articles. Obituaries. Burnt grass. A stone with the date of my grandparents' plane crash written on it.

"Dear God." The words tumbled from my mouth. The piece wasn't a painting.

I rushed forward and switched on the nearby samovar lamp. Light washed upward, illuminating the piece, verifying what my eyes could barely believe. The townscape was a collage, created out of layers and layers of paint, gesso, paper, and scraps—e-waste like computer chips and keyboard pieces, pieces of photos, strips of newsprint and fast-food wrappers, cufflinks, silver chains, doll eyes, slashes of paint, lines of ink—all coming together to create an intricate scene when viewed from a distance.

Unbelievable. The work of a genius.

And I knew who the artist was.

When I'd interned at Christie's auction house in New York City, I'd seen this artist's work. More than that, I'd also spent time with it when I occasionally helped as a greeter or did odd jobs at Zaninelli Funeral Home in Greenwich Village. The owner, Jimmy, was a collector of outsider art. Three collages by this very artist hung in his office, the pride and joys of his collection.

Vespa was the artist's name. She was an elderly recluse who hadn't tried her hand at art until the age of sixty-four. By seventy she was touted in the art and gallery world as the Grandma Moses of the Twenty-First Century. At first glance her pieces appeared to be quaint scenes of rural life, like Moses's work, almost idyllic. On second look they revealed unflinching glimpses into brutal reality, drug abuse, gambling, gruesome deaths: nightmarish vignettes rumored to be inspired by Vespa's own tumultuous life. Her work was astonishing, mysterious, and worth—well, individual pieces had sold for twice the value of Anna's saltbox home, fancy window boxes and all.

I turned toward her and Tuck, pointed at the piece. "Wh—where did your mother acquire that?"

Anna's gaze went to her feet, as if embarrassed or ashamed, or maybe uncomfortable. "I should have put that away before you came. It's . . ."

As her voice trailed off, I tried to make sense of her reaction. Contemporary—and even more often—outsider art wasn't everyone's taste, and Vespa's pieces were far from mainstream. Did Anna dislike the style or the unsettling details of the piece, or was there a different reason for her discomfort?

She looked up, clutching at her scarf with one hand, like a toddler kneading a security blanket. "My brother made it." Her voice faltered. "I realize it—it's unusual. He was in an accident." Her speech loosened, words flowing like blood from a fresh wound. "He was hit by a car twelve years ago. He was living in New York City at the time but had come home to Shelburne to visit me. He suffered a traumatic brain injury."

"Sweet Jesus," Tuck said. "I'm so sorry."

She nodded. "It was a hit-and-run. Left him intellectually limited. He has an apartment in a facility with an art therapy program. He never did crafts before that."

I opened my mouth, but nothing came out. Despite what she was saying, it looked like a Vespa to me. Her brother hadn't made it. I'd bet on it. I was also willing to bet, assuming it was Vespa, that it would sell in the blink of an eye. But I couldn't bring myself to contradict her, not considering her brother's situation. It was overwhelming to even think about having something like that happen to someone you love.

Tuck rested a hand on her arm. "I can't imagine how diffi-cult it's been for you."

Anna's breath hitched. "It was terribly rough on my mother."

I glanced back at the townscape, then turned to Anna. "Would you mind if I took a closer look?"

She wiped moisture from the corners of her eyes. "Go ahead, feel free."

Taking out my jewelers' loupe, I returned to the piece. I bent in closer than before and used the loupe's magnification to study the very center. I could make out scratches on a link of silver chain in the shape of the letter 'V'—the exact way Vespa tradi-tionally marked her work.

Tuck and Anna fell silent. I looked over my shoulder to see what was going on. They were watching me, waiting for me to say something. One thing was for sure: debating who'd made the piece with Anna wouldn't do any good. There were any number of possibilities. Her brother could have purchased the piece and given it to his mom to store. Maybe her mom had bought it from a friend who needed money. It didn't fit in with her mom's overall taste—that was undeniable. Maybe Anna was lying. Maybe her brother was a thief. The list went on and on.

I steadied my voice. "Would you consider selling it?"

Anna fingered her scarf. "I wish I could, but it would break my brother's heart if he discovered I'd sold or even given it away." She looked down again. "He's easily upset."

Tension pinched in my neck and shoulders. The townscape would probably spend most of its life hidden away in a closet, like it was nothing more than a piece of out-of-season decor, a plastic Santa or Thanksgiving platter dragged out and dis-played when her brother came over for dinner. The piece deserved to be treasured and shared, to be loved by people who truly appreciated it.

I gave a small, tight nod. Arguing would only alienate her— and the last thing I wanted to do was hammer a wedge between us. "If you change your mind, please offer it to me first. I'd be happy to buy it or sell it for you on commission. I really do love it."

"Of course," Anna said, though I could see in her eyes she had no intention of parting with it.

I stole another look at the townscape. *No way, I couldn't let this go at that.* "Pretty sure" wasn't good enough. I needed to know for certain if I was right about it being a Vespa piece. If it was, and especially if it was an unknown or lost work, bringing it to the attention of the art world would go a long way toward restoring our reputation and putting our business back on the map, even if we didn't end up directly involved in selling it.

"Would you mind if I took some photos? I'd really enjoy studying it some more."

"Go ahead. According to my mom, it's a city here in Vermont. Brattleboro. Bellows Falls." She shrugged. "My brother's therapist says doing crafts helps him cope with confusion and stress, to put the past behind him and move forward."

"I've heard a similar thing," I said calmly. But my calm was as superficial as it had been all those years ago when I'd spent time in my own therapist's office.

Chapter Three

As soon as we were in the privacy of the Volvo and headed toward home, I told Tuck about my suspicion that the townscape wasn't what Anna claimed.

He raised a hand, palm out, to quiet me. "I hear what you're saying, but we can't afford to jump into this half-cocked. The last thing we need is to offend Anna and have her running around telling people we're insensitive know-nothings."

I took a fresh grip on the steering wheel. There were other possibilities. Before I'd created the memory box with my therapist, she'd shown me pictures of them on Pinterest. I glanced at Tuck. "I suppose the therapist Anna's brother goes to could've shown him examples of Vespa's work. He could've copied her style."

"That would fit with what Anna said."

The memory box I'd made filtered back into my mind. I'd been exposed to artists all my life and learned basic techniques as a child. Still, my box had ended up looking amateurish compared to the ones on Pinterest. I pressed my lips together, shook my head. "The therapist angle's a nice pat answer, but it doesn't make sense. The townscape is remarkable. It's not something an inexperienced person could make—and Anna said her brother never did art before he started therapy. Besides, the signature on the collage is a 'V' as in Vespa. Not a 'G' for Gorin."

"Gorin's probably Anna's married name. Her brother's surname could be Valentine or Van Helsing." He said it lightly, not to pick on me, but because he was Tuck, and Tuck preferred to keep things upbeat.

"Or Vladimir the Vampire," I countered.

Tuck swiveled in his seat, his expression growing more serious as he looked directly at me. "I'll admit I don't know much about Vespa. Do you know when she first appeared on the art scene? She's a newer artist, right?"

I mentally flipped through what I could remember. "A decade ago, maybe. I'd have to check to be sure. Why?"

He rubbed his chin. "If Anna's brother started doing art soon after his accident, that would put the two events in the same general time frame. What if he had a natural talent? What if we have this the wrong way around?"

Catching his drift, I laughed. "Are you suggesting he could *be* Vespa—that a guy creating gritty noir collages decided it was a good idea to market them in the disguise of a little old lady?"

Tuck waved off the idea. "Alright, so that theory's a bit too outlandish." His voice gentled. "I'm not saying you're wrong about the collage being by Vespa, or about who she really is. It's just that on more than a few occasions, I've let my desire for something to be better than it really was cloud my judgment. We purchased some nice items from Anna and made some good will by helping her out. Let's play it safe, forget the townscape, and move on. It's not like she's going to sell it anyway."

I sighed. "You're probably right." Tuck wasn't the only one guilty of wishful thinking. Only last week, I'd fallen in love with a hooked rug at Fisher's Auction. I'd arrived at the sale too late to preview the piece up close. Then, in the heat of the auction, I'd overbid, only to discover, once I had it in my hands, that the rug was a new reproduction. No question about it, desire and adrenaline could lead to wrong assumptions.

As I pulled onto the main road, I tapped the gas, speeding up to join the flow of traffic. But what if the collage was as good as I thought? What if it had been made by Vespa, not Erik? If Anna was willing to let us sell it for her on commission, we wouldn't have to risk a dime, and we could walk away with enough to solve our financial problems.

Tuck chuckled. "You're not giving up, are you?"

"Not quite yet. I'm going to send the photos I took to my friend Jimmy Zaninelli. I'm not an expert on Vespa's work, but he owns several of her pieces. He'll be able to tell us if the collage is worth investigating."

* * *

Once we got home, I sent the photos to Jimmy, with an explanation saying the woman who owned the collage claimed her brother had made it but that I thought Vespa might be the real artist.

He immediately texted back. *Fantastique! Looking forward to studying them.*

I answered. *I'm dying to know what you think.*

Might take me a day or two to get back to you. A City Council member died. His wake's this afternoon. Another tonight. Church service tomorrow. Wish you were here. I'd ask you to help. I'm completely exhausted already.

If I were in the city, I'd be happy to lend a hand. Which I would. Helping out at Zaninelli Funeral Home had paid great and been a cream puff job, though not particularly regular. I added, *There's no hurry. Get back to me when you can.*

For the rest of the day and into Sunday, I managed not to bitch too much about how long it was taking for Jimmy to respond. Instead, I focused on constructive things like selling the perfume atomizer I'd bought off Anna to a customer of ours in Texas—cheap price, fast sell, like I'd planned.

Okay, I might have driven Kala crazy by talking incessantly about the townscape, Vespa, and outsider art in general while we finished sorting the jewelry and moved on to scouring the shop for pieces that would sell quickly online. It would've felt strange not to talk about the collage. I mean, no matter who made it, stumbling over an amazing work of art like that was thrilling.

Early Sunday evening, I left Tuck and Kala to their own devices and headed to Shane's cabin in St. Albans for a barbecue and sleepover. Shane was a close friend with a capital "B" for benefits, as well as my ex-probation officer. We'd met a few years ago after I took bad advice from my mom and unwittingly bought a stolen collection of duck prints and stamps from a stranger, then sold the collection to a woman who turned out to be an undercover police detective. I was charged with selling stolen property but got lucky and ended up getting probation with no jail time. Our mutual attraction was immediate and eventually crossed the professional line. Since I'd returned to Vermont, we'd reconnected. He was now Detective Shane Payton with the state police. He was kind and smart, and most of the time straightforward. We shared a lot of common interests, in and out of bed.

Anyway, when I reached the cabin, Shane came jogging around from the backyard to greet me. He had on faded jeans and a white T-shirt that clung to his sculpted chest and six-pack. His short, curly hair looked even more rebellious than usual, sandy-brown curls sticking up like little devil's horns. It was enough to make a woman forget about barbeque altogether and just move on to dessert.

"Hope you brought your swimsuit," he said.

"I kind of forgot it." I gave him a sexy smile.

He grinned like a kid who'd won a blue ribbon at a fair. "Sounds promising."

I retrieved a bowl of potato salad from the passenger seat, my donation to the meal, then we headed around the outside of his cabin to the poolside deck. Tiki lights glimmered, reflecting in the water. Votive candles and a bottle of wine sat in the middle of a table for two.

"Wow. You went all out." I set the potato salad down on a minibar next to the grill and sniffed the air. "Something smells delicious."

"Steak kabobs. There's a green salad in the fridge, and strawberry shortcake for dessert." He nodded at a bowl of berries sitting on the minibar. "That is, if you don't mind slicing those while I keep an eye on the meat."

"No problem," I said.

As I settled down on a stool at the bar and began cutting up the strawberries, he walked over to the table and picked up the bottle of wine. "Cabernet—Charlotte Village Winery. Want a glass?"

"You sure know the way into a woman's heart." My chest tightened from the truth of it, but I counteracted the swell of emotion with a laugh. "Either that, or you're buttering me up for something."

He smiled, then brought a glass over to me. "The only thing I want right now is to hear more about that house call you went on."

Excited to have a new audience for my babble about the townscape, I stopped slicing and sat up taller. Earlier, when Shane and I had talked on the phone, he'd been in a hurry. I'd promised to tell him about our trip to Anna's when we got together.

"It was a referral from Janet, who works for Felix Graham." I skipped over the part about the rotten-egg stink in the shop when Janet arrived and the bad news about the septic. I was happy to not talk about that for a while. Instead, I got right to the townscape and my feelings about it. "I swear, it looks like a Vespa. Tuck is worried it's a matter of wishful thinking. Still, he's as curious as I am."

"Did you take any photos?" Shane asked.

"Yeah. They don't do the piece justice, but I'd love your thoughts." Eagerness jumped inside me as I took my phone out and brought up the images.

He set down his wine and took the phone. "You said it's a collage?"

"If you keep going, the last few photos are close-ups. You'll be able to see what it's made from—computer junk, doll eyes. It's worth a mint. If it's what I think it is."

"Impressive." His voice deepened. "Have you considered it might be stolen?"

My excitement plummeted. Always the cop. "They're not that kind of people."

"How about the brother who supposedly made it? What kind of person is he?"

"I don't know much about him. But the collage was hanging right where anyone could see it. You'd think if it was stolen, they would have stashed it somewhere before we arrived. I mean, we're art and antique dealers. For all they knew, we might have recognized the piece and turned them in."

"Did the brother know you were going to be at the house?"

Shane had a point there. "I'm not sure. He doesn't live with Anna." For a second, the men's slip-on shoes in Anna's hallway and her quick justification passed through my mind. She'd said he didn't live with her. Could the slip-ons in reality belong to someone else?

Shane shut off the phone and handed it back. "It's up to you. Personally, I'd forget about it. There are lots of other pieces of art out there to invest your money and time in. No need to take a risk."

I gritted my teeth. Why couldn't he just be excited by the possibility that we might have stumbled onto something special? Heat seeped up my neck, a slow burn of anger. I grumbled under my breath. "It's not for sale, anyway."

"That's probably for the best," he said.

As Shane went to the grill and checked on the kabobs, I snatched up the paring knife and began hacking the strawberries into chunks. As irritated as I was with him, the chance of the collage being stolen had passed through my mind when I first saw it. I also understood where Shane was coming from. After I got off probation, my record had been expunged. That gave me a fresh start and allowed me to get internships at museums and top-notch auction houses. However, an expunged record didn't mean that every person on the planet had forgotten about my brush with the law. There were still a lot of local people who remembered the incident, and my mom sitting in prison for forgery only added to their contention that I was a lowlife. You know, like mother like daughter? Given the chance that the collage could've been acquired in a less than honest manner, it might've been wiser to give it wide berth to start with.

* * *

Dinner was wonderful, the wine relaxing. It didn't take long for my frustration with Shane and thoughts of the townscape to retreat into the back of my mind. Later, our moonlit skinny-dip led to a hot time in bed. Then I spooned against Shane and fell into an exhausted, blissful sleep.

But a second later—at least it felt like a second—I bolted awake, the townscape once again front and center in my mind. I checked my phone: three in the morning, hours before either of us had to get up. Still, no message from Jimmy.

I squeezed my eyes shut, trying to stop the whirring thoughts. I counted to a hundred. I stared at Shane's left forearm, thrown up over a pillow. That forearm was tattooed with a cartoon devil. He had an angel on his right one.

I focused on his back. Muscular. Deep caramel-colored tan. A single kiss on the nape of his neck could rouse him, ready for another round of—

My subconscious yanked my thoughts back to the townscape. I needed to study the photos again, see if I'd missed something that could prove whether it was a Vespa or not. If I found something, I could point it out to Shane in the morning. It wouldn't mean the piece wasn't stolen, but it might convince him I was right to think the mystery was worth investigating.

I crept out of bed, pulled on my panties and tank top, snagged my phone from the nightstand, then tiptoed down from the loft to the living room. A man-size recliner sat in front of a window, streaked with moonlight. I curled up in it, legs tucked underneath me, and brought the photos up on my phone. I enlarged them. Lightened them. Darkened them.

I rubbed my eyes. Either the photos were worse than I'd thought, or the piece wasn't as good as I'd been convinced of in the heat of the moment. Stinking wishful thinking.

No, I chastised myself. *I was right. It was special.*

Maybe.

Before I could second-guess myself again, I texted Jimmy. *Have you had a chance to look yet? Sorry to be a pest.. I'm dying of curiosity.*

"Ahem." The sound of Shane clearing his throat broke the stillness of the room.

I looked up. He stood a few yards away, dressed in nothing except his boxer briefs. He frowned. "You okay?"

"Ah—I couldn't sleep."

He stepped closer, voice a low demand. "What's going on?"

"Nothing, really," I said.

My phone chimed. At this hour? Undoubtedly Jimmy getting back to me. It chimed again.

Shane eyed the phone "Answer it. I'm guessing this is about the collage."

I looked down, ashamed by my obsessiveness. "I know. I should've waited until morning. It's my friend Jimmy. Honestly, I didn't expect him to call right back."

"Go on, answer. I'll make coffee." Shane turned away and walked toward the kitchen, long strides that rapidly put distance between us.

I answered. "Hey, Jimmy. I didn't mean to wake you up."

"Darling, I'm the one who should apologize. That funeral— oh, my goodness, it was a madhouse." Even over the phone, Jimmy's dramatic flair was unmissable. He'd grown up in Greenwich Village, and more specifically in the artsy LGBTQ community. Owning a local funeral home that celebrated the lives of so many members of that community—and becoming renowned for his collection of cutting-edge outsider art—had only made him embrace his roots with more vigor.

"So, what do you think?" I asked.

"First of all, don't ever take up photography as a profession. Seriously, darling, the photos are that bad."

"Sorry. I was in a hurry."

"Let me take another look."

As he fell silent, I listened to Shane rummaging around in the kitchen. The fridge opened. Dishes clinked. The smell of brewing coffee filtered into the living room.

I waited another second, then nudged Jimmy, "Is it a Vespa?"

"It's certainly interesting. You said it's signed?"

"Yeah, there's a 'V' on a piece of silver chain."

"How about themes? Vespa's work is like Kahlo's. You're familiar with Frida Kahlo, the Mexican artist?"

"Somewhat," I said, a bit sheepishly. My studies had focused on New England folk art, but I had enjoyed her work in passing.

"Like Kahlo, Vespa's works repeated themes from her life. Brutal crime. Anguish. Blood. Money. Family."

"The townscape certainly had those things, and more."

Jimmy made a little clicking noise with his tongue, as if thinking. He let out a long breath. "I wouldn't give up on this piece being a Vespa quite yet. Look at it in person again, and take note of the smaller details, the intricacies of the objects used to create it. See if you can find out more about this woman's brother."

I glanced toward the kitchen. Yeah, just what Shane would prefer not to have me do. Still, he worked in law enforcement and wasn't someone whose livelihood depended on coming up with unique pieces of art and antiques to sell—or someone who knew exactly how hard it was to do on a daily basis. Not that either of us were wrong. It was just two different ways of looking at the same subject.

Getting up from my chair, I turned my back to the room and looked out the window. Moonlight bathed the grass and trees, shimmered on the pool. I held the phone closer. "It really bothers me that the woman who owns the piece might not know what she has. She doesn't even like it. If the piece is real, it deserves to be treated with respect. She could handle it carelessly, unintentionally damage it."

Jimmy's voice hushed. "Darling, are you sure it's not stolen?"

I groaned. *Not this again.* "There aren't any red flags, other than that it turned up in an unlikely location."

"The cleverest criminals are the ones you'd least suspect," he said.

His ominous tone swept a chill up my arms. "What are you thinking? Are there other stolen Vespa pieces floating around?"

"I've been out of the loop for the last few months—but I haven't heard any rumblings."

Beyond the window a fox trotted past the pool and vanished into the darkness. I'd hoped Jimmy might put my mind to rest. Instead, he was channeling Tuck and Shane and making me more uneasy.

I lowered my voice further. "I really don't think that's the case here."

"Just saying, ask some more questions. And take more photos. If it ends up being a real Vespa, you damn well better give me the first crack at buying it. I'll give you a more than healthy finder's fee."

"You'll be the first to know."

"Good. I'll be waiting to hear more," Jimmy said. "If you get additional pics, send them my way."

"Will do."

As we said goodbye, Jimmy didn't ask and I purposely avoided saying who owned the townscape. It wasn't that I didn't trust him to not undercut me. But other collectors and dealers would be quick to do exactly that if word of a potential Vespa slipped out. Besides, not sharing names or addresses of a piece's current owner was expected decorum.

Leaving my phone on the end table, I went into the kitchen. Shane sat at the marble-topped island. A stick of butter and a sliced loaf of banana bread waited on a plate in front of him. Soft country music drifted in the background.

He put his coffee down and smiled. "Did you get your questions answered?"

"Not totally." I headed for the coffee pot, fixed a mug, then joined him at the island. I certainly wasn't going to bring up that Jimmy had also mentioned the possibility of the piece being stolen.

However, there was another aspect of the townscape mystery that squirmed at the back of my brain, thanks to Jimmy making me think about Frida Kahlo's unsettling artwork and personal struggles. What if Anna was right and her intellectually disabled brother had created the townscape? If that was the case, then Shane might have personal insight that could help.

I picked at the edge of my thumbnail, throat tightening as I struggled for the right way to broach the subject. Why were mental health issues so difficult to talk about, even with people you were close to?

Shane nudged the banana bread toward me. "Have a slice. My mom made it."

His mom. I stared at the bread, moist slices mottled black and cream. Whatever being or spirit was responsible for coincidences, they certainly were working overtime today. It was his mom I'd just been thinking about. A few years ago, she'd had an accident at work that resulted in a traumatic brain injury. At the time, Shane had been in his early twenties and on the fast track to becoming a state police trooper. He'd put aside those plans and taken the probation job so he could move home to help with her care.

I took a slice, broke off a piece, and chewed it slowly. I swallowed, had a sip of coffee, then met Shane's eyes. "Have you ever heard of brain injuries bringing on artistic abilities?"

His brows pulled together. "What do you mean?"

I took a breath, then hurriedly explained, "I know you think I should walk away from the townscape, but there are lots of possibilities other than it being stolen. The guy who allegedly created it was hit by a car and left intellectually disabled. Do you think someone like that could unintentionally copy or imitate the style of a masterful piece in detail? He supposedly never did art before the accident."

He sat back in his chair, rubbed at the stubble on his jaw. "Are you talking about an artistic savant?"

"I guess I am. It seems improbable, but it's not impossible, right?"

He shook his head, as if amused by my befuddlement; then he frowned slightly, and his voice turned serious. "I read a few articles about brain damage and savants when my mom was at her worst. It's been known to happen, though I don't recall anything specifically about imitating other artists. But at the time, I wasn't paying that close attention. All I wanted was for Mom to have even a somewhat normal life again."

I met his gaze. "I'm glad it turned out as well as it did."

"Mom was lucky."

I took another bite of bread, mulling things over. "Personally, I think it's more likely that his sister's wrong about who made the collage. I mean, I can't count the number of times people have told me their great-great-uncle created a piece of mass-produced Victorian furniture, despite there being a manufacturer label on the back of it."

"This man not being the artist makes more sense to me too," Shane said.

I slid my hand along the side of my coffee mug, feeling its warmth. I quieted my voice. "I'm sorry I woke you up. I sent Jimmy the photos you looked at a few days ago. I was dying to hear back from him. He said they stank."

Shane chuckled. "They weren't very clear."

I grimaced. "Yeah, I get that now. I should take some new ones. But before I even consider having anything more to do with the piece, I'm going to do some serious research, make sure everything's on the up and up."

I left it at that. *Research* was an innocent enough word to get past Shane. Besides, it wasn't like I planned to do anything illegal. As far as the whole stolen possibility went, if I caught a whiff of something fishy, I'd back off and tell Shane about it.

Chapter Four

When I got home later that morning, I parked in front of the shop and went inside. The warm glow of the store's vintage lighting brightened the furniture and showcases. Music murmured softly—*Songs from a Secret Garden*, Tuck's favorite album. The egg smell was temporarily gone thanks to the septic tank being pumped. However, he and Kala were nowhere to be seen.

"Anybody home?" I called out.

The shop was divided into a combination of larger open spaces and private nooks and crannies, a labyrinth of eye candy for people to meander through. We currently displayed furniture, primitives, and folk art in the front. The showcases of silver and collectable sat in the middle, near the checkout counter. Our art gallery was in the rear, just past the door that went into Mom's art studio. Upstairs, the balcony-like space opened onto a view of the entire first floor. A door off it led into the book loft.

"Up here," Kala's voice echoed from above.

I hurried up the stairs. Tuck stood with his arms folded, supervising as Kala hung the diminutive oil of Madonna and Child next to a grouping of other oil paintings. Clearly, they'd been busy for hours. The balcony's previous country look had been replaced with an elaborate montage of Oriental rugs, spun brass pieces, and velvet-upholstered chairs.

I gave an enthusiastic thumbs-up. "Looks like a Russian tearoom."

"That's the idea," Tuck said. His voice turned teasing. "Wild night?"

I shrugged. "More like an early morning."

Kala snickered. "Testing out the good detective's handcuffs again?"

I laughed. It was easier to play along than resist their razzing. I glanced at Tuck. "I talked to Jimmy. I need to get some clearer photos to him, but he thinks the townscape is worth investigating." I waited a heartbeat, then went on. "Shane says there are known examples of brain trauma leading to someone becoming an artistic savant. Interesting, huh?"

"Very much so," Tuck said.

Kala rested a hand on a hip. "So? Where do you want to begin our search?"

"If you're done up here, I'd like to have you work some of your internet magic."

She rubbed her hands together, like a bottle digger eager to dive into a new honey hole. "Ready and willing."

"Okay, then. Before we do anything else, I'd like to rule out the possibility of the townscape being a stolen Vespa piece. There's no sense in pursuing it further if that's the case." I held up a finger to keep her quiet as I continued. "I want to keep everything aboveboard. No deep dives into anyplace illegal, got it?"

She widened her eyes, like a child proclaiming innocence. "Whatever gave you the idea I'd do something like that? I'll

41

start with a general search, then the FBI's National Stolen Art File, then Interpol—only stuff available to the public."

Tuck spoke up, "We don't even know if Vespa made it."

"That's why you and I are going to talk to Anna's brother, find out firsthand if he's capable of creating a collage of that skill level. If he's not, then we'll know Anna was either mistaken or lying."

"How do you propose we find him? We don't know where he lives or even his name," Tuck said.

I grinned. "I've got an idea."

* * *

Most likely because I'd spoken with Jimmy earlier, a way to discover the brother's name had come to me on the way home from Shane's cabin. It wasn't foolproof. But then again, was anything?

While Kala settled down in the book loft with her laptop, I went downstairs with Tuck. He took on the shopkeeper role, watering the assortment of houseplants that were displayed in the front window along with furniture. As a carload of customers pulled in, he stopped his chore, greeting them like long-lost friends as they walked inside.

I blocked out their chatting, sat down at the shop's desktop computer, and started my search by googling: *Obituary daughter Anna Gorin Vermont*.

When I'd occasionally worked at Jimmy's funeral home, I'd sometimes helped clients write obituaries for their loved ones. Obits often included information about surviving family members, such as Anna *and* her brother.

A bunch of paid ads for funeral services popped up at the top of the page. Mostly LegacyAngel.com with a list of various towns.

I narrowed my search by adding *Scandal Mountain Gazetteer*. I should have thought of the *Gazetteer* to start with. The local newspaper covered the Champlain Valley region. It was run and owned by the infamous Lefebvre men, three generations of guys living together without any women in sight—grandfather, father, and adult son Tristan, who I'd been friends with in high school. If journalists came in flavors, the Lefebvres were horseradish: predictably unsubtle, tenacious, and country to the core. Their journalistic zest, along with free obituaries and Vermont news that couldn't be found elsewhere, had led to the *Gazetteer* thriving in print as well as digital form while other papers floundered and died.

I hit "Enter," and an obituary headline surfaced. "Gotcha!"

Tuck and the customers swiveled to look at me.

I cringed. "Sorry. Just a little excited."

As I pulled up the full obituary and started scouring for Anna's name, the tap of Kala's footsteps came down the stairs and over to me. "You found the brother?"

"Maybe. Give me a second," I said, voice hushed this time.

Instead of focusing on finding Anna, I circled back and started reading from the beginning.

Scandal Mountain/Shelburne—Katja "Kathy" Smirnov Volkov passed away on March 27.

I skimmed past the bio and went straight to the important part.

Survivors include her daughter, Anna Volkov Gorin, and her son, Erik Volkov. Katja is predeceased by her parents and her husband, Alexander Volkov.

"Erik Volkov." I said the name aloud, getting a feel for it. "'V' for Volkov—or Vespa. That's certainly an odd and inconvenient coincidence."

"You can say that again," Kala said.

Her voice faded into the background as Anna's words came back to me. *My brother made it . . . He was hit by a car twelve years ago . . . He has an apartment in a facility that has an art therapy program. He never did crafts before that.*

Snagging my phone from my pocket, I transferred the photos I'd taken of the townscape to the desktop computer, then blew them up larger. No matter if the photos were crap or not, that didn't change the fact that the piece was amazing.

"This whole thing is really baffling," I said.

Kala leaned closer to the computer screen. "I'm no art expert, but I just scanned through a bunch of Vespa's collages, and this sure looks similar, at least as far as style goes. Vespa's a woman, right?"

"Yeah, in her seventies." As I studied the photos again, I rested an elbow on the counter, chin propped up on my fisted hand like Rodin's *The Thinker*.

My mind went to my mom. Before the forgery arrest, she'd been a renowned copyist, creating look-alikes for collectors who preferred to keep replicas on display and the real masterpieces stored in vaults. She'd sometimes done work on referral for Felix Graham's top-shelf customers, as well as for our own. My birth had delayed Mom's studies, but she left me with my grandparents and went off to art school in her mid-twenties, attended copyist programs at The Met and the National Gallery of Art. She had decades of training and experience now, not to mention having grown up surrounded by art and visiting artists. That kind of training was what it took to copy a masterpiece or even to replicate a famous artist's style—or so I'd always thought.

I straightened back up and looked at Kala. "I guess it's possible that an artistic savant could unintentionally mimic Vespa's style."

She shrugged. "Couldn't say. My job's making sure the townscape doesn't fall into the stolen Vespa category. So far, I haven't found any mention of it."

"You mean no mention of it being stolen?"

"Not just that. I haven't come across any Vespa pieces that look exactly like that specific townscape, or even articles that mention it."

Glancing back at the computer screen, I thought about what Jimmy had said concerning artists' work reflecting themes from their personal experiences. "What if Erik experienced hardships similar to Vespa's?"

"And is an artistic savant, mimicking her style, who just happens to have the same initial as her?" she added.

"It does seem far-fetched. But we're talking outsider art. By definition, the people who create it and their circumstances are out of the norm—atypical geniuses who are one in a million." I met Kala's eyes. "Would you mind searching a bit more? If we found a match for the townscape, it would make untangling this situation so much easier, though there is an outside chance it could be an undocumented Vespa. "

"No problem. I've got a few more places I'd like to try." She hesitated. "Do you want me to hunt down Erik's accident, just for curiosity's sake?"

"Maybe later. For now, stick with looking for the townscape. One step at a time." I wiped a hand over my face. As thrilling as the possibility of the piece being a real Vespa was, the idea of it being an original work created by Erik in a similar style made my head spin. That was, assuming the townscape wasn't an exact replica of a Vespa piece, and especially if Erik had created other more unique pieces. They'd be worth a ton to him, and potentially to the gallery owner or art dealer who discovered him and launched his career. To someone like us.

No question about it. We had to locate Erik. Talk to him— or better yet, see if there were more examples of his other works. Or "crafts," as Anna called them.

I nibbled my bottom lip. Unfortunately, the obituary hadn't listed where Erik lived, though traditionally such information was included for every family member. I supposed it could have been an oversight, or perhaps his or Anna's preference. But I did know one thing: Anna said he *quite often* came to her house for dinner. I couldn't believe that would happen unless he lived somewhere local.

Chapter Five

F irst thing the next morning, Tuck cornered me as I was coming out of my bedroom. It was just before eight. I was headed
downstairs to make coffee, and he was still in his pajamas. His
finger went to his lips, silencing me. He pulled me down the
hallway to his three-room suite and shut the door behind us.

"I want to show you something," he whispered. We stood in
his darkened library—the rolltop desk, the club chairs, and even
the books on the shelves unchanged since the suite had belonged
to my grandparents. A humid-jungle aroma drifted through the
doorway to his bedroom. It would have struck me as odd, except
I knew the smell came from beyond that room, from a makeshift plant nursery in Tuck's private bathroom.

He walked to the rolltop desk, pushed up the tambour. A
chocolate frosted cake sat on the desk's writing surface. It was
decorated with raspberry-pink birthday candles and the likeness
of a see-no-evil monkey.

"It's Kala's birthday?" I asked, surprised.

"When you were with Shane the other night, she made me
watch *Happy Death Day*." He cringed. "A sorority girl reliving
her birthday over and over. Creepy killer in a mask."

"Why didn't you just say no?" Kala loved horror movies. A few weeks back, her obsession with the feral hog movie *Razorback* had even gotten my imagination working overtime.

Tuck waved off my comment. "I slept through most of it. Afterward Kala let it slip that today was her birthday."

I counted the candles. Twenty-two. "Is that her age, or is there an extra for good luck?"

"Twenty-one today," he said with confidence.

"So the bartender at the Jumping Café was right to question her ID."

"She mentioned being surprised by that. Mustn't have been your garden-variety fake."

I laughed. "I would assume not, knowing Kala and all her mysterious friends and skills."

He closed the desk's tambour. "She hasn't gotten any gifts or cards, at least in the snail mail. So, I thought we could have a little party. I'm planning on build-your-own tacos for dinner. If you go into town later, would you mind picking up a bottle of tequila? I forgot to get that—and limes."

"No problem. I'm just glad she told you about the birthday. If she'd mentioned it to me, it might have gone right over my head. I've been pretty preoccupied."

"Anything I can do to help?"

I thought for a second. "Do you think Janet might know where Anna's brother lives? Janet said they were friends, right? It's not like we can call every assisted living place within a hundred-mile radius or like they'd reveal the names of their residents to a stranger for that matter."

"She might know." A devious sparkle twinkled in Tuck's eyes. "A while ago, I promised to give Janet a lipstick plant."

I nodded. The plant offer had been intended as a thank-you for previous information she'd given us that revealed a suspect in the theft of the decoys we were now auctioning in November had been with Graham instead of where she claimed on the night the birds were stolen.

"Well," Tuck went on, "I forgot about the plant when she was here the other day. You could take it down to Graham's shop, talk to her while you're there. It might be better than calling."

"What if Graham's there?" I asked. Even if I set aside the possibility of Graham being involved with Mom's arrest, his connection to the decoy theft was more than a little unsettling. Sure, at one point I'd been a suspect as well and had even been questioned by the FBI Art Crime Team. And, sure, Graham had stopped at our shop to visit since then and acted as if there wasn't a trace of bad blood between us.

I looked at Tuck and smiled. "On second thought, if Graham's there, I'll just treat him like we're best buddies. It might be fun to give him a taste of his own two-faced, slippery medicine."

* * *

Even before our shop opened for the day, several customers appeared. A good sign, especially on a weekday and with our shop not being on the main road. Every cent that came in was desperately needed, and it looked like the promotion Kala was doing on social media was starting to pay off. In turn, that success also made her less grumpy about failing to find a Vespa piece that matched the townscape, at least so far. She still had a few long-shot auction catalogues and art magazine articles she wanted to check.

I texted Shane and invited him to Kala's surprise party, then headed down the driveway with the lipstick plant in the Volvo's passenger seat. As I came to a stop before turning onto the street, a pink compact car chugged out of the drive across the way. The swanky home at the other end of that driveway belonged to René St. Marie, a real estate developer, a friend of Felix Graham's, and a general muckety-muck who'd love nothing better than for us to be forced to sell our property so he could snap it up. However, René wouldn't have been caught dead behind the wheel of a compact car, let alone a bright pink one.

I studied the driver. Halo of fuzzy blonde hair. Glasses with oversized frames. René's sister, Celine St. Marie—my mom's best friend.

I tooted the horn and waved. Though I doubted she recognized me, she fluttered her fingers my way. She'd always fit the cliché mold of a flaky artist and had become more so as she slipped into her mid-forties. Her encaustic art was extraordinary, inspired—so she claimed—by messages she received from angels. She took her religion and calling as an artist seriously, volunteering for art programs at tons of institutions and events.

As she continued down the street, a thought came to me, and I gave a hoot of excitement. If Janet couldn't tell me where Erik lived, I'd try a different approach—namely, locating the art therapist he went to. And Celine might just be able to help with that, given how many art programs she was involved with.

I pulled onto the street, following her car at a polite distance as she chugged past the grass airstrip where my grandparents' plane had crashed.

Taking a deep breath, I let the memory of those horrifying moments slip into my mind. Most often I tried to block them out when I drove by the field. But after looking at the townscape, it felt wrong to ignore the harder parts of life that the past ten years and therapy had failed to drive from my mind. I could still hear the hum of their distant plane. See it emerge from behind a veil of white clouds and descend toward the airstrip. Then the crash and explosion, and my running across the field in hopes of saving them from the flaming wreckage, running without end, as if in a nightmare, powerless to help.

I clenched my teeth, shoved the memory back, and focused on Celine's pink car, creeping along in front of me. I breathed in, counted to ten, let the air out slowly. Yeah, no matter what the therapist believed, making a silly memory box and burying it hadn't helped me forget. Not in the least.

The thought of my ex-therapist brought up a new possibility. She was technically a grief counselor, but it was likely that she'd know the names of local therapists who specialized in working with people with disabilities like Erik's. The only problem was I had no idea if she was still in the area. Plus, I had zero interest in reconnecting with her. Sure, I'd stalked her online right after our sessions ended, but she'd vanished from social media about a month later. I wasn't surprised. She had more than her own fair share of issues, including a lack of professionalism and an intrusive ex-husband. More than once, her ex had walked in on our sessions and dragged her out into the hallway to "talk" as he called it. *Browbeat* was the word I'd have used. If it had been me, I wouldn't have tolerated being treated that way.

I wrinkled my nose and crossed the idea of locating and talking to her off my list, then went back to contemplating a more workable game plan. Once I got to Graham's antique shop, I'd ask Janet where Erik lived. If that didn't work, I'd fall back on talking to Celine about art therapy programs. Or simply do a Google search for programs in the area.

Celine's brake lights came on as she reached the end of our street. She stopped, then pulled out and went toward Scandal Mountain village. Her turn signal came on. It blinked nonstop as she chugged past umpteen side roads and houses, the church, and the park. Eventually, she veered into Quickie's Quick Stop.

I started to drive past but swerved into Quickie's at the last second. Why postpone talking to her?

I parked close to the store's front door, and as Celine approached the entry, I jumped out and waved. "Hi, Celine."

"Ah—nice to see you?" Her eyes, magnified ten times by her glasses, didn't hold a trace of recognition, though we'd last spoken less than a month ago.

"I'm Edie Brown, Viki Tuckerman's daughter. We have the antique shop across the street from your brother's house."

She beamed. "Oh, how nice. I heard you're living at home again."

"For a while, at least until Mom comes home." I got right to the point. No need to confuse her with small talk. "Do you know any local art therapists?"

She stroked the gold cross that hung from a chain around her neck. "There's Elvis in St. Albans. A lot of people love him. And—" She waved off the rest of the sentence. "If you include Burlington, there are quite a few to choose from. You could ask my brother. René will know them if they belong to the Vermont Chamber of Commerce."

I resisted the urge to make a face. Even the thought of talking to René St. Marie was as repugnant as the idea of chatting with my ex-therapist, especially since René was more than likely to tell his buddy Graham what I'd been asking about.

I tried a different tactic. "How about Erik Volkov? Do you know him? He's a local artist. He does amazing collages—landscapes, townscapes."

"Doesn't sound familiar."

"Are you sure?" In retrospect, I could see that having this conversation wasn't one of my most brilliant ideas. If Celine couldn't recall me, how could she remember someone she might have only briefly run into?

She tapped her temple with a finger. "I'm not good with names or faces, but I remember art."

My pulse quickened. I took out my phone, brought up the best photo of the townscape. "Does this help? Have you ever seen this work?"

She peered at the phone, squinting. She pressed her lips into a thin line. "Hmm . . . It reminds me of Vespa. She's a famous outsider artist. Are you familiar with her?"

"Yeah," I said. That really wasn't what I wanted to hear, though perhaps it was just as valuable. Celine did know art.

She looked skyward for a heartbeat, then continued, "Other than that, it doesn't look familiar."

"That's okay," I said. I tucked the phone back into my pocket. "I really appreciate your trying to help. Next time you're at René's house you should come up to our place for a visit. Tuck would love to see you. We could have tea, sit down, and really talk."

"That would be wonderful." She hesitated. "If you'd like, I can ask René about art therapists for you. He really does know a lot of people."

"No," I said, sharper than I'd intended.

Her eyes widened. "Oh, sorry."

I shook my head. "I'm sorry. I didn't mean to snap at you. It's just . . . this is a personal mental health matter." It seemed like the appropriate moment for a lie. I took out a business card, handed it to her. "Do you mind giving me a call if you remember any art therapists or anything about Erik Volkov?"

"Of course, I will," she said.

We hugged goodbye, then I got back in my car and continued toward Golden Stag Antiques & Gallery. If I'd thought Celine was a slow driver, then an army of her clones were now on the road. By the time I reached Burlington and pulled into Graham's store, my jaw ached from clenching my teeth in frustration. As tense as I was, it was a good thing Graham's Mercedes SUV wasn't anywhere to be seen. Being nice to him was the last thing my mood called for.

I got the lipstick plant from the passenger seat and went inside.

Golden Stag was a spacious store with loads of consigners, as well as Graham's own massive inventory. As usual, the fragrance of spiced oranges hung in the air. Chandeliers and Tiffany-style lamps cast glimmering light over everything. Customers swarmed around the showcases and displays, which was a bit depressing since it made me wonder if the flurry of business at our shop might simply reflect a general uptick in people antique shopping, instead of Kala's promotion efforts.

A middle-aged man I'd never seen before stood behind the checkout counter. He eyed the lipstick vine in my hand, then asked, "Can I help you with something?"

"I was looking for Janet. Is she here?"

He gestured to the right. "She's that way. In the art gallery."

"Thank you."

As I walked toward the gallery, the neurons at the back of my brain tingled and prickled from the nearness of so many wonderful antiques. Blue decorated stoneware. Shaker boxes. Primitive and formal pieces of furniture that were to die for.

A wide doorway separated Graham's art gallery from the rest of the shop. As I stepped inside, my mind flashed back to the New York City galleries I'd visited. Despite being part of a larger shop, Graham's art displays were no less impressive. The first room was reserved for Vermont artists. There was a cow painting by Warren Kimble, an awesome Stephen Huneck dog bench, two breathtaking Emile Gruppe oils.

I closed my eyes for a moment, imagining how the townscape would look here among the other works of art. It deserved to be treated with honor and admired. If Erik was its creator, then he deserved be recognized as well. I smiled. So would the person who discovered him and the townscape—with recognition, respect, and financial reward for bringing it and him to light.

Janet's voice echoed out from beyond a partition wall. I walked around it, then came to a fast halt.

Janet wasn't the only person on the other side.

Graham turned to look my way. Salt and pepper hair slicked back. Raspberry-pink dress shirt casually unbuttoned at the collar, showing off a gold chain. I held in the urge to sneeze as the reek of his aftershave infiltrated my sinuses. *Damn.* I'd been so sure he wasn't around.

His upper lip quivered as if he hated the idea of even faking a smile; so much for him maintaining the mask of friendliness he'd put on when he'd visited our store. "Edie Brown, isn't this a treat."

I offered a watery smile. "Your shop looks great. Busy too."

"As always."

I jutted my chin, indicating the area I'd just left. "You have some truly wonderful pieces."

He shrugged as if the art were no big deal. "We've been working in conjunction with several other galleries." He walked in my direction, as if to pass by on his way out of the room. When he reached me, he bent close, seemingly to give some fatherly advice, and whispered, "This is what happens when you maintain a good reputation and can afford quality."

Anger roared through my body. I glared at his back as he strode away. *Self-satisfied, egotistical ass.*

Janet's voice broke through my anger. "I'm guessing the lipstick plant's for me. It's beautiful."

Not having to fake my smile this time, I handed the pot to her. "I'm glad you like it."

"I didn't want to say anything the other day. I thought Tuck had forgotten his offer."

I grimaced. "We both had."

My gaze was drawn to what she and Graham had been working on when I'd arrived. A variety of contemporary art pieces laid out on a worktable, waiting to be hung. Mostly encaustic paintings like Celine's work, and some abstract collages.

The sight of the collages sent an illogical surge of fear into my blood. My pulse hammered. Sweat dampened my armpits, though the collages were bright and cheerful, nothing like the townscape. *Graham doesn't know the townscape exists,* I told myself. Graham had walked away from the chance to connect with Anna. But that didn't change the fact that the piece was still at her house, and Graham would be there in an instant if he learned of its existence.

I glanced at Janet, suddenly unsure whether asking her about Erik was a smart thing to do. It took very little provocation for her to spill Graham's private dealings to us. What if my questions piqued her interest and gave her a case of verbal diarrhea? What guarantee did I have she wouldn't give in to her excitement and blab to Graham about this conversation?

I stood up taller. I was just being paranoid. Janet had never done that in the past, at least that I knew of.

Stepping closer to her, I lowered my voice. "When we were at Anna's, she mentioned a brother, Erik, who lives in assisted housing. Do you happen to know him?"

Janet nodded. "He's come here a few times with Anna. Both of them and their mother were at our open house last winter." She hugged the lipstick plant closer. "He's a rough-looking man, tall and tattooed, with big knobby hands. Younger than her, probably in his early forties. He bought their mom this tiny porcelain figurine, a ballerina holding a bouquet of violets. Not that expensive. Just not the sort of thing I thought a man like him would even notice. His mother cried when he gave it to her—right there in front of the other customers."

"Oh, my gosh. I might have cried myself if I'd seen that." I smiled slightly, remembering the dampness at the corners of my grandmother's eyes when I'd given her silly but heartfelt gifts as a child, such as snowmen created out of pinecones and twigs.

Janet's gaze went to the other room, as if she was checking to make sure we were still alone. She hushed her voice even further. "Graham didn't appreciate an elderly woman crying in the middle of his open house. He also didn't like seeing Anna's brother in the store."

"Because of the way he looks?" I guessed.

She sighed. "Not just that. Anna'd told me a few weeks earlier that he lived in a special facility partially because he was emotionally unpredictable. I made the mistake of telling Graham that."

I pressed a hand to my lips, saying nothing for a heartbeat. That didn't bode well for Janet keeping secrets. And it didn't bode well for Erik's stability either. Still, she'd given me the perfect opening. I chose my question with care and asked as nonchalantly as possible, "Is the place he lives local?"

"Shelburne, maybe. That's where he and Anna grew up. I don't think he's in Scandal Mountain." She frowned. "Why?"

I swallowed dryly, then shrugged. "Nothing, really. They seem like a close family."

"They are. She told me she would've invited him to live with her if it weren't for his issues."

"Are you saying he's violent?"

Her powder-pink lips pressed into a rosebud. "I don't know. I assume that's what she meant when she said 'unpredictable.'" She toyed with the lipstick plant's leaves for a moment, then added, "I like Anna. I'm not saying she's a liar. But I got the feeling there was another reason she didn't want Erik to live with her, that his issues were sort of an excuse."

"I wonder what it could have been?" I said.

Janet shrugged. "I have no idea. I could be wrong about it too."

I glanced to where a customer was wandering toward us. I smiled at Janet. "I should get going and let you get back to work." I'd learned a few things, but drawing out the conversation wasn't going to get me any closer to locating Erik, any more than my visit with Celine. On top of that, the more I tipped my hand by digging for information, the more I risked piquing Graham's interest, if Janet was as loose-lipped as I now feared.

I rolled my shoulders, easing a knot of tension. I really didn't have a reason to feel too downhearted. Janet had confirmed Erik didn't live far away. I had a general idea what he looked like now. There had to be a way to find him. But how?

Chapter Six

I glanced up from my phone to where Tuck stood on the other side of the kitchen, grating cheese for Kala's surprise dinner while she was still manning the shop. "Celine was right," I said. "There is an art therapist named Elvis. Jasper Elvis in St. Albans. There are a bunch of others if we include the Burlington and Shelburne areas."

Tuck stopped grating. "We could take the straightforward route. Stop by Anna's house with a basket of African violets to thank her for selling us such beautiful things, start up a conversation, and ask where her brother lives."

"I'd rather keep the violet idea in reserve for when we want to stop in and take more photos, or if we decide to approach her again about selling the townscape. Can you think of anyone else we know who works in a care facility of any kind, or is even related to someone who does?"

We simultaneously said, "Pinky!"

Pinkney Woods—or Pinky as she preferred to be called—worked as a runner at Fisher's Auction House as well as bartending at the Jumping Café. She also happened to be a member of the Fisher family, which meant she was related to a full third of Scandal Mountain's population, not to mention the rest of the county. If she didn't know someone, no one would. As a bonus, Pinky and I had gone to high school together. She'd liked me then—and perhaps even more so now, after my family's various encounters with the law.

An uneasy feeling flipped in my stomach as I called her number. The only downside to Pinky was that she never did anything for free. A few weeks ago, she'd given me vital information when I'd been searching for the stolen decoys—just like Janet had done. But in Pinky's case, I had to buy several obscenely overpriced stuffed animals in exchange for the help. Granted, the money went to a local fundraiser. However, I'd drawn the line when Pinky also wanted me to set her up with Kala. If Pinky wanted a date, she was on her own.

Pinky answered on the first ring. "Hey, Edie. What's happenin'?"

"Nothing much. Tuck's making a surprise taco feast for Kala's birthday. How about you? You working?"

"Not tonight. By the way, Jack told me he refused to serve Kala because of the fake ID thing. Bastard. I told him to mind his own business. He's been all hyped up and using a UV light to check IDs since he took some Zoom course on how to be a mega-bartender."

"Tell him she's legally twenty-one now." I quit making small talk and got down to business. "You don't happen to know someone by the name of Erik Volkov? He lives at an assisted living place around here."

"Can't say that I do," she said.

"How about anyone who works at an assisted living place or regularly visits one, like a nurse or hairdresser or someone with a therapy dog?"

"I've got an older cousin who drives a Special Services Transportation Agency bus. You know, for disabled and senior citizens. Edgar's always telling stories about the residential care homes on his route."

"Can you ask him if he's ever heard of Erik? He's probably in his forties. A tough-looking guy with tattoos. All I need to know is where he lives."

"I could, if—"

As she fell silent, I braced myself. This wasn't going to come cheap. At least she wouldn't ask why I wanted the address.

"Alrighty, I'll call him," she said, without hinting at the cost. "It'll probably be tomorrow before I get back to you."

"Ah—that's fine. Thanks." As I hung up, I turned to Tuck.

"Something wrong?" he asked. "You look puzzled."

"Seems Pinky's throwing us a freebie. That kind of worries me."

My phone pinged. A text from Shane.

Sorry, Edie. Can't make it to the party.

Work? I asked.

Just got called in. Can't say more.

Hope it's nothing serious.

Me too. Wish Kala happy birthday from me.

Will do.

I set my phone on the table and looked at Tuck. "Guess it's just going to be the three of us. Shane can't come—" I stopped talking as the phone went off again.

Tuck chuckled. "You're Grand Central Station tonight."

"Pinky probably just realized she forgot to name her price."

I checked the Caller ID. *Jimmy.* I answered immediately. "Hey, I'm glad you called."

"Get any new photos of the townscape yet?" he asked.

I pulled a chair out from the kitchen table and sat down. "I've been focused on locating the woman's brother—or even the therapist he goes to."

"Check your email," he said. "I'm sending you something right now."

"What is it?"

"I went to Sterling Gallery today." He sounded super excited.

I ventured a guess. "They're the gallery that represents Vespa?"

"The one and only. They have a place in Vermont too—Manchester. But you knew that already, right?"

Embarrassed, I shifted sideways in my chair. "Not really."

He tsked. "Darling, you need to pick up your pace. Sterling is huge. New York. Vermont. Denver." He hushed his voice. "I took a few photos of her work when no one was looking. We don't need anyone asking questions, right?"

I nodded. "Good idea. It'll be a big help to have more images for comparison."

His voice lightened. "I also thought you'd like to know there's an invitation-only opening of Vespa's work this Saturday. In Manchester."

"Really?" Okay, this was very interesting.

"Guess who has an invite?"

"You're going?" It would take Jimmy a solid four hours to drive north to Manchester from his home in New York City. It wasn't that outlandish a distance, but I was surprised considering how busy his funeral home had been.

"I'm calling it a perk for all the overtime I've put in. Driving up to Vermont on Friday. I don't have a plus-one yet . . ." He let

63

his voice trail off. I could almost see him standing there in his office, examining his manicured fingernails for a second while he dramatically drew out the tension before continuing, "You interested?"

"Of course, I am."

"Good. Between now and then, see if you can get some better photos of the townscape." His voice turned teasing. "If you can't, I just might have to track down that woman and her brother while I'm in Vermont and see the piece in person."

"Don't worry," I said cheerfully, though I was taken aback by his none too subtle threat, tongue in cheek or not. "I've got something in the works right now."

"Fabulous, darling. Look at the photos I sent you. Once I book my hotel, we'll make plans to meet up."

"Perfect. Talk to you soon."

This time when I hung up, the phone remained silent, but the pounding of my heart slammed loud in my ears. When Jimmy and I had talked before, he'd been courteous enough to not even bring up the subject of Anna's name or address. He was my friend, a man I'd help at the drop of a hat. I trusted him completely. But in the world of collectors, I'd seen closer friendships ruined over smaller prospects. If the collage turned out to be a Vespa, it would be worth a fortune—and Jimmy's teasing comment left me wondering how far he'd go to own it.

Chapter Seven

Kala walked into the kitchen a few minutes later. Her gaze went straight to the platters of grated cheese and veggies spread out along the counter. She grinned broadly. "Tacos! My favorite."

"Happy birthday!" Tuck opened a cupboard door and took out the cake. I guess he knew she'd hunt it down if he didn't reveal it ASAP.

Her eyes went wide. "For me?"

He laughed. "Of course. Who else would it be for?"

I retrieved the bottle of Villa One tequila I'd hidden under the table. "Happy twenty-one."

She snatched the bottle. "Wow. This is really good stuff. Thank you."

While she opened the bottle and poured three shots, I told her and Tuck an abridged version of Jimmy's phone call.

"One thing I can guarantee," Kala said after I finished, "the townscape isn't a known Vespa piece or a reproduction of one. I've searched everywhere. It's one of a kind."

"That's fabulous news," I said. I was thrilled she'd had a chance to complete her search despite the shop being busy. I took a shot glass, raised it in a toast. "Here's to fruitful searches. May the rest of the puzzle come together, and soon!"

"Here, here," Kala cheered.

Tuck lifted his glass. "Let's not forget the real reason for this party. Happy birthday to you, Kala."

She poured another round of shots, then we all fixed our tacos. We'd just sat down at the kitchen table to eat when a Toyota Camry winged up the driveway and parked by the path to the house.

Kala bounced from her chair and went to the door. "You didn't tell me you invited guests."

"We didn't," I said. "Well, I invited Shane, but he has to work."

I swiveled to look out the window. I didn't recognize the car, but there was no mistaking the woman climbing out of the driver's door: Pinky.

She strutted down the walkway, her rooster comb of spiked blonde hair keeping time with her stride. She was carrying a magnum bottle of something.

Kala stepped back, grinned at me. "You really didn't invite her?"

"I mentioned we were having tacos for your birthday. That was it, though."

Her eyes glistened. "We should invite her to stay. There's plenty of food, and she's not boring for sure." She opened the door and motioned Pinky inside. "Perfect timing—come in, come in."

Pinky thrust the bottle at her. "Happy birthday. Special bubbly for a special woman."

Kala ogled the bottle's label. "Dom Perignon." Her smile widened. "Hope you can stay for dinner. Tuck made more than enough."

"Wouldn't dream of saying no." Pinky turned to me. "My cousin Edgar called. That guy you're looking for lives in Milton. Checkerberry Manor, the ugly place on Route 7. Enhanced living for disabled people."

It took me a second to realize I'd heard right. I knew where she was talking about, and she was right about the ugly part. Three stories, concrete and gray siding. I couldn't believe she'd found out so easily. "Your cousin really knows Erik?"

"Knowing people's his job. You can't just pick up a disabled person, then take them back to the wrong place."

Tuck jumped into the conversation. "Wasn't Checkerberry involved in a scandal a few years back? Something about cutting corners?"

"That's the one. A paraplegic guy fell and lay in a hallway all night. They were sued big time. Edgar says the owners and staff have been hyper-careful since then, nurse on duty all the time."

"Enough about that." Kala ushered Pinky to the kitchen. "Fix a plate. After dinner we're having cake and watching *Death Day 2K*. You like horror movies?"

"Who doesn't?" Pinky said.

Kala grinned. "Finally, someone with taste."

"*Death Day*'s lightweight," Pinky continued. "More funny than scary."

"Exactly. Do you like *Razorback*?"

Tuck leaned across the table toward me, voice low. "Sounds like we might be able to escape movie night this time."

"Thank God," I said. Maybe I shouldn't have resisted playing matchmaker for Pinky.

All through dinner, Kala and Pinky talked nonstop. I took out my phone, munching my food while I brought up my email.

Normally, I stuck with our household's "no phones at the table" rule, but I couldn't stand not looking at the photos Jimmy sent.

There was no mistaking the first photo as anything other than a distant shot of a Vespa collage, a beach scene titled *Family Outing*. The next one homed in on the center of the collage: a husband, wife, and two children—a boy and a girl—sitting at a picnic table, eating sandwiches. The husband faced away from everyone else, looking out toward an algae-green lake. The sandwich in his hand hemorrhaged fifty-dollar bills and droplets of blood.

I shuddered, then studied it again. There were other odd details. The girl appeared normal, but the boy's hands were wrapped in bloody gauze. The mom's lips were stitched shut.

The next photo was a close-up. According to Jimmy's note, it was of the sandwich. The slices of bread were created out of little bleached bones. The fifty-dollar bills were newsprint. The blood was plastic-coated wire.

"Earth to Edie," Tuck drew my attention away from the photo. "Something interesting?"

"Yeah," I said. I glanced to where Kala and Pinky had finished their tacos and moved on to doing another tequila shot. This wasn't something I could discuss with Pinky around. I also needed to look at the photos on a larger screen. I wrapped my last taco in a napkin and got to my feet. "I'll be right back."

Cradling the taco, I hurried out of the kitchen and down the hallway, past our formal dining and living rooms and the door to the first-floor study. Then I sped up the front staircase to my bedroom.

The early evening light slanted across my desk. As I waited for my laptop to come to life, I looked out the window, trying to imagine the scene before me as a collage: shredded bits of sponge for the tree canopies, dyed green and arched to form old maples and young elms. A vintage rhinestone bracelet would work to imitate the evening light reflecting off the antique shop's windows.

I rubbed my neck. Nothing was impossible, but it was hard to believe anyone—even if Erik was an artistic savant, which was a long shot in and of itself—could so closely replicate Vespa's style and techniques. Not even someone like Mom, who was a master copyist, at least when it came to paint.

Refocusing on the job at hand, I set to work downloading the photos from Jimmy's email—a total of twelve images. Besides the beach scene, there was a collage of a railroad station, reminiscent of the townscape in tone and theme. Jimmy was right. The photos I'd taken had been poor at best. Still, like my photos and unlike the images of Vespa's work I'd seen online, Jimmy included extremely close-up shots that allowed me to view what I assumed had gotten him excited.

Identical small "V's" were scratched into both pieces. Actually, in the case of the beach scene, there were a bunch of "V's" disguised as stylized seagulls, some right side up and others upside down, all perfectly symmetrical. Both pieces also featured a man looking away from the viewer. I'd noticed a similar man in Anna's townscape, standing in an alleyway near a puddle of blood. At that time, I'd guessed he was relieving himself. I wasn't as sure about that anymore. In these, the men's hands were fisted at their sides. Still, even with the subtle variation, these reoccurring details led me to believe the townscape was more likely an unknown Vespa or a reproduction of one rather than something created in her style or purely from Erik's imagination.

I raked a hand over my head, reconsidering that thought. I couldn't make sense of it. Why was Anna so certain her brother had made it? Had he lied to her? Had she lied to us?

I rubbed a chill from my arms as Jimmy's tongue-in-cheek threat came back to me. He'd be in Vermont on Friday. That gave me three days to untangle what was going on. I had to talk to Erik Volkov as soon as possible.

Unfortunately, I suspected the staff at Checkerberry Manor weren't going to simply welcome me with open arms and point me in Erik's direction.

Chapter Eight

Checkerberry Manor—according to their website—specialized in service-enriched, long-term housing for physically and/or intellectually disabled adults, especially veterans. Studio and single bedroom apartments. Nurse on staff 24/7. Cafeteria. Activities. Safe and secure living.

If nothing else, it was clear I wasn't going to simply march in and visit Erik without getting past a variety of security measures, notably locked entries and a staffed front office. However, a closer read of the website gave me an idea. They offered tours to families of potential residents.

I filled out their online tour request form, stating that I'd be in Milton tomorrow. Did they have any available times? I used our real names, Tuck's and mine, in case they checked to see if we were legitimate people, then I got creative, stating we were searching for an assisted living facility for Tuck's out-of-state—and very fake—sister. I hit "Send" just before I went to bed, and was surprised to wake up in the morning to a response from a woman by the name of Yvette.

We have a two o'clock slot available. Would that work for you?

Yes. Thank you so much, I emailed back.

* * *

At quarter to two, we pulled off the highway and into Checkerberry Manor's parking area. The bland style of the three-story building and its location were a huge clue as to the financial status of the residents who lived there. Shelburne, where Erik grew up and I'd earlier assumed he might live, was a wealthy community. The lavish assisted living places there undoubtedly catered to a well-off clientele. Milton, on the other hand, was a more average town, and by the looks of it, Checkerberry Manor housed people with meager bank accounts.

As I maneuvered the Volvo into the overcrowded visitor parking area, Tuck pointed to where a Mercedes sedan was just backing out. The car's deep, metallic-red color glistened as the sun reflected off it, as dark bloodred as the puddle in the townscape.

I claimed the vacated spot as the car moved off, then glanced at the clock on the Volvo's dashboard. "We're still a little early, but I think we should go in. We can look around the lobby while we wait."

"Like in case there's any residents' art hanging on the walls?" Tuck said.

"Exactly." One of the photographs on Checkerberry's website had showed an exhibit of the residents' artwork. I couldn't tell if any were collages. But if a piece by Erik was hanging up in a public space, it might instantly solve the entire mystery.

We climbed out of the car and started down the sidewalk toward the front doors. Only a few yards ahead of us, a white-bearded man in slacks and a short-sleeved shirt rested a hand on the back of an elderly woman in a dove-gray sweatsuit, compelling her to walk in the same direction we were going. Her sparse wisps of hair sprayed out in all directions.

"No, no, no," she moaned. "I'll miss my bus."

"It left five minutes ago. In the future, be out here on time. We can't afford to keep calling a taxi just for you." He stopped as they reached the entry's automatic glass door and grasped her by the hand, then attempted to wave an ID card in front of an access control panel.

The impatient tone he'd used on the woman struck me as unprofessional. Still, as he finally got the ID to work and the door began to slide open, I didn't come to the woman's defense. Instead, I hurried forward and made sure the door didn't slide shut until they were safely inside; then Tuck and I followed. It didn't seem like a good idea to make a scene over the way a staff member handled a resident when we needed them to like us in order to achieve our goal. Besides, he wasn't being that mean, and I imagined having to deal with the same problem over and over again could be frustrating.

The man waited a second until the door closed. Then he released the woman and pointed across the lobby to a line of stiff blue chairs. "Wait over there and don't move." As she hurried to do as told, he swiveled to us. "Is there something I can help you with?"

Tuck stuck out his hand. "I'm Angus Tuckerman. We have an appointment for a tour."

The man's face transformed from exasperated authoritarian to kindly Santa. He flashed a smile. "Yes, of course. I'll tell Yvette you're here." He cleared his throat. "Sorry about that. She and the bus driver have an ongoing dispute about pickup times, among other things. It's a daily struggle."

Without waiting for a response, he left us, strode to a door that was near an unattended reception desk, and vanished.

Tuck bent close and whispered, "You think the bus driver he was talking about was Pinky's cousin Edgar?"

"Maybe."

I glanced toward the woman in the sweatsuit. She was slinking past a half wall that opened into a large common room. She took a few more hesitant steps, then raced down a nearby corridor.

The squeak of shoes against polished floor echoed behind me, drawing my attention. A black woman in a white blouse and stylish African print skirt emerged from the door the man had gone through. She hurried over and offered her hand to Tuck. "Nice to meet you, Angus. I'm Yvette. I'll be giving you the tour today." She looked at me. "Edie, right?"

I nodded. "We appreciate you doing this on short notice."

"No problem. We love showing off our facility." She eyed Tuck. "Your sister is currently living out of state?"

"North Dakota. We'd dearly love to have her closer."

"She's lucky to have family like you."

I pressed my lips together. Tuck was a pretty darn convincing liar.

"Come along," Yvette said. "First you'll need to sign the registry. No one comes or goes from Checkerberry without us knowing—residents, staff, or guests. It's just one of our many safety protocols. After that, I'll show you the communal areas and courtyard garden, then we'll go upstairs and visit a one-bedroom apartment and a studio. Both have walk-in tubs with showers."

I dutifully signed the registry—name and time of arrival. Then I hung back a few steps as she led the way into the common room, talking about a grand piano that sat in one corner, donated recently by someone or other.

"This"—she gestured proudly to a windowsill lined with bedraggled plants—"is our houseplant exchange area. Our residents propagate plants with the help of a volunteer from a local garden center. Extra plants are put here for anyone to take. It's a favorite with many of our residents and staff."

Tuck slid an unimpressed look my way. I had to agree, the houseplants were as sad as most of the room. Not that it was horrible—just large, plain, and slightly threadbare, more like an exhibition hall than a cozy gathering area. But that didn't matter. It had nothing to do with why we were here. We were here to see Erik.

Yvette lifted her chin, motioning to the sizeable courtyard beyond the window. "We're also very proud of our gardens."

I crossed my arms and resisted the urge to tap my foot in impatience as I looked out. She was right, though. It was nice. Shade trees and comfortable-looking outdoor furniture. A woman in sweats weeded a raised container garden. A pudgy, fifty-something man was watering tomato plants. Other residents were walking about or just sitting on benches enjoying the sunshine. But there wasn't anyone who fit the description of Erik that I'd gotten from Janet—tall, rough-looking, with tattoos and big hands.

I turned to Yvette, plastered on a smile, and jumped in with both feet. "When we're upstairs, can we stop in and say hello to Erik Volkov? We're friends with his sister, Anna Gorin. We promised her we'd say hello. She's the one who recommended Checkerberry Manor to us."

"Ah—" Yvette looked at me as if lost for words. Her eyes cut toward the office, then back to me, as if she was deciding how much she could technically share.

"Do you know which room is his?" I asked, letting a touch of my impatience leak out.

"I do. But I don't believe he's in," she said.

"You mean, he's gone out shopping or something?" Our timing couldn't have been worse.

She rubbed her lips. "Let me think . . . A few residents left after lunch for special activities. I don't think he went with them." Her expression brightened. "His uncle and aunt picked him up. You can't have missed them by more than a few minutes. I believe he's not expected back until after suppertime."

"Oh," I said. I didn't have to fake the disappointment in my voice. I also couldn't help wondering if it was the same relatives Anna had mentioned, the circling vultures who'd laid claim to the Persian rug and the samovar lamp.

Tuck spoke up. "Maybe we could at least get a peek at some of his latest art? We noticed on the website that you have an exhibit of residents' pieces."

"We actually don't have an ongoing display, though we probably should. Those photos are from our Artsy-August Craft Show. It's our largest event. Residents sell their arts and crafts to the general public—knit items, paintings, silk flower arrangements—all sorts of things."

"That sounds nice," Tuck said.

I crammed my hands in my pockets, finding it harder and harder not to look grumpy as we toured the cafeteria and then the apartments. A headache began to throb in the back of my skull. It wasn't like we could say, "See you later," and leave without her catching on that our story about Tuck's sister was a lie. That would mess up our chance to ever get back inside again, and it was starting to look like coming back later in order to see Erik's artwork was exactly what we were going to have to do.

As she pointed out a room full of exercise equipment, another place we might find Erik's work occurred to me. "Excuse me."

She looked my way. "Yes?"

"What about your art room? Can we see that?"

Tuck nodded. "My sister loves her crafts. It's the one thing that brings her joy these days—her therapy."

Yvette grinned. "We're especially proud of our art program. We used to do it in-house. Now our residents have the option of going by bus to a trained expressive arts facilitator, every Tuesday and Thursday afternoon. Some of our residents even choose to spend extended time there."

I frowned. "An art facilitator. Is that like an art therapist?"

"Not really. It's a multimodal approach, drawing, painting, music, dance . . . It's designed for relaxation and exploration in a safe space, therapy at a different level." She spoke rapidly, like it was a memorized spiel; however, her sincerity and excitement were real. "It furthers many of our residents' ability to communicate. I apologize for not mentioning it earlier. We're delighted we can offer the program."

"Interesting concept," Tuck said.

"Who's the facilitator? Is it someone who's here in Milton?" I scrunched my toes, waiting with raw anticipation for her answer.

She turned her attention to Tuck. "If you think Checkerberry fits your sister's needs, we should schedule a virtual meeting with her. We can go over the programs with both you and her in detail then."

"Is it Elvis in St. Albans?" I asked. It was the only art thera-pist's name I could remember off the top of my head. Hopefully, I'd hit the bull's-eye or at least draw out an answer.

"Dr. Elvis. He's quite the character," she said. "Do you know him?"

"Not really. I was just wondering." It came out tarter than I'd have preferred.

She gave me a practiced smile, then said to Tuck, "I think your sister would be very happy here. We live by the motto that our residents' comfort, safety, and privacy come first."

As we walked back toward the front entry, I replayed the conversations we'd had in my mind, determined to outfox her evasiveness and find a loophole.

I bit down on a smile. Yvette had said the trips to the art facilitator happened on Tuesdays and Thursdays. Tomorrow was Thursday. If Erik was truly into making art for therapy, he'd most likely go on the outing to the facilitator by bus. A transport bus that just might be driven by Pinky's cousin Edgar.

Chapter Nine

Not long after we returned home, I covered myself in bug repellent so the blackflies and mosquitoes wouldn't eat me alive, then walked down the driveway. Shane had texted to say he was coming by in a little while. I'd told him I'd meet him down on the road by the airstrip. I needed fresh air and some time alone to unwind. Tuck and I might have been riding high on the way home from Checkerberry Manor, but when we'd walked into the shop, Kala had met us with some not so great news.

Who was I kidding? The news was downright depressing.

The puddle of sewage sludge in Mom's secret garden had returned.

I couldn't figure out how it was possible. We'd just had the septic pumped. But a trip to the garden confirmed she was right. Sure, the puddle wasn't as massive as before—at least not yet. But the reek was nasty. To make matters worse, Tuck brought up a disturbing possibility I hadn't considered.

If the smell got any stronger, and the wind blew in the direction of René St. Marie's house, and if René figured out we had a failed septic, he'd contact the authorities and have it officially condemned. That would mean we'd have to move out of our home and close the shop until the issue was resolved—a situation that could well be the final straw for the business. In truth, there was a good chance we'd end up being forced to sell the property, something that would delight René to no end.

No ifs, ands, or buts about it: we had to move up the time line for getting the septic replaced before René St. Marie literally caught wind of our problem. In other words, we needed to come up with the cash and have the work done in the next week or so instead of at the end of the summer, as I'd planned.

Walking fast, I reached the bottom of our driveway, crossed the street, and headed along the left-hand side of the road. The crunch of my sneakers against the roadside gravel formed a lulling rhythm, interrupted only by the caw of crows up on the forested knoll that hid René's house from view.

The birds rose from the trees, black silhouettes against the blue sky, before they descended into the enormous bramble patch at the end of the airstrip.

I took a deep breath, almost afraid of what I'd smell. But there wasn't a trace of sewer stench in the air—not yet.

I rolled my shoulders to release more tension, then slowed my steps, focusing on the sounds and sights, savoring a bittersweet feeling as memories of the hours I'd spent hidden in the bramble patch unspooled in my mind.

The brambles marked the border between René's property and the grass airstrip that my family owned, though it was currently leased out. In the center of the brambles was a ravine that had been the town dump a hundred years ago. As a young teenager, I'd dug antique bottles out of it and sold them at the Jumping Café's weekend flea markets. René St. Marie would have had a fit if he'd known I was trespassing and scavenging on his land.

I sighed. Life and my troubles had certainly been simpler back then.

Still lost in thoughts of the past, I left off walking along the road and scrambled through the roadside weeds and down toward the airstrip. There were only a couple of small-engine planes parked on the far side today. It would be a lot busier in the autumn, when the trees took on their fiery hues, and tourists and photographers vied to get a bird's-eye view of the foliage.

I stopped, picked a handful of Queen Anne's lace and carried the bouquet to the spot where I'd buried the memory box. After all these years, I wasn't positive of the exact location. But I was close, and it felt right.

As I knelt and set the flowers on the ground, a lump formed in the back of my throat. In the distance the crows screamed again and took off, flying toward René's house this time.

I rested a hand beside the flowers, the earth warm against my palm. Not only had life and my troubles been simpler, but my grandparents had always been there to calmly nudge me toward the best path.

My mind went to when I was a freshman in high school, stubborn and convinced I knew everything. One time I was with a bunch of older kids, and we ended up at a camp in the boonies. The place was locked, but one kid claimed it belonged to his uncle. He jimmied a window, and we went inside. We played poker, drank, and ate everything in the place. I got home at two in the morning and snuck back into the house. I thought no one was the wiser, until the next day, when my grandfather slickered me into turning traitor. Not by confronting me, but rather by suggesting it was up to me to keep my friends and myself out of even deeper hot water by confessing to what we'd done. That was my grandfather: no yelling or panic, just calmly facing and solving problems as they arose.

The toot of a car horn brought me from my thoughts. Shane's Land Rover pulled over to the edge of the road. He waved at me from the driver's seat.

Turning away from the airstrip, I waded through the weeds to the road. I opened the Land Rover's passenger door, climbed in, and smiled at Shane. "I'm glad you could come over."

He rested a hand on the steering wheel and leaned over, offering a kiss. The sleeves of his oxford shirt were rolled up, showing off his forearms. I snuggled in close to him, letting his hands cup my face. His lips were warm against mine, gentle, parting enough to hint at desire. Man, I was lucky to have someone like him in my life—even if he ticked me off sometimes—no pressure, just friendship and hot times in bed.

Shane abruptly pulled back, nose wrinkling as if he'd caught a whiff of something nasty. My mind flew to the septic, but he said, "Trying to kill every bug within a hundred miles?"

I remembered the bug spray I'd used and laughed. "Not very sexy, huh?"

He winked. "Not anything a shower for two couldn't fix."

"Brat." I gave him a playful punch in the arm.

"What were you doing down there?" He jutted his head toward the airstrip.

"I was thinking how much easier life used to be."

His voice gentled. "Troubles with the townscape?"

"Actually, we're making progress in that area." I rubbed a hand over my face. It didn't seem right to burden him with more of my personal problems. Still, I gave in. "The other night when I was at the cabin, I needed a break from the stress, so I didn't say anything. But, along with all the bills my mom left behind and the property taxes, we now need to replace the septic system."

He cringed. "That is major."

"You're telling me. I'd use the commission from the decoy auction, but it's been delayed until November, and we can't wait that long."

"Tuck must have some savings or investment funds?"

"He used them to pay off Mom's lawyer fees. And I can't take out a second mortgage on the property. Mom did that last summer."

Shane's expression softened. "I've got cash left in my cabin fund. I can loan you most of what you need. No interest. Pay me back when you can."

The kindness and generosity of his offer sent a flush of warmth radiating across my face. I looked away for a moment. Mom would have jumped on his offer, but that's how she rolled—playing on guys' sympathy, then wiggling her way out when the relationship went sideways. I didn't want to treat Shane like that. Taking money was a big commitment. I valued the easiness of our friendship too much.

I looked back at him, drummed up a smile. "If this town-scape thing pans out, we'll be all set. We've located the guy who supposedly created it. Tomorrow we're hoping to talk to him at the place where he does art therapy." I purposely omitted the part about Erik and the facilitator not knowing we were coming.

"That sounds good," he said.

"I'm a little nervous," I admitted. I was grateful to be past the no-invitation part. "I talked to Janet down at the Golden

Stag. Apparently, the guy's 'emotionally unpredictable.' Whatever that means."

"What did you say his name was?"

"It's Erik," I said.

Shane put the car in gear, shifting it and, momentarily, the subject as well. "Are we headed up to your house, or would you rather go somewhere else, like the pub?"

"The house is fine. If you're hungry, we've got tons of leftovers from last night. I could make us taco salads."

"That would be great." He pulled away from the edge of the road. "What's Erik's last name?"

"Volkov—Erik Volkov. His surname is part of why I'm confused. Vespa uses a 'V' as her signature. But considering Erik's last name and that he's intellectually disabled, he could have adopted a similar one to hers without realizing what he was doing."

Shane glanced my way. "You've compared the townscape to Vespa pieces?"

"I've been studying photos. Kala's been searching the internet for an identical known Vespa townscape, or even a mention of it. So far she hasn't turned up anything." I hesitated for a beat, then added, "Saturday, there's an invitation-only opening of Vespa's work in Manchester. Jimmy's taking me as a guest. It'll give me a chance to look at Vespa's pieces firsthand."

"That sounds like a golden opportunity." He slowed, turned into our driveway, and then his tone became flat, hard to read. "Tuck's going with you tomorrow, right?"

I nodded. "Luckily, we've got Kala to watch the shop."

Shane slid his hand along the steering wheel. "I don't want to worry you. I'm the last person to believe all mentally disabled people are prone to dangerous mood swings or violence. But you'll want to take things slow. Talk quietly. Help this Erik avoid confusion by giving him an extra-long time to answer. If his demeanor starts to shift, leave immediately."

I turned away, looking out the passenger window as the gardens and house came into view. "I really feel bad for him and Anna," I said softly. "I can't imagine having a family member's life changed in the blink of an eye like that."

Shane hushed his voice. "When I worked for probation, occasionally a client would arrive in the middle of a mental health crisis no one was aware of. Seemingly out of the blue, they'd become irrational. Same thing can happen when you're arresting someone. Just be vigilant and open-minded, and stick close to Tuck."

"I will," I said, and I meant it.

Shane's tone lightened. "I'll be curious to hear what you find out from him. I have to say, I'm surprised the art therapist is letting you stop by during a session."

My thoughts froze, guilt over my omission coming on strong. "It's not really a therapy session. The person's an art facilitator . . ." I went on, making up reasons a professional would let strangers into a session. They all sounded like nonsense to me.

Shane nodded, as if accepting every one of them, though I found that hard to believe, given he was normally over-the-top perceptive.

Chapter Ten

My cooking skills were somewhat limited, but for once my taco salad bowls came out perfectly crisp and airy. Add to that Tuck's homemade salsa and fresh sour cream, and Shane was impressed by the meal. Frankly, I was too.

But despite that achievement, I couldn't shake my growing anxiety about tomorrow. It even overshadowed any thought of the septic. What if the therapist wouldn't let us speak with Erik? What if he wasn't there? So many questions. Too many ways things could go wrong. The feeling didn't even subside when I walked Shane out to his car to say goodnight.

"Be careful tomorrow, Edie," Shane said as he brushed my jawline with his fingers.

I gave him a swat. "Don't be such a worrywart."

He shook his head, rubbed a hand over his angel tattoo, then said, "You don't make things easy for a guy."

I kissed his cheek. "I promise I'll let you know how things go as soon as I can."

"You better."

He got into his car. As he took off down the driveway and out of sight, I looked toward where the gardens and trees framed a distant view of Scandal Mountain Valley.

If it had been winter instead of the first of July, the leafless trees would have allowed me a glimpse of the street and his car as it went past the airstrip. But right now, all I could see were the hillsides and treetops, illuminated by the sunset while everything below was shadowed. Deeper in the valley, haze was rising. Above me, streaks of vibrant blue and raspberry saturated the sky.

I breathed deep, filling my lungs with cool evening air. I loved this place. I couldn't imagine having to let it go. But if something didn't turn around—

Clenching my hands, I forced that thought from my mind. Enough stinking thinking. Enough doom and gloom. Tomorrow was going to work out. It had to. That's all there was to it.

I turned on my heel and beelined to the shop, to make sure Kala had set the alarm and everything was locked up tight for the night. Then I went back into the house. There was only one way to ensure nothing would go wrong tomorrow, and that was to make certain our plans were as seamless as possible.

I found Tuck and Kala upstairs in his suite. He sat at his rolltop with several books open in front of him. Kala was looking over his shoulder.

She turned and smiled at me as I walked over. "Tuck's been teaching me the basics of valuing books."

"We've got a fast learner here," he said. "You'd think she'd been in the book biz for years."

Kala beamed. "That's me—a natural."

I laughed, then asked. "Have you heard back from Pinky yet?" Kala had called Pinky soon after Tuck and I returned from Checkerberry. She'd asked Pinky to find out from her bus-driving cousin where the art facilitator's office was and what time the group from Checkerberry Manor would arrive there.

"Edgar still isn't answering her calls," Kala said. "Pinky's getting pretty pissed."

"I hope she doesn't kill him before he answers our questions. We need that information."

A slow, devious smile played over Kala's lips. She shut the book in front of her. "There is an easier way to do this. If you want, I could take a little remote looksie at Checkerberry Manor's computer records. The therapist's contact information should be there."

"You mean, hack into them?" I held up my hands, warding off that suggestion. "Absolutely not."

She frowned. "I know the other day you said to keep everything aboveboard. But I have this friend who could—"

Tuck interrupted. "I'm with Edie on this. Nothing illegal."

"I suppose you're right." Kala glanced my way. "I did do some extra research already. I was going to tell you earlier but didn't want to say anything in front of Shane."

My eyes widened. "You *already* hacked into something?"

"Not that. I tracked down Erik's high school yearbook. It was online—available to anyone." She looked up for a moment, as if summoning what she'd learned from thin air. "Twenty years ago, Erik Volkov graduated from Champlain Valley High School. Nothing remarkable. He did some amateur boxing. Local gym, no big deal. Sixteen years ago, he graduated with an accounting and finance degree from Fordham University in New York City."

"Fordham?" Tuck said. "Erik couldn't have gotten in there without getting good grades in high school."

Kala shrugged. "Not valedictorian, but not bad. After Fordham, he drops off the face of the earth. No social media accounts—not even LinkedIn. No online presence at all until his mom's obituary."

"What about his accident?" I asked. I might have told Kala to hold off looking into Erik before, but I was glad she hadn't listened. The more we knew before tomorrow, the better prepared we'd be.

"The accident's the weird part. I used everything Anna told you—twelve years ago, home from New York City, staying with her and their mom in Shelburne. Hit by a car. Traumatic brain injury. I assumed it happened somewhere in this area. But nothing. There were other people hit by cars that year—and by trains and one tractor. But no Erik Volkov."

"That is strange," I said.

Tuck waved off the idea. "There may have been a reason his name was withheld from public records. His family or the police could've requested it for privacy's sake or for safety. We also can't assume it was really an *accident*, right?"

"Are you suggesting someone hit Erik on purpose?" I couldn't deny the possibility had passed through my mind before. Janet's description of Erik, along with the criminal-type activities depicted in the townscape, had led me to assume he'd traveled with a rough crowd, the sort that didn't hesitate when it came to murder and revenge. Honestly, the newer information about him being a Fordham accounting and finance graduate seemed far-fetched.

"I'm not suggesting anything," Tuck said. "Just bringing up a possibility."

Kala raised her voice. "Shane could probably find out more about the accident."

I glared at her. "Yeah, he'd just love me asking for something like that." The last thing I'd ever do was ask Shane to risk his job by digging into police records for me, public or not.

Kala folded her arms across her chest. "I'm betting Shane's at the root of the 'no hacking or dark web' rule."

"Partly," I admitted. I glanced at the carriage clock on top of the desk. Almost ten. I looked back at Kala and rested my hands on my hips. "I think it's time to try Pinky again, don't you?"

"Sure, I suppose." Kala took out her phone and put it on speaker. Pinky answered after two rings, "Hey, babe."

I scrunched in closer. "Tuck and I are here too," I said. It was only fair to warn Pinky that she and Kala weren't alone.

"Oh," she said, surprised. "If this is about Edgar, I haven't heard a frickin' peep."

"Is it possible he won't return your call at all?" Tuck asked.

Pinky snickered. "I should have said something before. Edgar's life is a soap opera right now. He's stuck between a new love and a pissed off soon-to-be ex-wife. His wife's filed for divorce and put the house up for sale, but she and her lawyer are still hunting for reasons to totally take Edgar to the cleaners."

"Like proof he's been cheating?" Kala asked.

"Exactly. He probably left his phone on the bus and is hiding out at his girlfriend's place." Her voice quieted. "He'll surface in time for work. But we might not hear back tonight."

"Thanks for trying at least," I said.

"No problem. If I hear back from him, I'll let you know right away."

Kala hung up with a cringe. "So, what are we going to do now?"

I rubbed my hands over my face. "I think we should assume we're not going to learn the location of the facilitator or the exact time of the session from Edgar. Although we do know it's after lunch. Yvette told us that."

Kala tilted her head. "You could do a stakeout, like the police. All you and Tuck would have to do is park across the street from Checkerberry before noon, wait until the bus arrives, then follow it."

"That's probably our only option," I said.

Tuck cleared his throat, then focused his attention solely on me. "Before we go any further down this stakeout rabbit hole, I should mention that we have another complication. Do you remember Kelly O'Keeffe?"

I flipped through my mental file of names I'd heard over the years. I vaguely recalled someone by that name visiting my grandparents. "From Dublin? The size of a Volkswagen. Deals in rare books?"

"That's the guy. I emailed him photos of our first edition *Finnegan's Wake* last week. He's in Boston right now. He's planning on driving up tomorrow to see it. If he buys, it'll put five-thousand dollars in our pocket."

Five thousand. I did a quick calculation. It wasn't enough to help with the septic, but it would take care of our monthly bills. "That's great news," I said before I realized something else. "But if you're going with me to the facilitator's office—"

Kala rolled her eyes. "You don't need to sugarcoat it. I'm the book newbie. Tuck needs to stay behind and handle the Irish Volkswagen." She stretched her arms and grinned like a preening Cheshire cat. "On the other hand, I'm very good at sweet-talking therapist types."

I eyed her. One of these days, we'd have to have a talk with Kala about her past. Dark web skills. Hacking. Therapists. I met her gaze. "Erik and the therapist won't be the only ones there. It's a group session, so there'll be other clients." I remembered what Janet had said about Erik being emotionally unpredictable, and Shane's advice. "We'll need to take it slow. Be ready to leave if things go sideways."

"I can bring Taz," she suggested cheerfully. "Just in case."

"Absolutely, not." Taz was Kala's nickname for her military-grade Taser, and I couldn't tell by her tone whether she was kidding or not.

"If you insist." She rested a hand on her hip. "You do realize no one's going to let us past the office while a session's going on."

Tuck got up from his chair, paced toward the fireplace, glanced at a painting of an angel that hung on the wall, a beautiful encaustic piece by Celine St. Marie. He turned back to Kala and me. "If I can have a fake sister who needs assisted living, why can't one of you be looking for an expressive arts workshop for yourself or for a great-grandmother? That might get you a peek at Erik's group in action."

Kala wrinkled her nose. "That's kind of a lame plan, don't you think?"

"Do you have a better suggestion—other than Taz?" I asked.

"Not really." She flopped down on the desk chair Tuck had deserted. As she leaned back and gave the chair a spin, the light from the desk lamp glinted off the see-no-evil monkey brooch pinned to her bandana.

"I've got it!" I grinned. "We'll take boxes of junk jewelry with us. Stuff the therapist's clients can use for collages and whatever else they're making. That's how we're going to get in—a fake great-grandmother and a jewelry donation."

Chapter Eleven

J ust before noon, we drove into the VFW parking lot across the road from Checkerberry Manor and parked. We had a good view of Checkerberry's entrance from there, and the VFW was closed, so we wouldn't draw suspicion if we had to wait a long time. The largest problem was the Volvo's ancient air-conditioning. The day was hot. There was no shade in the parking lot. By the time one thirty rolled around, the car was as sweltering as a sauna.

I leaned forward, wiggling my shoulders to unstick my shirt from my spine. "I feel like a steamed clam."

Kala fanned herself. "I think my hair's wilting."

"But you're okay with staying a while longer, right?" I asked.

"Well, I'd—" She abruptly looked away, out the window toward the farther lane of traffic, then gestured wildly. "There it is!"

It took a moment for me to spot the minibus, trundling northward behind a tractor trailer. The bus's brakes squawked as it turned into Checkerberry's parking lot. As it crept toward the building, a dozen or so people trickled out of the facility's front entry to meet it—someone in a wheelchair and an elderly woman with a cane. A tall, larger man in a black baseball cap brought up the rear of the group. Maybe Erik.

Still watching the bus, I wiped my hands on my pants, drying off sweat. " You know, I think I'm going to strangle Pinky's cousin if I ever meet him. When he got to work this morning, he must've noticed her messages. Why not call her then?"

"Maybe Pinky offended him. She can be pretty *pushy*." Kala stressed the last word as if to give it extra meaning.

I took my eyes off the bus and glanced her way. I didn't like the sounds of that. "Pinky hasn't been pushy with you, has she?" Too forward. Too handsy. I could see it happening.

"Nothing this girl can't deal with," Kala said.

I laughed. Maybe Pinky had met her match. "Just remember, if you ever need backup, I'm here for you."

"Same here, though that guy of yours seems pretty domesticated."

I waved that off. "We're not like that. Just keeping it casual."

"Sure, you are," she said with a snicker.

My face heated and I lowered the side window to get some extra air. Kala was wrong. Shane and I had a good low-key thing going on. No promises. No strings, like one of us owing the other one money. Besides, I wasn't foolish enough to think I was good long-term relationship material for someone in law enforcement. Eventually, the fun times would come to an end, and he'd move on.

I glanced back at the bus, still sitting in the parking lot. "What do you think is taking so long? It looks to me like everyone's seated."

"Let's just hope it moves as slowly once it gets on the road," Kala said. The road between us and Checkerberry was actually

US Route 7, a main artery by Vermont standards. Today it was super busy, a steady flow of cars, pickups, and larger vehicles rolling along in a nonstop chain of traffic. She added, "And that it's the right bus."

My mouth went dry. "Don't even suggest that." More than one bus. Why hadn't I thought of that before now?

The bus inched forward through the parking lot. It stopped at the edge of the road, waiting for a break in traffic. I put the Volvo in gear and drove to the VFW's exit. All I had to do was stay put until the bus pulled out, see which way it went, then follow as close as possible. If it wasn't the right bus, we'd find that out when we got to its destination. At this point, there was no time to rethink.

In a burst of power, the bus launched forward, crossed traffic and headed south, back the way it had come. I glanced to my left at the oncoming traffic, eager for a break so I could join the flow. A car was coming, followed closely by another. Next came a bread truck and a van.

"Damn," I muttered as the bus kept moving down the highway, slowly disappearing over the crest of a hill.

"We're going to lose it," Kala groaned.

A mid-size U-Haul was coming now and behind it an SUV. Between the two was a tiny gap in the traffic, nowhere near as big as I'd have normally chosen to zing into.

"Hang on." As the U-Haul passed, I floored the accelerator and squealed into the gap.

The SUV's horn blared. I glanced in the rearview mirror long enough to see the driver give me the middle finger.

"Tha—that was close," Kala stammered.

"Did you want me to wait another hour?"

I pressed on the accelerator, keeping pace with the traffic. As we reached the top of the rise where we'd last seen the bus, I spotted it again, about ten cars ahead of us, still heading south. We weren't as close as I'd have preferred, but at least we hadn't totally lost track of it.

The U-Haul in front of us swerved toward the centerline, almost crossing it before returning solidly to the proper lane.

I tapped the brakes, putting more distance between it and us. It veered close to the edge of the road, then back to the middle.

Kala gripped the edge of her seat. "What the hell's wrong with them?"

I ground my teeth. "Idiots have probably never driven anything larger than a compact car."

"They could be texting. Or drunk," Kala said.

"Could be."

The U-Haul's brake lights blared red as a pickup pulled into traffic ahead of it, further lengthening the distance between us and the transport bus.

I wiped a bead of sweat off my face, then took a fresh grip on the steering wheel. Less than a quarter mile ahead was an intersection with traffic lights. Route 7 continued onward, but a turning lane headed west toward the interstate ramps and the Champlain Islands. If we got in the wrong lane, we'd lose the bus for certain.

"Can you tell if it's going straight or turning?" I asked Kala.

"I can't see anything with that stupid U-Haul in the way."

I gritted my teeth, rolled a set of mental dice, and stayed in the straight-ahead lane.

As the U-Haul veered into the turning lane, I spotted the bus continuing straight. "Thank God," I said, too soon. The bus slid through a yellow light that turned red before we reached it. I thumped the steering wheel. "We'll never catch it now."

"We have to be close," Kala said. "It's not like they're going to transport people for hours, at least for something like this. How many local art facilitators are there, anyway?"

Tension cramped my neck and shoulders. "You'd be surprised. In this direction alone, there were two or three places that did that kind of thing."

"That's better than dozens."

"Yeah, I guess."

The light turned green and the traffic snaked forward, moving slightly faster as the space between vehicles lengthened. As we went around a bend in the road, I caught a glimpse of the distant bus. I'd traveled this route hundreds of times. Ahead, the highway forked again, one artery heading east into Colchester Village and the other continuing down a hill toward Burlington.

Unfortunately, we lost sight of the bus again before we reached the fork.

Kala took out her phone, swiped her finger across the screen a few times, then held it out for me to see. "Try left. There's a therapist who does artsy stuff down that way."

I took my eyes off the road long enough to glance at her phone. I couldn't see the website's details, but I recognized enough from my own search to vaguely remember it.

"Left it is," I said.

I slapped on my turn signal, crossed traffic, and headed into Colchester Village. I passed Claussen's Greenhouse and Perennial Farm, the spot where I'd always bought birthday presents for my grandfather. Tuck's definition of heaven on earth. As I drove by a grade school, my gut began to whisper we were on the right track, though logic said it wasn't anything more than a healthy guess.

The cramp in my neck began to pinch in earnest as we drove another block. There weren't many businesses now. It was mostly private homes.

"There's the sign!" Kala motioned at an older two-story building.

It was a white clapboard structure, previously a schoolhouse, judging by its overly tall windows. A line of cars curled around it, waiting at a drive-up window that had been added onto the front. Next to the drive-up was an enormous sign in the shape of an ice-cream cone.

"An ice-cream parlor?" I said, confused.

"Not that." She pointed at the entry to the building's parking lot.

A smallish, conservative sign read:

The Well-Being Center
Rejuvenation for spirit and soul

I swerved into the parking lot. It was narrow and jam-packed with cars. But there wasn't any sort of bus to be seen or any additional signage other than for the ice-cream parlor.

I glanced at Kala. "Do you see it?"

"Maybe it's around back."

She was probably right. The parking lot wasn't only narrow and packed with cars, it also hugged the building so close it was impossible to see what was in the rear.

I swallowed a lump in my throat and for a heartbeat wondered why we were even doing this at all. *Money for the septic and to keep the business from going under,* I told myself—the finder's fee we'd get from Jimmy if the townscape turned out to be an unknown Vespa, or the even larger amount that could come from discovering Erik as a new outsider artist, an artistic savant.

I scowled. Of course, those things were vital. But there was more to it than just that. The townscape and its provenance deserved to come to light, to be revealed to the world. Fostering that would put our business back on the map. It didn't mean just cash for now. It meant we'd have a future as long as we outlived our current money issues. Not to mention, Mom would have to accept that I was more capable than she thought.

I set my jaw and tapped the accelerator, speeding up as I zoomed around the building's rear corner—

An elderly woman stood dead ahead.

"Watch out!" Kala screeched.

I slammed on the brakes. "Yikes!"

There were people everywhere, filing out of the bus, wandering across the parking lot. A man pushed a wheelchair . . .

The Volvo skidded sideways, stopping only a second before it collided with the elderly woman. She was small, with wisps of sparse gray hair. I'd seen her getting onto the bus at Checkerberry. And now that I saw her up close, I suspected she was also the woman in the sweatsuit the white-bearded man had been wrangling at Checkerberry the other day, though I didn't recall her having a cane.

"You could have killed someone," the man pushing the wheelchair shouted.

I raised my hands in an apology. What else could I do at this point?

The man glared, then hurried to propel the chair out of the way toward a small modular building, previously hidden by the schoolhouse's larger structure. A dozen other people were walking in the same direction, including a stocky blond man in a bus driver–type uniform—and the tall guy in the black baseball cap that I hoped was Erik. The elderly woman with the cane now toddled behind them all.

"Jesus, that was close," I said.

Kala nodded. "I thought the old lady was a goner."

I squeezed the Volvo past the bus into a parking spot on the other side of it. "Yeah, not exactly the entry I wanted to make."

I swiveled in my seat, looking at the modular building, more like a temporary school classroom than anything else. I figured it was going to take some fancy talking to get inside and see Erik, but if the art facilitator had witnessed me almost running over her clients, my chance of getting in might have gone from difficult to impossible.

Chapter Twelve

Kala and I decided to wait a few minutes, to give the facilitator time to get the session started, and to give our adrenaline a chance to subside after the close call. While we sat there, the stocky blond guy in the bus driver–type uniform emerged and strutted off in the direction of the ice-cream parlor.

I turned to Kala. "Do you think that's Edgar? He kind of looks like Pinky."

Kala snickered. "It's lucky you didn't mow him over. She would've skinned you alive."

"You can say that again." I took a deep breath. "Ready to go inside?"

"Ready as I'll ever be."

As Kala swiveled to open the car door, I noticed a lump at her waistline. "Is that Taz?"

She grinned sheepishly. "Better safe than sorry?"

I pointed at the glovebox. "That stays here."

She grumbled but did as I asked while I retrieved our so-called scrap jewelry donation from the Volvo's backseat. I handed her two shoeboxes full of beads and glittery stuff. I took the larger box I'd assembled with the townscape's elements in mind—vintage copies of *Life* magazines, typewriter keys, and electronic odds and ends from our kitchen junk drawer, along with some cufflinks and lengths of silver chain. If Erik was the creator of the townscape, the goodies would draw him the way yard-sale signs were irresistible to me.

I stood up as tall as I could and strode confidently with Kala past the bus and up to the building's glass entry doors.

Block letters expanded on the information from the sign out front:

Well-Being Center—Rejuvenation for spirit and soul
Dr. A. S. Meadows, PhD, ATR-BC
Expressive Arts Facilitator and Registered Therapist

Gripping my box of goodies closer, I did a quick mental run-through of the spiel I'd prepared about our donation, then reached for the intercom button. But before I could press it, the automatic doors whooshed open of their own accord.

I glanced at Kala. A smile tugged at her lips. Apparently, luck was with us—or someone had simply forgotten to secure the door.

As the door began to slide shut, we raced inside. The diffused scent of lavender filled my nose. A tinkle of harp music reached my ears. The chill of subarctic air-conditioning sent goose bumps across my skin.

Rubbing my arms to warm up, I looked around. I expected to find myself in a waiting area or at least to see a reception desk. But there was nothing other than the empty corridor we stood in, with automatic glass doors on our end as well as the farther one.

To our right, a door stood open. I peeked inside. Two leather chairs sat in front of a flattop desk. Nearby a blue couch and upholstered chairs formed a semicircle under a window curtained with dream catchers and half-dead spider plants.

I shuddered as the dying plants reminded me of the first time Mom had left me at the therapist's office, a month or so after my grandparents' deaths. That therapist's name had been Alder Scranton. She was supposedly the most up-and-coming young therapist in the area, a specialist in grief counseling.

"Call me, Alder," she'd said with a pert smile. "I hear you're going through a rough time?" Without waiting for an answer, she'd glided away from me, her bohemian-style skirt floating around her as she took a watering can off the top of a file cabinet, then strolled to where a pot of spider plants sat dying on the windowsill. I'd been glad she'd noticed the plants' life-or-death situation, but even at that fledgling stage of our relationship, her laidback style struck me as unprofessional. Everything about her fit the same mold, from the softness of her voice to her feathery earrings and messy-bun hairstyle. However, it only took me two visits with Alder Scranton to realize those things were a well-oiled facade, casual airs designed to put clients at ease, draw out emotional responses, and unlock secrets—even to inspire pity for her as an empathic woman struggling to help others through difficult times.

"Pssst." Kala's voice pulled me from the past.

She stood a little ways down the corridor, holding the boxes of junk against one hip. She nodded at a closed door.

Leaving the thoughts of my less than standard therapy experience behind, I hurried to her. Through a window in the door, I could see the Checkerberry group. Most of them sat at tables, gluing things onto sheets of cardboard and into boxes, drawing with crayons and markers. An older man swayed to the harp music. The elderly woman I'd almost run over was staring out a window. I couldn't see the guy in the ball cap or anyone matching Erik's description, but the room was quite large, and the view through the window limited.

A college-age guy in a turquoise T-shirt and cargo shorts glanced our way, then hurried to where a purple-haired woman sat on top of a desk with her skirt puddled out around her. He whispered something in her ear.

"Here goes nothing," Kala murmured, as the woman slid down from the desk and glided toward the door and us.

She was in her mid-forties. Her hair was gathered in a messy bun. As her face came into view and I saw who she was, I wanted to run for the front door. Her hair might've now been purple instead of blonde, but she dressed and moved with the same calculated nonchalance as the last time I'd seen her. *Dear God, I should have seen this one coming*, I thought.

Kala touched my hand. "What's wrong?"

I swallowed back the knot in my throat. "That's—my ex-therapist."

"You're kidding."

"I wish."

As Alder Scranton—now Dr. A. S. Meadows, PhD, ATR-BC—reached the door and opened it, her eyes widened the same way mine had.

She recognized me, no question about it.

Chapter Thirteen

"Edie Brown, what a nice surprise." Alder stepped into the corridor, leaving the door open behind her.

I took a fresh grip on my box and pulled back my shoulders, feigning confidence. Nearly a decade had passed since my last visit with her. I wasn't a teenager torn apart by witnessing the death of two people I loved deeply. I wasn't the girl who shouldn't have had to endure a therapist staring out the window or sharing her personal problems when she should have been listening—not to mention the arguments I'd witnessed between Alder and her ex-husband. I wasn't the high school senior who had finally escaped from therapy by convincing my mom that Alder had *cured* me of my grief.

I pasted on a smile and shifted into play-acting mode. "It's great to see you. I was so excited to hear you were doing well." I motioned at Kala. "This is my friend, Kala. She wanted to talk to you about her great-grandmother."

Kala smiled, so genuinely it could've fooled even me. "We're looking for a group program—something to lift her spirits."

"You've come to the right place," Alder said, but her flat tone made me wonder if she was already suspicious.

Kala craned her neck, peering around Alder and through the open doorway behind her. She quieted her voice as if to keep the conversation from traveling beyond our circle, "I'm so glad we came while a session's going on. It does look like what I was hoping for. Do you mind if I sneak in and take a peek at what they're working on?"

Alder's smile wavered. "We have a policy—"

I jumped in and took over the sales pitch. "We brought some costume jewelry and other things we thought your clients could use." I motioned at Kala's boxes. "I've never forgotten the memory box you had me make. It helped so much."

Kala opened the lid on the top box and angled it so Alder could see inside. She gave it a shake, like an auctioneer tempting the audience with an item up for bid. "You do such important work for your clients and their families," she said.

The corners of Alder's lips twitched. "It's not much, but we try."

I bit down on my own smile. Kala was playing this just right. There was nothing Alder loved more than flattery, except maybe money and sharing her woes.

Kala held the boxes out toward Alder. "I'd say you do a lot more than try."

Alder hesitated, then took them. "We don't usually allow people in during sessions. But technically this isn't a closed group. I'm sure they'd love to show you what they're working on."

As Kala and I had preplanned, I hung back while she and Alder went inside first. My box wasn't for general use. It was just for Erik.

I walked forward, far enough that I could see the entire room. But Erik—or at least the tall guy I assumed might be him—wasn't anywhere to be seen. Which made no sense. It wasn't like Alder would let him wander around the building during his session. Unless, perhaps, he'd gone to the bathroom.

I tapped Alder on the shoulder. "Do you have a restroom I could use?"

"They're down the corridor near the end on the right-hand side," she said.

Box in hand, I headed back into the corridor. When I'd been in therapy, Alder had always let me take off when I needed a bathroom break. Truthfully, I'd abused those moments of freedom, dawdling to use up as much of my assigned therapy time as possible.

I glanced into the rooms on either side of the corridor as I walked toward the restrooms. There were couches and chairs, coffeepots, and all kinds of stuff in the rooms, but no people. When I reached the bathrooms, I discovered two, single occupancy, side by side. I checked the first one. It was unlocked and vacant. Same for the second.

Frustrated, I blew out a breath and turned away. The door to the room across the corridor was closed, but through its window I could see what appeared to be a table haphazardly draped with a plastic drop cloth. A paint tray and brush sat on top of it, along with a stack of newspapers. It looked like someone was preparing to repaint the room's walls, but maybe, if I was lucky . . .

Crossing my fingers, I tiptoed across the corridor. As I neared the door, I could see an easel off to one side. A square canvas striped with red and black paint sat on it.

A flutter of excitement came to life in my belly. *Please, let this be what I think it is.* The beginning of a collage. I could only hope.

I leaned close to the window, checking to see if anyone was inside. Finding it empty, I eased the door open and hurried to the piece. The canvas was a sheet of somewhat thin board. A base layer of newspaper had been applied, then overlayed with rough strokes of black and red paint and some gray as well. Here and there, the paint had been wiped off, allowing words from the newspaper to bleed through. Lines sketched with a pencil foreshadowed a person and a building that would eventually appear after the addition of more layers. It wasn't the work of an average person. It was too precise, yet free-form and naturally balanced at the same time.

I stepped back, tilting my head, studying it. I closed my eyes and brought up a mental image of the townscape. Beneath the buildings and people, below the bits of e-waste and jewelry and this and that, it seemed like the piece's initial layers had been newspaper and paint—just like this.

I set down my box of junk, took out my phone, and snapped a photo of the piece, and then another and another, careful to not rush like I had done at Anna's house. If this piece was nothing, the photos wouldn't matter. But if it was the foundation for a collage, documenting it would be a huge help when it came to comparing Erik and Vespa's work—that was, assuming Erik had made this. I still hadn't found him—or more correctly—the guy in the baseball cap that I hoped was him.

Satisfied I had enough good shots, I picked up the box and went back out to continue my search. There weren't any more rooms, so I walked to the glass doors at the end of the corridor. They didn't automatically open as I approached. However, when I pressed the latch, they did, letting a wave of sweltering air bully its way inside.

I stepped out onto a deck. Under its wide roof, an assortment of picnic tables sat in the shade, a good place to draw, using a pad of paper and markers. But it wouldn't work for someone creating intricate collages with gesso, paint, and tiny scraps of this and that.

Near where a vine-covered lattice walled in one side of the deck, a ramp led down onto the lawn. From there, a worn path went to a shed up close to a cinderblock garage. The shed was the sort of building where lawnmowers and garden tools might have been stored, except in this case a tarp-covered lawnmower sat beside it. A she shed? An artist's studio?

I looked over my shoulder, to make sure no one was watching from the corridor. It wasn't like Kala could distract Alder forever. Eventually, my prolonged absence was bound to be noticed.

Leaving the deck behind, I jogged down the ramp to the shed. Though I could see a sliver of the parking lot and even part of the bus, it was surprising how secluded the spot felt, distant even from the whir of traffic on the road and the buzz of people at the ice-cream parlor.

I rapped lightly on the shed door.

A sparrow fluttered up from the building's drip edge, but no sounds came from inside.

I took a breath, rapped again, then called out, "Hello? Anybody in there?"

Nothing. Not even a bird this time.

Holding the box with one hand, I wiped a dribble of sweat from my temple. If someone was watching from Alder's building, they'd probably think I needed a good head shrinking myself, knocking on an empty shed, talking to Mr. Nobody.

I reached for the shed's latch—

A man's voice boomed behind me. "Lookin' for someone?"

Chapter Fourteen

I wheeled around. A tall, bulky man was stomping toward me. His eyes were dark and pinched, his face weathered and pitted with acne scars. One cheekbone was slightly concave. He wore a stained sleeveless T-shirt and low-riding sweatpants. I guessed he was around forty. It was hard to be sure. But he had on a black baseball cap, and his arms and hands were heavily tattooed and as splattered with paint as his work boots. Behind him, the side door into the garage was now open. I could make out a table cluttered with jars of paint, hand rollers, and other tools of the collage-making trade. There was a box full of rags. A pile of old newspapers.

His eyes narrowed even further. "Didn't you hear me?"

I blinked at him. Emotionally unpredictable, Janet had said. Shane warned me to be careful. Take things slow. Talk quietly. Give him time to answer. Err on the side of caution and don't meet with him alone, a suggestion I now wished I'd followed.

Forcing back my fear, I locked my knees and met those hard eyes with a smile. "Are you Erik Volkov?"

He froze, then frowned. "Do I—I know you?" His stutter was unmissable, his accent slightly Russian.

"I'm Edie Brown. I'm—" I started to say I was a friend of Anna's but then thought better of it. I didn't need Anna discovering that I'd been here. I held out the box to him. "I brought something for your art."

He folded his arms across his chest. "Don't need anything."

"It's free. A gift." I nodded at the garage. If it was his workshop, there were likely to be more pieces in there. "Why don't we go inside. You can take a look. You might find something you like."

He glanced toward the deck and the main building, then eyed the box again. "Why give to me?"

"It's stuff I don't need." As he stepped closer and peered into the open box, I caught a whiff of garlic and onions, stale sweat. I sweetened my voice and tried a different tactic. "I saw the piece you were working on inside. It's amazing. I'd love to see what else you're working on. Seriously, I like art."

"Not art," he grumbled.

"Can I look? Just for a minute. Please?"

He stepped aside as if to invite me into the garage. All right, I knew he was just shifting his weight. But I pretended to read his movement wrong and rushed past him, through the doorway and into the garage, before he could stop me.

The place was built like a military bunker: concrete walls, no windows. Industrial lighting hung from the beams. There was a cot and some mismatched living room furniture. A fire extinguisher. A coffee maker. An apartment-size fridge. It wasn't as chilly as the main building, but it was cooler than the outdoors. Clearly there was an air conditioner somewhere. Most importantly, in the center of the garage bay closest to me, a collage the size of a picture window lay across a table made from plywood and sawhorses. Even from a distance, I could see the piece was far from finished. It was, however, as impossibly intricate as Anna's townscape and identical in many ways to the piece I'd seen inside.

My hands shook from excitement as I set my box down next to the jars of paint and hand rollers. On trembling legs, I walked around the pile of old newspapers and toward the piece.

BANG!

My heart jumped into my throat as the door slammed shut behind me.

I swung around. Erik stood between me and the windowless door. My eyes darted to his knuckles, as big and dark as black walnuts. The tattoos on his right hand spelled out the word *Death*. The letters on the left hand read: *C-m-e-p-tb*, perhaps Russian, I assumed.

Those darkened knuckles bent his enormous fingers into meaty fists.

A flash of the townscape filled my mind: A man standing in an alleyway near a puddle of blood. I felt myself go pale. Was Erik out here alone because it was safer than him working with everyone else?

I gulped a breath. *No*, it wasn't fair to assume things like that. Erik hadn't done anything to warrant my fear, at least not yet. I just needed to be cautious. Watch him closely.

Erik stomped over to where I'd left the box. As he looked at its contents, his fisted hands went reflexively behind his back, like a child in an antique store who's been told to look and not touch. Obedient. Curious. If anything, afraid and a bit withdrawn. Not someone out of control.

I steadied my voice. "Will any of those things work for you? I hope so."

"They are—great." He looked my way, hands now at his sides.

I smiled and took one step backward, then another, easing myself closer to the makeshift table and collage. I had to get a good look at it. Make sure it was as amazing—and Vespa-like—as my instincts were claiming. Better yet, I needed photos to study later.

Slowly, I turned to look directly at it. Brightness washed down from the overhead lights, glinting off ridges of paint and coils of plastic-coated wire. It highlighted pencil-sketched faces and strips of newspaper, slashes of paint, fast-food wrappers, jewelry . . . It was closer to being finished than the piece inside. Still, it had a ways to go.

I cocked my head, gaining a different perspective on the piece. It looked to me like it was going to be a cutaway of a three-story building—a glimpse into the tenants' lives. Even at this stage, it was awe inspiring, meticulous work by impossibly skilled hands—an artist in his own right, or perhaps he was unintentionally reproducing Vespa's works or copying her style, I still wasn't sure. It wasn't like I had a reference guide to all her work tucked away in my head. Plus, there was the matter of the townscape. If it was a reproduction of an unknown Vespa, then where had Erik seen it?

My heart beat faster. There were so many questions to ask and so little time. I had to make each one count. I looked away from the collage and at Erik. "Where do you get your ideas? From magazines? Art exhibits? The computer?"

He rubbed his lips, kneading them like they were scraps of cloth destined to become a detail in one of his works. He glanced over his shoulder at the closed door, then said, "Dr. Meadows."

I clenched my teeth, keeping my reaction to myself. Hearing her name shouldn't have come as a surprise, but it had in that moment. I took a breath, then spoke slowly, "Dr. Meadows shows you pictures of art?"

"No. I—" His accent became stronger as he struggled to speak. He rapped a knuckle against the side of his head. "I had accident. Dr. Meadows—uses art to help."

"You copy ideas from Pinterest?" That's where Alder had showed me photos of memory boxes. I'd previously wondered if that was where Eric might've seen Vespa's work, though it seemed like a Pin of the townscape was something Kala would have uncovered in her search.

"Not about what goes in," Erik said. "Making collage gets confusion—nightmares—out of my head. Therapy."

I nodded. I wasn't sure he'd totally understood my question, but I didn't want to frustrate him by asking the same thing again. "Do you sign your pieces?"

He frowned. "Why?"

"You have a 'V' in every piece. 'V' for Volkov—or Vespa?"

His lips clamped together like a vault sealed shut.

I gentled my tone. "It's okay if you do. My mother's an artist. Sometimes she uses other people's signatures." Dear God, I never dreamed I'd ever say that to anyone.

Sweat beaded on his forehead. He sidestepped toward the door as if to open it and invite me to leave. "I need to work now."

"Okay—" I glanced around, hoping to spot another collage. I hadn't even taken one photo. I had to buy more time. "Before I go, do you have any other pieces I could look at? I really like this one. Are there others here or inside, like in Dr. Meadow's office?"

He stared at me as if I'd asked the most nonsensical question in the world. "Why would there be? Healing is letting go. Moving on."

I remembered Alder telling me I needed to bury the memory box at the airstrip as a way of letting go and moving past the horror of witnessing my grandparents' death. That made sense. But Erik's pieces were different. His collages were real art. Besides—"But you gave one of them to your mother, right?"

"Mama's gone." His voice strained as he said it, deep and so full of sadness that the tone went straight to my heart.

I quieted my voice. It went against my previous plan to keep any connection to Anna a secret, but the truth felt right now. "Anna showed me the townscape you gave to your mom. It's beautiful. That's part of why I came. I wanted to meet the man who made it."

Erik's brow wrinkled. He rubbed it with a knuckle. "Alder says it's wrong. I make lots for therapy. For letting go. Not for giving—"

He went silent as a knock came at the door.

I held my breath, waiting to see what he would do. I needed more time. I needed the person at the door to go away. I needed Erik not to answer it.

He called out. "What do you want?"

The door brushed open. And Alder sashayed in.

Chapter Fifteen

Alder stood in the doorway, hand on a jutted hip as she glowered at me. "Your friend's ready to leave. She's waiting inside."

I looked at Erik. His head was bowed, gaze on the floor like a child guilty of defying a parent's rules. For a moment, I felt compelled to react the same way to her intrusion into our conversation, but instead I pulled my shoulders back and stepped toward her. "Sorry you had to come looking for me. I lost track of time."

"Let's go," she said. Her voice was level, but her face was pale.

I smiled at Erik. "It was nice to meet you." I needed to ask him more questions and get photos of the collage he was working on. But I didn't want to raise any red flags about why Kala and I had stopped by, and complying with Alder was most likely the only way back in.

Alder flagged her fingers at the doorway, indicating for me to leave first. I did as she asked, scurrying out of the garage and letting her herd me back the way I'd come. As I went up the ramp past the lattice half wall, Alder rushed ahead of me, then swiveled back and blocked my path.

"What in the name of God were you doing out there?" Her chest rose and fell as she took fast, sharp breaths. "Erik's a patient. He . . . he's easily disturbed."

"Ah . . . I was—" I struggled for a believable excuse. "It was too cold in the building. The air-conditioning. I went outside to warm up. Erik saw me. We started talking." I blinked as if confused by her panic, then risked stepping into client–patient privilege territory, her use of the word *disturbed* having brought back up the question of Erik's stability. "Are you saying he's dangerous?"

Her voice turned shrill. "That's none of your business." She puffed out another breath. "Tell your friend—Kala—she needs to find a different place to take her great-grandmother. I can't have her or you around here. You never were respectful to me, Edie Brown."

Heat prickled up my arms, but I wasn't about to let her bullying get to me. There was too much at stake, like finding out for sure if Erik was unintentionally replicating Vespa's work or if he was an undiscovered outsider artist who just happened to have a style similar to hers. There also was the huge question about what had happened to the other collages he'd made.

I dropped my gaze to my feet, faking submission. "I just wanted to bring you those boxes and help out Kala."

"I don't need your donations." Her voice lowered, just above a whisper. "I heard about your trouble—arrested for selling stolen property. Your mother's in prison for forgery. I don't need or want to be connected to people like you."

I clenched my teeth, holding back the urge to defend myself as I pushed past her and marched toward the automatic glass door. As it slid open, I glanced back and snapped, "Nice to see you again too, *Doctor*."

After all this time, Alder hadn't changed. Not one bit. And it seemed I hadn't either.

* * *

All the way home, I raged to Kala about my encounter with Alder and the manipulative stuff she'd tried to pull during our therapy sessions, about her self-absorption and her bickering with her ex. I might have even thrown in a thing or two about my mother's similar behavior, stuff I generally didn't share with anyone other than Tuck and Shane.

By the time we got home, I was overheated, sweaty, and grumpy.

Tuck stood at the counter, packing books for shipping, including the first edition *Finnegan's Wake*.

"You sold it?" I asked. The thought of 5K instantly vanquished my bad mood.

Tuck nodded. "You can say that again. I told O'Keeffe if he bought a few more, I'd personally deliver them to Ireland free of charge."

"Sounds like an excuse for a vacation to me," I said with a smile.

"You and Kala could come. We could write it off as a business expense." His tone became somber. "I showed him your grandfather's copy of James Connelly's *Labour in Irish History*. He offered five hundred for it. It's a fair price . . ."

As Tuck let his voice trail off, I gritted my teeth. I knew where this could lead, first one book and then another, then my grandma's sterling silver and the artwork off our living room walls. I'd told Tuck selling Grandpa's books was out of the question. I didn't want to do it. But I also couldn't afford to be stupid, not with the septic situation hanging over our heads. "Go ahead—sell it. It's not like the book's going to Felix Graham. Grandpa always liked O'Keeffe."

Tuck nodded, then frowned. "I assume by the looks on your faces when you walked in that your visit didn't go so well?"

A dull ache pressed inside my chest. "Good and bad." I told him about Erik's therapist being none other than Alder. Then I went into the part about Erik. "No matter what, I'd put Erik in the savant category—assuming Anna wasn't lying about him having no training in art before the brain injury. I'm still not sure if he's unintentionally replicating Vespa's work or if his pieces are only inspired by her style, or even just coincidentally reminiscent of hers."

"Sounds to me like you made lots of progress," Tuck said.

"That's what I tried to tell her." Kala wriggled in next to Tuck and swiped a peppermint from the bowl beside the cash register. "She's upset because Erik claims he creates them purely for therapy, then lets them go and moves on."

I clarified. "Erik said he doesn't keep any of them or give them away except for the townscape Anna has, which he freely admitted to making."

"Then we know the townscape's provenance for sure," Tuck said.

"Looks like it, but it doesn't make the situation any less screwy."

Tuck raised his eyebrows. "So then, what happened to the other pieces he made?"

"That's the million-dollar question," I said.

Kala unwrapped the mint and popped it into her mouth. "I could see Alder making Eric burn them in some kind of therapeutic ceremony, like a wicker man ritual for art. You didn't happen to see a firepit in the yard when you were back there?"

"No, thank goodness." My brain engaged, possibilities forming fast. I pulled up a stool and sat down across the counter from them. "Alder could be writing a research paper about creativity and traumatic brain injury. She could be stashing Erik's work so she can use it to support her study when the time comes." It made sense and it was less horrific than the thought of his collages being burnt. "Publishing a paper on something like that would be a major professional achievement for her. It would give her prestige and draw people to her business like crazy."

Tuck rubbed his freshly trimmed beard. "Have you considered that Alder might be taking his work and selling it as real Vespas?"

"We can't rule that out, but I don't think so."

Kala scoffed. "Why not? She could be brainwashing or hypnotizing Erik into making forgeries. There's this movie—*Get Out*—starring Daniel Kaluuya. He goes to visit his white girlfriend's family. Her mom's a therapist. She hypnotizes him. He gets totally messed up—"

I jumped in before she could sidetrack the conversation any further. "The brainwashing part might be true, but Alder's not capable of pulling off a forgery scam."

"What makes you so sure about that?" Kala asked.

"To pull off that kind of scam, someone needs to be skilled at boosting other people's egos to make them feel good about what they're buying. Alder's all about putting people down to build herself up. She'd make a better mark than a con artist."

Tuck slid a look my way. "Kind of like someone else we know?"

I nodded. He meant my mom. Self-absorbed. Easily victimized by flattery or belittling. Personality faults that made it easier for me to believe Mom was at least somewhat innocent of the forgery charge.

I reached across the counter, snagging a peppermint. The plastic crinkled as I unwrapped it. I couldn't undo the screwup I'd made by not asking Erik what happened to his pieces before Alder interrupted us, but that didn't mean I was done trying to unscramble what was going on—not by a long shot. My gut said someone was using Erik, and that wasn't right.

Still holding the unwrapped candy, I leveled my gaze on Tuck and Kala. "Tomorrow morning, I'm going to visit Anna, try to get another look at the townscape and snap new photos. If I can compare good images of it with the photos I took yesterday of Erik's work in progress, I'll have a solid foundation for doing a comparison when I go to the Vespa opening on Saturday. Then we'll have a better idea if Erik's replicating Vespa's collages or style, or if his art comes purely from his own head."

"Sounds like a solid plan," Tuck said.

I put the peppermint in my mouth, savoring the refreshing coolness as I built up courage to say the rest out loud. I knew it was a good idea, but even the thought of it left me cringing. I quieted my voice. "Before I do anything, I need to talk to Mom."

Tuck's eyebrows arched in surprise, but he kept his smile in check. I knew what he was thinking. He was delighted and astonished, and afraid to say the wrong thing. My feelings toward Mom had mellowed since I'd started considering she might've been set up. However, it didn't mean that everything between us was as warm and cuddly as a basketful of puppies.

Still, Mom's innocence or guilt or her personality weren't what was important right now. It was that she was a copyist by trade, forgery's legal kissing cousin. As such, she might have unconventional suggestions about what to look for when comparing Erik's and Vespa's work. It went against my grain, but it only made sense to ask her for advice.

* * *

"Edie, sweetheart," Mom said a few hours later when I answered her scheduled call from prison. "It's wonderful to hear your voice. Is Tuck out for the evening?"

"He's here too. I have something I want to talk to you about before he gets on." Normally, I'd let Tuck answer her calls, then he'd put the phone on speaker, and I'd say, "Hi." After that, I usually just listened in while the two of them talked.

"What is it, dear?" She sighed dramatically. "The powers that be turned down my request to paint a Monet-style garden on the walls of my cell. Can you believe it? It would make this place so much more bearable."

"I'm sure it would. By the way, do you remember Alder Scranton, the therapist you sent me to?"

"Of course. Such a nice, sensitive woman. You were a bit hard on her." She paused. "Did Alder ever get away from that awful ex-husband of hers?"

"I think so. She's going by a different last name now."

"That's good." She sighed, louder than before. "Can you believe they expect me to live surrounded by monochrome walls? It's bad enough that this place smells like disinfectant and body odor."

I pressed on. "Where did you first hear about Alder? How well did you know her?"

"That was a long time ago. Why?"

Tuck coughed into his hand, drawing my attention. He put a finger to his lips.

I nodded. *Yes. I know. Prison. Other ears listening.*

"She has a client and I'm thinking about buying some of his artwork." A simple, somewhat truthful reason seemed wiser than elaborating.

"I went to high school with her. Her family lived in Scandal Mountain at the time. As I remember, they moved to New York City not long after we graduated. I was jealous of that. But, at the time I had other responsibilities. As I recall, she had a gorgeous older brother. He was a senior when we were freshmen—"

"Mom, I don't care about her brother. It's Alder I'm interested in." I also wasn't interested in hearing for the millionth time how her fleeting teenage marriage and my appearance on the scene put the brakes on her dream of heading directly from high school to an art college in Paris.

"There really isn't much else," she said. "I ran into her at an art show not long after your grandparents' accident. I mentioned you were going through a rough stage. She'd opened a therapy office in Burlington. Why? Did something happen to her?"

"Not exactly. It's just . . . her client makes collages as part of his therapy, and I'm worried about the signature he uses. I think he may be unconsciously mimicking another artist and using the same initial. I don't want to buy something questionable." I said the last part for the benefit of any unseen party who might be privy to the conversation. Plus, it was true.

"That wouldn't be good," Mom said.

"Any thoughts on how I can figure out what's going on? His pieces are stunning."

"Did you check the back of the canvas? His full signature might be there in pencil. Move the piece around—natural light, artificial . . . sometimes pencil is hard to see. You could also simply ask the artist about his signature." She paused for a second. "Did you say 'initials' or 'initial,' like a single letter?"

"It's a single letter." I hoped she wouldn't ask which one. Telling her "V" would be a dead giveaway.

"Are you certain you're not seeing something other than a signature? When we're searching for a specific thing, our brains can play tricks on us—like by turning a sliver of moon into the letter 'C.'"

Heat washed up my neck. I'd seen a letter, not something else. "V's" on links of silver chain exactly like Vespa's trademark, upside down and right side up, always the same.

Mom went on, "A better approach is to forget about signatures. Instead, magnify the collages as much as possible. Compare the individual components. Are the brushstrokes confident or hesitant? What do the edges on the sections of paper look like—torn or neatly cut? Is there a sense of depth? Study the collages sideways and upside down. That will help trick your brain and make differences stand out." She was silent for a moment. "Don't forget the psychological aspects. Are there repeated dates, words, or numbers—letters besides the one you've been focused on? Do the collages' symbols and images match the artist's life story—or do they diverge?"

"Yeah, I may have kept my focus too narrow," I said. Maybe I knew most of what she'd shared from the time I'd spent

trailing my grandparents and from my classwork and internships. But she was right that I needed to worry less about the
"V" and spend more time studying other aspects of the pieces.

"Remember, if you look for a full signature on the back of
the piece and don't see one, it's possible Alder's client hasn't
added his signature to any of the pieces because he doesn't consider them finished or even works of art—or he could have been
planning on coming back to sign the pieces and just hasn't taken
the time to do it yet."

I closed my eyes and pinched the bridge of my nose. It was
impossible to miss that she was now referring to her own failed
legal defense: *Yes*, the painting in the trunk of her car was an
exact replica of Maxfield Parrish's *Afterglow*. *No*, she hadn't
intentionally created a forgery. *Yes*, she'd planned on adding her
own signature and marking the painting as a copy on the back.
She just hadn't done that at the point it was discovered.

"Mom?" I said, waving Tuck closer. Better to be done with
the conversation before she launched into a poor-me rant and we
nose-dived from amicable into argument. Mom might have
been set up for the forgery arrest, but that didn't mean she hadn't
been up to something when the trouble went down. I raised my
voice. "Tuck's dying to tell you about a book he sold today."

"Oh, of course." Her voice gentled. "I love you, Edie.
Remember, trust your instincts and your intuition."

"Thanks, Mom," I said, and I meant it.

Chapter Sixteen

The next morning, when Tuck and I pulled into Anna's driveway, I was surprised to find both of her garage doors open. Tables draped with white sheets lined one bay, their tops covered with knickknacks and tons of household items. Furniture and racks of clothes filled the other bay.

"Anna's been busy," Tuck said.

I grimaced. "Let's hope she hasn't already moved everything out there."

Our plan was to ask Anna if the 1947 copy of Peterson's *A Field Guide to the Birds* that Tuck had previously noticed was still available. He hadn't offered to buy it before because we already owned several better copies of the same book. Today, though, we hoped to use it as an excuse to get back into her mother's suite, where we could finagle a few new photos of the currently not-for-sale townscape.

Tuck craned forward, peering through the windshield. "I don't see any books in there. Do you?"

"I'm not sure." If the Peterson guide was out here instead of inside, we'd have to come up with a new excuse on the fly.

I pulled the Volvo up in front of the garage. As we got out, Anna emerged from the house's breezeway, carrying a cardboard box overflowing with used Christmas garlands. She smiled and cheerfully announced, "Almost finished."

"Looks great." I stepped into the garage, scanning to see what was there. Stacks of books covered a back table, most likely all the books from her mother's suite. *Damn it.*

Tuck took the box of garlands from Anna's hands and carried it into the first bay. "I'm surprised you got everything set up so quickly."

"My uncle and a cousin stopped by. They helped with most of it."

An image of circling vultures popped into my head. "Are you talking about your uncle who was interested in the Persian carpet?" I couldn't see the rug anywhere in the garage. If he hadn't taken it, then it would be the perfect thing to use as an excuse to get back inside. "Did he end up buying it?"

"His wife—Evita—was beside herself with excitement when she saw the carpet and the samovar lamp."

Tuck set the garland box on a table. "You had an older Peterson guide. I've regretted not offering to buy it. Is it still available?"

I did a double take. What the heck was he doing? Hadn't he noticed the stacks of books on the back table?

Anna's eyes brightened. "I put it aside with the other book you said was special. It's right over here." She edged into the maze of tables to where a half dozen books sat next to a metal cashbox. "I priced it exactly as you suggested."

I bit my tongue to keep from saying anything. Owning another Peterson wouldn't be the end of the earth, but we couldn't afford to spend money frivolously right now, especially if it wasn't going to get us inside.

While Tuck made his way over to check out the book, I skimmed the bays again, looking at what was there and trying to remember what had been in the suite. Tea sets. Ballerina figurines. Nesting dolls . . . even the old treadle sewing machine and worktable. Anna couldn't have possibly brought everything out already, or had she?

As I studied the table of books again, it came to me. Her uncle had taken the Persian carpet and lamp, but she hadn't mentioned the bookcase he'd had dibs on—ugly with newly replaced stained-glass panels. I shuddered. I really didn't want to spend money on it, but . . .

I swallowed my pride and walked over to where Tuck was counting ten-dollar bills into Anna's hand, then injected as much enthusiasm into my voice as I could muster and said, "Did your uncle decide to take the narrow bookcase too? The one with the stained-glass panels?"

If her eyes had brightened at the mention of the Peterson guide, they now beamed. "Evita didn't care for it, and I forgot to ask them to move it out here while I had their help. You're interested in it?"

The back of my throat pinched as I lied, "I found a spot in our store where it would be perfect for a display. I'd give you—"

"Three hundred dollars," Tuck said. No doubt he feared I'd lowball the offer, knowing how much I disliked the piece.

"That's more than generous." She glanced at the Volvo. "I'd prefer if you took it right now. Do you think it'll fit in your car?"

"No problem," I said. This was becoming an expensive facade. But apparently Tuck had become as convinced as I was that this whole thing could pay off big for us.

The pinching in the back of my throat tightened even more. What if Aunt Evita had fallen in love with the townscape, the way she had with the rug and lamp? Anna hated the collage. She might have asked Erik if it was okay to pass it on to a family member.

I dismissed that thought. The townscape was amazing to me, but it was large and not the sort of piece just anyone would hang on their wall. It would take a true connoisseur of contemporary and outsider art to want it, someone like Jimmy.

With that thought having relieved some of my tension, my steps lightened as we went up the walk and into the house. Without prompting from Anna, Tuck and I exchanged our shoes for slippers. Today, the black slip-on dress shoes were missing, and with them Anna's need to justify their presence. *"There's no one else here,"* she'd said the last time. *"Those belong to my brother. He comes over quite often for dinner, prefers them over slippers."*

But if Erik kept the slip-ons here to wear when he visited, then why were they gone today? There weren't any shoes by the door other than mine and Tuck's, so it seemed unlikely Erik or anyone other than Anna was in the house.

Mulling over the possibility that Anna could've been lying about the slip-ons, I trailed her and Tuck to the suite. As expected, it was all but empty now, only a few plastic totes and scattered items remaining. Anna led us to the bookcase. A handful of volumes lay on the bottom shelf.

Tuck opened the case's door. "I can't remember if I looked at these the last time. Do you mind if I take a minute to go through them again before we carry the bookcase out?"

"Take all the time you need," she said. "If there's anything you'd like, just speak up."

As Tuck took out the first book, opened it, and began to explain to Anna in detail the difference between first editions and first printings, I took advantage of not being in the limelight and padded to the nook where the townscape hung. I couldn't wait to lay my eyes on it again. It was such an amazing—

The wall was empty.

I stared, not wanting to believe it.

I swiveled toward Anna and Tuck, voice going taut. "What happened to the collage?"

Anna squinted at me. "Why?"

I backpaddled. "I was just wondering. Uh . . ." I offered a curated slice of the truth. "I studied folk art in college. I know you don't care for the piece, but I loved it. Your brother is amazingly talented."

"Aunt Evita likes it too."

My stomach dropped. "You gave it to her?"

Anna folded her arms across her chest. "Not yet. It's in the bedroom."

I pitched my voice lower. "I know your aunt's family. Family should come first, but . . ." I'd tipped my hand more than was wise, and my brain scrambled for some sort of truthful cover. "I was going to offer to hang it in our shop's gallery as part of a one-person show. We'd invite collectors to see it. Seriously, your brother could make a living with his art." At this point, the only thing I could do was pretend like I didn't have any reservations about the townscape being totally original. I had to stop Anna from giving it away or, at a minimum, slow down her decision long enough for us to finish researching.

She shook her head. "You don't understand. Art isn't a profession for Erik. It's a way to pass the time, that's all."

"Seriously, Anna. He has a special talent. It could change his life, and maybe even yours." My voice strained as I struggled to remain calm. "What he's creating is called outsider art—works made by people who live outside the mainframe of society and don't have formal training. Your brother wouldn't even have to come to the show if he didn't want to. We'd sell the piece for him."

"He doesn't need to get wrapped up in something like that. He's had enough disappointment and stress in his life."

I took a breath. "Could I at least take some more photos? The ones I took the other day didn't come out very good. I'd like to show the piece to a friend of mine who specializes in outsider art. Would that be okay?"

"I'm not sure . . ."

Tuck rested a hand on Anna's shoulder, his eyes twinkling as he turned on the charm. "You might as well humor Edie. Let her take the photos. She doesn't give up easily."

Anna's eyes went to the bedroom doorway, then to me. "All right. Honestly, I think my uncle hopes I'll refuse. I even heard him and Evita arguing about it when they thought I was out of earshot." Her voice turned firm. "Take your photos, but no more talk about shows or artistic savants. My brother doesn't need to get dragged into something like that."

"I understand," I said, though I wanted desperately to keep arguing in favor of her at least keeping the piece. "Thank you, Anna."

I turned on my heel and hurried into the bedroom. The townscape was propped up against a wall near the bed. I pulled open the drapes, revealing a sliding glass door that went out onto a small terrace. The light it provided was perfect, bright but diffused. Now I just had to focus on the mechanics of taking good photos and not allow myself to get distracted enjoying the piece—which wasn't easy with every neuron in my body prickling and tingling from the joy of just being close to it again.

First I took a series of shots from across the room with the overhead light on, then without it. I moved closer, snapping photos every few steps. As the images of people and the street vanished, and the collage's components became visible, my hands began to tremble from excitement. I decided to find something to use as a tripod. I found a box—hassock size, duct-taped shut and labeled *Field and Stream*. It was sturdy and heavy, exactly what I needed, though it was odd that I didn't recall seeing it the last time I was in the room.

Once I'd pulled the box into position, I set the camara on top and began to photograph the townscape in sections, moving left to right, concentrating solely on the layered construction of the piece.

Satisfied that I had enough photos, I put my phone away and knelt closer, scouring for dates, letters, words, or numbers that stood out, just like Jimmy and Mom had suggested.

I sat back on my heels, giving myself slightly more distance as I let my mind take in the shapes and lines and colors, the depth, the composition. Puddles. Slashes of paint. Ragged stripes. E-waste. Food wrappers. Jewelry. Doll eyes . . .

The world around me fell away as I searched for subtle and involuntary artistic fingerprints, personal quirks my mother continuously worked to overcome in her career as a copyist: brushstrokes, smears . . . things I knew about as well as the ones she'd mentioned in our phone call, elements I could commit to memory that might mark Erik's hand and distinguish his work from Vespa's.

I brought to mind the unfinished collages I'd seen in the empty room and the garage at Alder's Well-Being Center. Stunning work. Impossibly intricate and meticulous. *Artistic savant* was the term Anna'd just used—

I snapped from my focus.

Artistic savant?

I'd never mentioned the possibility of Erik being a savant to Anna. When Tuck and I had visited the last time, she'd referred to his collages as a *craft*, as matter-of-factly as if he were using store-bought kits to decoupage sunflowers onto welcome signs.

"Well, well, well," I said under my breath. If it wasn't Tuck or me, then at some point since our last visit, Anna had talked to someone about Erik and his artwork, someone she believed and trusted. Someone from Checkerberry Manor—or Alder, perhaps? Or the person who wore the black slip-ons, assuming they weren't Erik's. Maybe the uncle or Aunt Evita? Someone experienced enough with art to recognize the brilliance of the townscape.

With that thought whirring in my head, I studied the townscape again, and a tiny detail jumped out at me from the window of a laundromat. *A date.*

June 1

I got out my jeweler's loupe to make sure I wasn't mistaken. The date was on a torn piece of newspaper. The paper had been painted over with white and then only *June 1* was wiped clean. Faint traces of the newspaper's other words and numbers remained, ghosts beneath the paint.

June 1. On a laundromat window, but not part of a "Closed for Vacation" sign or anything that made sense within the scene. Just a miniscule detail standing alone in a collage awash with images and letters.

I shivered. When I'd made my memory box, I'd included a scrap of paper with *July 10th* written on it—the date my grandparents' plane crashed. In less than a week, it would be ten years since that day. It seemed impossible that so much time had elapsed. It also seemed impossible that *June 1* didn't hold some special meaning for Erik, especially if it didn't have meaning within the context of the collage.

Was it the day he'd come home to visit Anna and been hit by a car? Kala had failed to dig up any mention of the accident online, but now it seemed that finding a date might make a difference.

That was, assuming Erik wasn't replicating a Vespa.

Chapter Seventeen

S hane called just before suppertime and asked if I wanted to
have dinner with him at the Jumping Café. I was all for that,
and not surprised when I arrived to find the place even busier
than usual. After all, it was Friday night and the beginning of
the long Fourth of July weekend.

My stomach grumbled at the mouthwatering smell of pizza
and burgers as I wriggled past the line of people waiting to be
seated in the café's restaurant. When I got to the pub side, where
we'd agreed to meet, I went up on my tiptoes, looking over the
sea of people in hopes of spotting Shane.

Pinky and Jack were tending bar. With his ready jokes and
rainbow unicorn T-shirts, Jack was generally a lot of fun, though
he was the guy who'd declared Kala's ID fake. Tonight, he was
busy pouring pitchers of beer for the waitresses. Pinky was mixing drinks six at a time. Perhaps she was a savant too, at least
when it came to creating drinks on the fly and keeping her finger
on the pulse of the community.

She handed something in a martini glass to a familiar man
sitting at the bar—Felix Graham. Our land grabbing—and currently particularly troubling—neighbor, René St. Marie sat on

the stool next to him. I clenched my teeth. Two slippery eels chumming it up at my favorite pub.

Out of the corner of my eye, I spotted Shane, waving at me from a booth near the restrooms.

I made my way over and slid in across from him. "How did you manage to score a booth? It's crazy busy." The only bad thing about the Jumping Café was their no-reservation policy.

"You've got Pinky to thank for that." He lowered his voice. "I'm not sure I like her doing favors for me."

I laughed. "Did she ask if you were meeting me?"

"As a matter of fact, she did. Why?"

"Don't worry. She's not looking for future police favors. It's me she's cozying up to. Actually, her long-term goal is to get Kala in her debt."

"Romance?" He picked up the pitcher of beer in front of him and nodded to the empty glass by my place setting. "Want some?"

"Sure. And before you ask—*yes* to pizza. I'm starving." I glanced to make sure Pinky was still behind the bar, then added, "As far as the romance goes, Pinky's hot to trot, and Kala's resisting at this point."

"I can't imagine Pinky taking 'no' for an answer," he said.

"Well, she's going to have to get used to it or try a different approach when it comes to Kala." The beer glass cooled my fingers as I took a sip.

Shane rested back in his seat, looking at me intently. "Did you talk to Erik Volkov?"

"Not for as long as I'd wanted, but I did get some new photos." I took out my phone and brought up the file where I'd collected the various images of collages, then handed it to him. "The unfinished piece is something Erik's working on. There are new photos of the townscape. I'm all but certain Erik made it. Also, there are some photos Jimmy sent me of Vespa's artwork in Sterling's New York gallery."

I sipped my beer while Shane studied the photos, swiping from one image to the next and back again. "I'm not sure I have this right. Which ones were made by Vespa?"

He held out the phone, and I showed him which images Jimmy had sent. "Pretty similar, huh?"

"Most definitely. They're damn creepy too."

"Yeah, hyperrealistic. My mom and Jimmy suggested I look for reoccurring details, symbols . . . stuff like that. I spotted *June 1* in the townscape on a laundromat window. I think it's significant. Maybe the date of Erik's accident." All right, I'd told Kala earlier that the last thing I wanted to do was ask Shane to dig up accident records for us. I still wasn't about to do that, but it didn't mean I couldn't approach the question indirectly.

"What do you know about Anna's family?" Shane asked.

Surprised that he'd skipped right past my mention of the date, I replayed his question in my mind. His tone seemed almost too smooth. Was he hiding something from me, or was it my imagination? I squinted at him. "She and Erik grew up in Shelburne, Vermont. They're Russian. At least, Anna told me her mother was from there, and her father was in the import business. Why? What are you thinking?"

"Just curious." He stopped talking, massaged his devil tattoo, then switched the subject again to how hungry he was as the waiter arrived to take our order. We decided to split the Friday night special, Moonlight in Vermont pizza: local sausage and cheeses with caramelized onion crescents and wild mushrooms.

When the waiter left, I shrugged off my unfounded suspicion and shifted to something I was dying to get Shane's reaction to. "I discovered something else when I went to see Erik—a weird coincidence."

Shane went still. "Something bad?"

"The expressive art facilitator that Erik goes to?"

He nodded. "Yeah?"

"You remember me bitching about the therapist I went to after my grandparents died?"

His eyes widened. "Are you saying they're one and the same?"

"You got it. The one and only Alder Scranton."

He frowned, thought for a second. "You didn't realize who she was when you made arrangements to look in on Erik's session?"

I looked down at my beer, bubbles rising around the edge of the glass. I took a long sip, buying a moment to come up with a benign answer. The trouble with fibbing is that it most often calls for more fibs later on. I wiped the corners of my mouth, then said, "I didn't make the arrangements. Kala did. Alder also goes by a different last name now—that was the real fooler . . ." I kept going, breezing past the fact that neither Kala nor I had really called ahead, then on to a CliffsNotes (and partly made-up) version of my looking in on the session. I totally skipped the part about Alder finding me in the garage and the nasty after-party that proceeded. Once again, that would've exposed my initial fib.

"It must have been hard seeing Alder again." He reached out and squeezed my hand. "You had some legitimate beefs with that woman."

"You're not kidding." I spoke faster now, relieved to be past the lying and eager to discuss other aspects. "That wasn't the only part of the visit that bothered me."

His hand withdrew. "What else happened?"

"Erik claims all his finished collages are gone except for the townscape."

"Gone? Where? What do you mean?"

"I don't know. He says he makes them purely for therapy. I'm worried they might've been destroyed as part of some cathartic ceremony. You know, releasing the past by burying them or burning them."

"All of them? You don't think he even kept a few favorites?"

"Not according to him," I said.

"And you're a hundred percent certain he created the townscape?"

"Erik says he did. I don't think he's lying. I mean, I all but saw him working on a similar piece." I shrugged. "There are other possibilities too. Maybe Alder's keeping them—"

I stopped talking as the pungent odor of a familiar aftershave wafted our way. I glanced in the direction of the smell. Felix Graham was talking to people in a booth a few yards away. He noticed me looking, said a quick goodbye, and came over to us.

His salt and pepper hair was recently cut and freshly moussed. One too many buttons of his shirt were undone, exposing a swatch of graying chest hair and gold chain. His gaze went to Shane. "Nice to see you're getting some time off before the busy weekend."

"I imagine it'll be a busy one at your shop as well," Shane said.

"Should be. Saturday, we're being featured on the *Morning Show*. A live remote about diversity and Independence Day as reflected in folk art—weathervanes, quilts, paintings . . . We're revealing some newly discovered masterpieces."

"Sounds wonderful," I said. Okay, I was jealous. But I'd been featured on the same TV show last month, so I couldn't begrudge him that much.

His thin lips curved into a snakelike smile. "Janet tells me you paid Anna Gorin a visit. Did you find anything interesting?"

My breath stalled. Damn it. Why couldn't Janet have kept it to herself for at least a few more days? I shifted in my seat, faked a smile. "We bought a little of this and that. A nice Peterson guide, a piece of art . . ." I let my voice trail off, then took a slow sip of beer and watched for his reaction to the last item.

A twitch at the corner of his eye told me the mention of art had caught his attention, though his scoffing tone denied it. "I hear bird books and paint-by-numbers are all the rage on eBay nowadays," he said.

Heat flashed up my neck and arms. I gritted my teeth and kept my smile in place. "It's an oil painting," I said placidly. "Russian. Madonna and Child. Not that valuable, but sellable."

"Well, isn't that nice. Goodie for you." He looked over his shoulder as the waiter walked up from behind him with our pizza. "I guess this is my cue to leave you two alone."

"Say 'hi' to René for me," I said, to make it clear I was aware he was seated with our neighbor.

He smiled. "Will do."

Once he and the waiter were out of earshot, Shane refilled my beer glass. "If I didn't like Graham before, I like him less now. He's one smug piece of work."

"Just be glad René wasn't with him."

Shane's voice softened. "You're still planning on going to Manchester tomorrow?"

"Yeah, to the Sterling Gallery with Jimmy. Why?"

He shrugged, totally casual. "Just promise me you'll be careful."

My mind went back to earlier when I'd questioned whether his nonchalance was fake or not. Maybe it wasn't my imagination. He had told me to be careful the other evening before I'd even gone to the Well-Being Center. "What are you worried about?"

"Humor me, and promise you'll tell me everything when you get back, about the art, who was at the show . . . the whole nine yards."

"Sure," I said. I hated not wholly trusting Shane, but my intuition screamed he was keeping something to himself. Maybe I was wrong. Perhaps it was as simple as his protective nature working overtime. Still, I'd experienced firsthand how perceptive he could be back when he was my probation officer. Last month, I'd seen him in his role as a state police detective from the opposite side of an interrogation table. His current masked expression and self-contained posture reminded me of those occasions. And like then, I was keeping things from him now as well. I looked directly in his eyes. "Do you know something I don't?"

He cleared his throat. "No—not at all. I just don't want to see you get mixed up in something again."

I narrowed my eyes. "Tell me what's going on."

"I have a feeling."

"Gut feeling?"

He nodded, but I didn't believe it was that simple.

He was definitely withholding something.

Chapter Eighteen

Manchester was the quintessential Vermont tourist town, beautiful mountains and stately homes mingled with outdoor sports, galleries, and trendy shops. As I crept toward the center of town, along with the bumper-to-bumper holiday traffic, I couldn't help but feel a pang of sympathy for Jimmy. My frustratingly slow drive down from northern Vermont was undoubtedly faster than his trip up yesterday on the busier roads from New York City.

When I reached the center of town, the traffic became even more restrictive. A hodgepodge of tents and canopies crowded a small parking lot on the right-hand side of the road, a street fair of some sort. A band was set up on the sidewalk. People rushed in and out of stores. Despite the congestion, the energy of all the activity lessened my frustration and filled me with a renewed sense of exhilaration. It was nearly six thirty, early evening, and a half hour after I'd promised to meet Jimmy at the gallery, but I was almost there. Soon I'd be able to judge firsthand whether Erik was replicating Vespa pieces or her style, or if his work was just reminiscent of hers.

I drove through an intersection, past a historic building with a mansard roof that held an impressive-looking bookstore. Not long after that, the Sterling Gallery sign came into view, set at the end of a driveway skirted by lawns and clumps of statuesque birches, shadowed by mountains and foreboding storm clouds.

I followed a Mercedes with New York plates down the drive and around a sharp bend. Ahead, I spotted the gallery building. It resembled a classic Vermont barn, except it had windows the shape of skyscrapers, terraced walkways, and an enormous portico created from jutting steel.

Not far from the portico, Jimmy's silver Porsche was backed into a parking space. He half sat on the hood, with his legs crossed at the ankles, as if posing for the cover of *GQ* magazine's best-dressed issue—cornflower blue slacks and jacket, blond hair carefully tousled, trademark huarache sandals. If I hadn't known Jimmy was still mourning his partner who'd died a few years ago, I'd have found it hard to believe he was single, let alone not attracting a flock of eager men right there in the parking lot.

I pulled into the space next to him and got out. "Sorry I'm late."

"Don't worry about it, darling." He gave me a hug and a kiss on each cheek, then stepped back and swept an approving look over my outfit: a black sheath dress worn with modest heels and a Navajo squash blossom necklace I'd inherited from my grandma, sterling silver with turquoise. "You look magnificent," he said. He rested a hand on my upper arm. "Tell me, have you learned anything more about the townscape?"

"Did you get the new set of photos I sent you?" I asked. *Vespa didn't make the townscape,* I wanted to say. I'd tell him eventually, after I was certain what was going on, and after I had a contract with Erik to introduce his work to the world at our gallery. That was, if Erik was creating the collages from his own imagination.

Jimmy's hand moved to the small of my back, steering me toward the portico. "Of course, I got the photos I was wondering about more recently. Did you find out anything else about the artist? What's his name?"

"Nothing new yet, unfortunately."

Jimmy sighed, disappointed. I suspected it was as much over me avoiding his last question as the lack of new information. "We can talk more after the show. I'm dying to hear what you think. I'm not joking, Edie, the townscape looks like a Vespa to me."

In front of us, other guests funneled toward the gallery's entry, mostly older couples dressed to the nines or in sporty Orvis casual. A family group who appeared to be Japanese stopped to take photos in front of a stone urn brimming with plum dahlias and silvery sedum. There were younger and artsier people mixed in, colorful hair, baggy A-line dresses, graphic T-shirts, and artfully ripped jeans.

As we reached the portico, Jimmy slowed his steps and whispered, "See the woman going inside right now? Jet-black hair. Metallic gown."

I looked toward the doorway. My best guess was that she was somewhere around sixty. She lifted her chin and strutted inside like a sparkly flamingo on a Fashion Week runway. Everything about her said, *"I'm here—feel free to kiss my rings."* A slightly older man walked beside her. He reminded me of a digital pet portrait I'd seen of a bulldog in a tuxedo, titled the *Dogfather*, a parody of the movie *The Godfather*.

"She's a major contemporary art collector," Jimmy went on. "I've run into her at New York openings before."

"Her husband doesn't look thrilled to be here," I said.

"Don't let looks fool you. He's as much of a collector as she is. Rumor has it, he and his son are heavily involved with the

NFT art market. We're talking double-digit millions. Buying and selling."

"They won't get any competition from me," I said, and not just because that level of buying was way out of my league. NFTs—nonfungible tokens—were a digital art form that didn't do a lot for me, despite Christie's and other auction houses I admired jumping on the bandwagon. NFTs were also reputed to be heavily connected to money laundering. Maybe my Dogfather impression wasn't far from the truth.

He nodded in their direction again. "The son's there right behind them."

I eyed the forty-something guy trailing along, a compact bull of a man, thick limbed with no neck, an oversized watch, and a bulky chain necklace. He looked more like a bodyguard than a family member, following in his parents' wake.

Jimmy took his hand from my back. "I don't think they care about the art at all. It's about bragging rights and investments, being seen as high society."

"It's the same with certain people and antiques," I said.

As we stepped through the doorway, we were greeted by a bone-thin woman in white chiffon. She checked Jimmy's name against a list, then let us move on, through the entryway and into the gallery's towering front room.

Light poured down from the beams above, spotlighting individual people as the crowd wandered deeper into the building. To our left, the crackle of electricity and flashes of glare came from a wall comprised of vintage TV screens. On one screen, a weeping woman held a winking baby. On another, a psychedelic QR code exploded into a sandwich that hemorrhaged fifty-dollar bills and droplets of blood. My mind went to the photos of

Vespa's work Jimmy had sent me. I'd seen the same sandwich in the beach scene. No surprise that Vespa had embraced crypto art. It fit with her style, and there were millions of dollars to be made. Plus, there were a limited number of collages even someone at her level could physically create. Not that I was an expert, but it seemed to me, one every couple of months would be a lot.

Still—I scowled at the digital art—it was a bit disappointing to see NFTs had infiltrated the Vermont gallery scene. It felt gimmicky, a money grab that took away from the gallery's classiness, though I suspected Kala would have loved it, TV screens and all.

The Dogfather and his no-neck son stationed themselves in front of the bleeding sandwich, blocking my view. I elbowed Jimmy and nodded at them.

He smirked. "Told you."

Somewhere deep within the building, the pulse of electronic music started up, throbbing hard enough that I could feel it through my shoes. As we joined the flow of guests heading toward the sound, a waiter offered us flutes of champagne. I took one, swirling the glass and breathing in its spiced pear scent before taking a sip. The flavor ranked with the best I'd ever tasted.

On either side, the walls drew close together, forming a short tunnel that undoubtedly led to the exhibit rooms. The wall to our left was decorated with an enormous black and white image of Grandma Moses, taken in the 1940s: a tiny woman in a pinafore apron and below-the-knee dark dress, white hair coiled into a gentle bun. Like her artwork, Grandma Moses was the epitome of rural quaintness.

On the wall opposite Grandma Moses was an equally immense colored photo of a petite older woman with Dolly Parton hair and large dark-framed glasses. A bright, hornet-yellow top snugged her oddly conical breasts. Yoga pants sheathed her birdlike legs. The placard next to her photo read: "Vespa: Grandma Moses for the Twenty-First Century."

I couldn't help smiling. The comparison was that perfect. Two small, mischievous-looking women, self-taught artists who had launched successful careers in their senior years. Two women whose art depicted rural and small-town life. Quite often, Moses used what she had on hand to create her works—leftover canvases, matchsticks, and pins to paint tiny details; glitter when she wanted to make snow sparkle. Likewise, Vespa's collages were a mixture of ready materials—the junk jewelry, fast-food wrappers . . . But beyond that point, their art transformed into mirror opposites. Moses painted direct and vivid but innocent versions of life in the early twentieth century, whereas Vespa's collages dove into the dark underbelly of twenty-first-century life with unabashed and horrific frankness.

I bent closer to Jimmy. "You know, I never thought about it before, but this is the first time I've seen a clear picture of Vespa's face. She's usually shadowed or turned away from the camara."

"That's part of her mystique," he said. He lifted an eyebrow. "You do know why she's called Vespa, right?"

"She's Italian like the Vespa scooters?"

He laughed. "Half right. *Vespa* means 'wasp' in Italian."

I looked at the photograph again. Big glasses. Large chest and narrow waist. Black and yellow clothes. I smiled. I could see it now. Plus, her collages did have a sting to them, especially compared to Grandma Moses's work.

Jimmy took me by the arm. "Before we do anything else, I want to introduce you to Sterling—the gallery's owner." His voice hushed. "Never hurts to make connections."

"That would be great." I'd been so focused on the chance to see Vespa's artwork, I hadn't stopped to consider the other benefits that could come from the visit. Jimmy was right: networking was vital in the arts and antique world, and the payoff could be huge.

As Jimmy towed me through the milling guests, I caught glimpses of Vespa's pieces, enormous, ominous, and especially startling against the gallery's stark white walls. Not just collages, but also a handful of small oil paintings that reminded me composition-wise of Celine St. Marie's encaustic angels. Only Vespa's oils were smaller, and the figures were common people—grim, tortured souls.

Jimmy located Sterling standing in front of a wall-sized collage and surrounded by a group of fawning patrons. He was about Jimmy's age, with chiseled features and a white jacket over a Banksy street-art T-shirt.

I whispered, "He's really handsome."

Jimmy nodded. "Sexy as hell—and married to a woman. Six children. Two cats. One dog."

"I'm surprised."

"You're not the only one." He sighed. "He's a fabulous promoter, from what I hear. Artists do almost anything to sign with him."

Sterling fluttered a hand at us as we approached. "Jimmy, glad you could make it."

Jimmy whisked me over. "I have someone I'd like you to meet. This is Edie Brown. She's from up north—near Burlington. Her family's been in the arts and antique business for generations—Scandal Mountain Fine Arts and Antiques."

His eyes widened, and the smile vanished from his face. "Brown?"

I froze. My mom. Maybe he'd heard about the forgery charge. Except Mom went by Tuckerman, her maiden name. Still, articles about her arrest had mentioned our shop. I straightened my spine. "I worked at Christie's for a while. Perhaps we met there?"

"That might be it." His smile returned. "Either way, any friend of Jimmy Zaninelli's is a friend of mine. Please, if there's anything I can ever do for you, call and ask for me."

My worry mostly subsided, though a pinprick of uneasiness made me replay his previous reaction. No question about it, he'd looked surprised to hear my name. But perhaps I was making a mountain out of a molehill.

Putting that train of thought aside for the moment, I smiled. "Thank you so much. I have more of an interest in contemporary art than my family has had before. Particularly folk and outsider art. I'm a huge fan of Vespa."

"Then, you're in for a treat. Vespa herself is here with us this evening."

"In person?" I glanced at Jimmy, my mouth falling open. I hadn't expected this. If nothing else, it totally eliminated the far-fetched idea Tuck had suggested when we were leaving Anna's for the first time. Namely, that Erik might literally *be* Vespa. I mean, photos could be faked, but a live appearance was a whole 'nother story.

"I had no idea she'd be here," Jimmy said.

Sterling preened, a hand flicking his sleeve as if to remove a bit of lint. "Here at Sterling Gallery, we enjoy surprising our patrons." He looked past us toward where a microphone stood on a stylish dais. "Speaking of which, I need to find my assistant. We're going to begin any second."

"It was great to meet you," I said. He fluttered his fingers, then swished off toward the dais, his most devoted fans trailing behind. I stepped nearer to Jimmy. "Did you notice how he reacted to my name?"

"Brown isn't exactly uncommon. He probably thought you were someone else."

"I guess," I said, though my gut wouldn't wholly let go of it.

I glanced at the Vespa piece Sterling had been standing under, now totally abandoned. Though it was a collage and not a painting, it reminded me of Edward Hopper's *Nighthawks*: late night, people sitting behind the window of a starkly lit restaurant. Only in this piece, the restaurant was a bar, and the street in the foreground wasn't deserted. Two drunk men were lurching into a black sedan. To one side, in an alleyway, a woman sprawled beside a dumpster. Blood pooled around her head. It was ghastly and mesmerizing—and unnervingly reminiscent of the bloody puddle in the townscape.

I stepped closer, looked deeper into the collage's image. Along with the woman, a man stood in the alley, his back turned to the scene. Hands fisted at his sides.

Two steps nearer and the scene vanished entirely as the collage's components revealed themselves. E-waste. Jewelry. Food wrappers. Pieces of chain and doll eyes overtop torn photos and newspaper. Familiar brushstrokes and slashes of paint. I didn't have to look for the "V." It was all there. Identical to what I'd seen in Erik's unfinished pieces and the townscape.

As my eyes scoured the piece for more connections, they homed in on a small date painted on the bar's plate-glass window: *June 1.*

For a second, I could only stare in stunned disbelief. Then I quickly snapped a few discrete photos. *Dear God. What the heck was going on?*

150

A woman's voice came through the microphone, silencing the gallery. "Attention everyone. If you'll all gather round, we'll get this very special evening started."

Jimmy rested a hand on the back of my shoulder, nudging me in the direction of the dais. "We should go over."

"Yeah. Of course," I mumbled.

As numb as if I were on auto pilot, I let Jimmy steer me to where the other guests were gathering. I didn't dare say anything to him about the indisputable similarity. I couldn't risk him revealing what I'd found until I knew for certain what was taking place. The piece I'd just looked at appeared to be made by Erik. Or was Erik's ability to copy Vespa's style just that good? Still, being an artistic savant didn't explain how he'd acquired such advanced-level skills when it came to using the tools and methods of collage making, physical techniques that were also identical to Vespa's.

A woman walked across the dais—Sterling's assistant, I presumed. She tapped her fingernail against the microphone, then her voice rose again. "Welcome to Sterling Gallery's celebration of Vespa—the Grandma Moses of the Twenty-First Century." She gestured to where Sterling waited at the back of the platform. "At this time, it's my pleasure to introduce you all to the first of our honored guests this evening, the eminent Sterling Meadows."

Meadows?

My body went cold as his last name echoed loud as a foghorn in my head. *Meadows.* Alder Meadows had gone back to her maiden name after getting divorced, just like my mom had done. *Sterling Meadows. Alder Meadows.*

I took a step backward, then another, edging away from Jimmy and hiding at the very back of the crowd. Sure, Meadows wasn't an uncommon name any more than Brown. I couldn't afford to make assumptions. I'd have to do some digging to make certain. But it seemed more likely than not that there was a connection between Sterling and Alder, especially given the link between Erik and Vespa.

My mind leapt to what my mom had said on the phone about Alder. *"We went to high school together. Her family lived in Scandal Mountain at the time. I remember they moved to New York City not long after we graduated . . . As I recall, she had a gorgeous older brother. He was a senior when we were freshmen."*

Gorgeous older brother. Sterling Meadows having a gallery in New York and Vermont fit. Even his age fit.

Sterling stepped up to the microphone. His voice rang out, filling the gallery, as cultured as crystal in a room filled with coarse earthenware. "It has been my honor and privilege to bring to you works by the finest folk and outsider artists from America and the world beyond. No one else reaches the level of importance today as Vespa—an artist of unparalleled raw talent, creative instinct at its most dynamic. She translates the reality of twenty-first-century rural life into unforgettable images. Without further ado, I'd like to introduce our own Vespa."

The woman in white chiffon who'd greeted us when we arrived emerged from a nearby doorway with an elderly woman leaning on her arm for support. From where I was standing at the back of the crowd, I couldn't see either of them very well, but Vespa appeared to be dressed exactly as in the photo. Tight honey-yellow top. Dolly Parton hair. Only tonight her hair was accented with a headband, and her fake eyelashes and heavy makeup were more apparent.

Applause exploded from the guests and employees. I joined in, the clapping of my own hands seeming to come at a distance as I struggled to get past what I knew in my heart was the truth. Sterling Meadows was Alder's brother. I could be wrong. But I didn't think so.

As the applause continued, Sterling left centerstage long enough for the woman to transfer Vespa to his arm. He walked Vespa to the microphone and stood with her as she gazed out, seeming to look through everyone like a sleepwalker searching an unseeable horizon.

Once the applause hushed, Vespa's quavering voice rose, "Art is suffering, not romance." Her gaze swept the guests. "It is the bleeding heart. It is the truth behind the facade we pretend is our existence. It is torn paper. Ungiven rings. Broken pieces that fall to waste in this world of computers and iPhones. It is what we see when we look away."

Murmurs of approval rippled through the room. The applause began again. When it subsided, Sterling bent toward the mic. "Thank you, Vespa, for your words of wisdom, a very special insight into your philosophy." He looked toward the audience. "Enjoy the show. Enjoy the champagne. Thank you all for celebrating the art of Vespa with us."

With that said, Sterling led Vespa back down from the dais and toward an open doorway.

The throb of electronic music returned. Waiters materialized with trays of hors d'oeuvres and more champagne. People circled round, snatching the finger food. Jimmy joined them, claiming a napkin and canapé as he chatted with a young collector.

I double-checked to make sure he wasn't looking my way, then hurried toward the doorway Sterling and Vespa had taken. Something strange was going on here, and I was damn well going to figure out what.

Chapter Nineteen

The room beyond the doorway was dark and black walled. Retro fiberoptic lamps spangled in the gloom like fireworks. NFTs strobed and crackled. In the flashing light, Vespa and Sterling were making their way along a line of a dozen or so guests, stopping to say a word or two, then moving on.

I licked my lips. Currently, the theory of Alder brainwashing or somehow enticing Erik into creating pieces in Vespa's style or even forgeries seemed more and more likely. She provided Erik's art to her brother. In turn, he was the con artist salesman the theory had previously lacked. It did explain why Vespa appeared to create so many pieces so quickly. The only stumbling block was the question of why Vespa hadn't noticed fakes mixed in with her real work. Then again, perhaps she had. Vespa was a tiny, elderly woman. Even if she was aware of the scam, she might be too frightened to do anything about it.

Careful to stay out of Sterling's line of sight, I moved closer. I needed to talk to Vespa. But how could I do that with Sterling around? And what should I ask her?

As I mulled over my next move, Sterling's reaction when we'd been introduced replayed in my head. Startled? Surprised?

A bead of cold sweat trailed down my spine. Perhaps his reaction had nothing to do with my mom's reputation. Alder might have told Sterling about finding me in the garage with Erik. She could have told him my full name.

I scooted closer to the edge of the room just as the woman collector with the flamingo strut and "kiss my rings" attitude paraded past with her Dogfather husband. I wasn't surprised to see them in Vespa's inner circle and was equally unsurprised when I spotted their no-neck son trailing a few steps behind.

A hefty middle-aged guy—dressed in black from his knit beanie down to his shoes—hurried to a nearby atrium door that led out onto a terrace. He opened the door, held it for Sterling and Vespa as they went outside, then blocked the exit with his bulk.

My breath hitched. Disappointment for me. Worry for Vespa. Where was Sterling taking her? And why rush off? *She's a recluse, not used to appearances,* the practical part of my brain whispered. *He doesn't want to give her a chance to tell anyone about the scam,* a louder voice inside me insisted.

As fast as a pickpocket at a flea market, I slipped past the other guests and went to a window next to the door. The view was obstructed by a waterfall of drapes. I eased them back a few inches and peered out into the evening light.

Right below the window, Sterling was helping Vespa into the rear seat of a golf cart. He placed a cane on her lap. She instantly latched onto it, like a parrot clutching its perch for dear life. I pressed my hand against the window glass, as though by my reaching out she would be able to sense my concern.

Sterling patted her hand, then kissed her cheek. As he went to kiss her other cheek, Vespa turned her head, and a thread of light from the window glinted off a brooch that studded her headband. A brooch in the shape of—

I blinked, unable to believe my eyes.

Leaning right up to the glass, I trained my gaze on the brooch as if it were an element in a collage, an element that could shed light on all the confusion.

The brooch was a monkey, hands raised to cover its eyes.

See No Evil—an exact match to Kala's brooch.

Chapter Twenty

For a second, I stood immobilized, watching as Sterling said something to the golf cart's driver, then stepped to one side. The vehicle took off, cruising up a gravel path, through the galleries' gardens, toward a cottage on the other side of them. Sure, it wasn't impossible for Vespa to have a vintage brooch identical to Kala's, but the probability of her owning one and wearing it in a similar manner to Kala's had to be astronomical.

Mystified and even more determined to figure out what was going on, I turned from the window and rushed back into the main gallery. I snagged a flute of champagne, then retreated to an alcove—a private spot with atrium doors on the far end that offered a view of a deserted terrace and evening-shadowed gardens beyond.

Dropping down onto a bench, I took out my phone and texted Kala. *Do you still have the monkey brooch?*

I set the phone on my lap and gulped a mouthful of champagne. It cooled my dry throat but did nothing for the confusion jumping in my stomach. What was taking Kala so long?

I looked at a Vespa collage that hung on a wall across from me. It was the size of a briefcase, far smaller and less intricate than any of the collages I'd studied so far, closer to the size of the small paintings I'd noticed earlier. Railroad tracks spanned the piece's foreground. Two dilapidated industrial buildings stood directly behind them. One was a single-story warehouse, white paint peeled down to bare concrete. The other was a tall, rangy wooden structure with ramshackle grain elevators, annexes, loading docks, and silos. There were no people or puddles of blood. Just generic feedstore and granary buildings, created in shades of black, white, and muted red. I'd seen similar structures in other artwork and in railyards throughout New England in real life. Very cool, but not unique.

Tilting my head, I studied it at an angle. Even with that slight change in perspective, I could see that Purina feed bags formed the background, the company's trademark red and white checkerboard all but covered with newsprint, paint, and ink. It lacked many of the details that reoccurred in the other pieces, but its stark, grim tone echoed them. Perhaps, it was an early work before Vespa's trademark small-town commentary had fully developed.

My phone vibrated against my lap.

Barely able to breathe, I snatched it up and read Kala's text. *Don't be mad. I lost See No Evil. I meant to tell you.*

I typed as fast as I could. *Where? When?*

Time shifted into slow motion, seconds becoming hours as I waited for her answer. A nerve began to twitch at the corner of my eye. Finally, she replied. *At the Well-Being Center. I think it fell off while I was talking with one of Alder's clients. Why?*

What did the client look like?

Remember the woman you almost ran over in the parking lot? The old lady with the cane.

Older woman. Wispy, sparse hair. Cane. I'd only seen her for a few seconds, but I'd never forget those petrifying moments. I also remembered the first time I'd seen her, when the white-bearded man was walking her back into Checkerberry Manor. She'd been dressed in a dove-gray sweatsuit. If only I'd paid closer attention to what she'd looked like, especially her face.

I envisioned Vespa: Dolly Parton hair, likely a wig. The eyelashes were unquestionably fake. Her oddly conical breasts could be falsies. Bright clothing. Heavy makeup. The woman at Checkerberry and the Well-Being Center lacked these things, but the two women's age, height, and small stature were similar. Both women used canes but weren't dependent on them. Before tonight Vespa had only appeared in shadowy photos that made it easier for her not to be recognized by people who might meet her elsewhere—like in a small, northern Vermont town.

Kala sent another message. *The woman was staring out the window while everyone else worked on their projects. I felt bad for her. She looked sad. I went over to cheer her up.*

My fingers trembled.

I think she's Vespa. She's wearing a monkey brooch that looks just like yours.

What! You're kidding?

I wish I were, I replied. Then I added, *And I wish I knew why someone as famous as Vespa is living at Checkerberry and making art with a bunch of amateurs.*

Yeah, it's totally strange.

I looked back at my phone, rereading Kala's texts. As I did, a possibility I'd failed to fully consider—or rather considered and then dismissed—struck me. According to Kala, Vespa hadn't been working on an art project at the Well-Being Center.

Was it possible Erik wasn't being used to forge or create pieces in a similar style to Vespa's work? What if his pieces weren't mixed in with hers? What if all the so-called Vespa artwork originated from none other than Erik Volkov and his own imagination?

What if the persona of Vespa—*Grandma Moses for the Twenty-First Century*—was a total sham?

Chapter
Twenty-One

My thoughts spun from the possibility—Vespa, a front. A total fake. When Sterling had mentioned that Vespa was at the gallery, I'd totally ruled out Tuck's far-fetched suggestion that Erik might literally *be* Vespa. But was it possible?

I still had a hard time believing it, considering his intellectual disability. But now I could see how an even more insidious plan might have come together, one that involved exploiting Erik and his talent. Alder could have noticed Erik's artwork someplace, like Checkerberry Manor's annual Artsy-August Craft Show, or maybe she'd gotten lucky and discovered him after he became a client. Either way, Alder would have recognized his talent as unique. She could've showed his work to Sterling, or he might have spotted it at the Well-Being Center himself.

Alder and Sterling Meadows. The therapist and the promoter. The perfect team.

I supposed it was even possible they'd been on the lookout for an outsider artist to cash in on, and that was exactly what they were doing to Erik.

Fabricating the persona of Vespa would've been a breeze—a reclusive, elderly outsider artist, haunted and scarred by images from her dangerous and turbulent past. The ideal golden child for art patrons to fawn over.

Still, that begged the question—assuming my theory was on track: Who was the elderly woman playing the part of Vespa? Was she another victim like Erik, or was she in on the scam? If she was intellectually disabled as well, that could explain her living at Checkerberry Manor. It also might make it easier for someone like Alder to manipulate her into taking on the role.

I glanced toward the far end of the alcove, to the atrium doors, the terrace, and darkening gardens. Though I couldn't see the gravel trail the golf cart had taken, I knew it was just around the corner of the building. It would only take a few minutes to walk to the cottage the cart had headed toward. Sterling was still here at the gallery, so Vespa—or whoever the old woman was—might be alone. Confronting her could well net me the answers I needed.

After gulping my remaining champagne, I looked to make sure no one was watching, then rushed outside onto the terrace. The previously foreboding storm clouds were now overtaking the sky, their gloom eclipsing the last of the evening light.

Yeah, a nasty storm was brewing. And it wouldn't be long before it and darkness arrived. But I couldn't let that stop me.

Two steps down, and I was on a path flanked by murky reflection pools. My internal GPS steered me past a granite sculpture of an armless woman, polished on one side and rough on the other.

Even before I reached the corner of the building, I could see that the trail as well as the cottage were indeed only a short walk from the gallery. I hurried through the eerie half-light toward the house, shortcutting across the dampening grass, sticking close to the clumps of birches and sculptured evergreens. Thank goodness I'd worn pumps instead of high heels.

A Wealth of Deception

A sudden gust of wind bent the trees and whipped my hair across my face. I began to jog. I wasn't going back, not after coming this far.

The dim outline of a fence and shrubs that formed a border between the gallery property and the cottage yard came into view. I slowed to a walk. Only two windows in the cottage were lit. Still, the closer I got, the more I began to question the wisdom of my idea, and not just because of the rapidly approaching storm. With the scam being so lucrative, was there really a chance that Sterling had left the woman unattended? Unlikely at best, especially if she lived at Checkerberry because she was perhaps mentally disabled.

A motion light in the cottage's front yard flashed on as the back door opened. I froze in my tracks. Three kids and a German Shepard raced out. They hadn't seemed to notice me, so I shrank back against an evergreen, hiding in the darkness of its shadow, not wanting them to be alarmed by the unexpected arrival of a stranger. The kids were around eight and maybe ten years old. Earlier in the evening, when Jimmy had mentioned Sterling's homelife—a wife, six kids, a dog, two cats—I hadn't been sure if he was serious or not. Now I was wondering if these kids were members of Sterling's family. The cottage clearly was part of the gallery property.

My mind filled with a memory from when I was around the same age as the kids in the yard. My grandparents had been in Canada on an antique-buying trip. Mom was home from art school, and we were in the kitchen, heating caramel sauce in the microwave for ice-cream sundaes. I could remember every minute of what happened like it was yesterday—see it, smell it, hear it.

The microwave timer had dinged.

And in that same moment, a car roared up the driveway. A stranger in a tweed coat jumped out, stormed through the twilight to our back door, and began pounding on it.

"You sold my wife a fake!" a man's voice shouted. "I want my money back, now."

I ducked down, hiding behind the kitchen counter. The door wasn't locked. Its window was only lightly curtained. There was no way he couldn't see Mom cowering against the microwave. No way he couldn't get in.

He pounded again, then tried the knob. As he thundered into our kitchen, Mom crept forward, face pale as she smiled sheepishly. "What are you talking about?"

"The *antique* barber pole you sold my wife. It's a fake. There're hundreds just like it on eBay."

Mom's voice trembled. "I–I didn't realize. I'm only watching the shop for my parents. They'd know all about it. I have no idea where it came from." She hesitated. "What did it say on the price tag? Antique or replica? It could have said replica. I might not have noticed."

He thrust out his hand. "Two thousand, two hundred and fifty bucks—plus sales tax. I'll take it in cash."

As Mom once more blamed my grandparents, anger simmered inside me. I tightened my hands into fists, blunt fingernails pressing hard against my palms. The man was a jerk. But Mom was lying, and it wasn't a white lie. My grandparents hadn't bought the barber pole. Mom had picked it up at the flea market the day before she sold it to the man's wife. She probably really thought it was old, and I suspected she'd already spent the woman's money as well. Before the ice-cream sundae idea had come up, Mom had told me she'd scored last-minute tickets to a concert at Place des Arts in Montreal. Bye-bye cash.

Clenching my teeth, I shelved that unpleasant memory and looked back at the yard.

The dog and kids were circling nearer to the fence and shrubs now, closer to where I was only partly hidden. No matter what was going on, it wasn't right to alarm them by confronting Vespa in their presence, any more than the man had handled the situation right that night in our kitchen. No question about it, the man had deserved his money back. No question, my opinion of my mom had nose-dived after hearing her blame my grandparents instead of shouldering the responsibility herself. Still, there was a right and wrong way to handle things—and getting kids stuck in the middle was wrong.

As the dog led the kids back closer to the light of the cottage, I dashed out from the evergreen's shadow, hurrying through the gusting wind and gloomy light to the golf cart trail. Its gravel crackled under my shoes. Droplets of rain pattered down, then stopped. This trip had gained me nothing. But now that I thought about it, there was someone who might have information about the old woman—Pinky's cousin Edgar.

I groaned. Just what I didn't need, to be even more in Pinky's debt.

As I neared the end of the trail, the aroma of smoke from an expensive cigar reached my nose, followed by the murmur of men's voices. One of them struck me as familiar. Sterling, maybe?

Curious, I dodged off the trail before they could spot me and took cover behind a heavily pruned cedar. A quick look confirmed one was Sterling, but the rapidly encroaching darkness and a pillar hid the other from my sight.

"Trouble?" the second man said. His accent was gravelly, maybe Russian.

"Nothing for you to worry about. You'll get your cut," Sterling answered.

"If you can't keep your own nose clean . . ."

As his voice trailed off, Sterling's went as hard and inflexible as stone. "Tell Elizaveta this isn't a good time. I'll call her."

The other man waited a beat to reply. When he did, his tone sent a sharp chill up my spine. "If that's how you want to play it. Maybe it's time for me to *visit* your sister again?"

"I said, I'll deal with it." Sterling's tone remained unflinching.

The man chuckled, a dry, harsh sound like bones grinding. "If you don't, she'll pay. More than last time."

I didn't hear their footsteps retreat, but the conversation went silent after that, and the atrium door on that side of the building whooshed opened and shut as if they'd gone back inside. What had they been talking about? Who was Elizaveta? What had the man meant by "*visit* your sister again"? A sister who was quite likely Alder.

With a whirlwind of new questions gaining momentum in my head, I raced back along the garden path, through the fading half-light and the encroaching storm, past the armless woman and the reflection pools. I slipped inside the building, pulling the alcove door quietly shut behind me. One thing was clear: neither man intended to back down. Of course, there was a chance their conversation had nothing to do with Vespa being a fake. I didn't know for a fact that my theory was true. But if I was right and they were, then it was possible that someone much more dangerous than me had caught onto the scam.

I took a deep breath, slowing my thoughts and steps as I went back into the gallery's main room. I needed to find Jimmy and get out of here.

Through the milling guests, I spotted Sterling on the other side of the room, walking beside the guy who'd blocked the door after Sterling and Vespa went out to the golf cart, the hefty middle-aged man dressed in black from his knit beanie down to his shoes. Had he been the man on the terrace with Sterling?

Sterling gestured at a small oil painting. The man smiled and nodded. Back when we'd first arrived and I'd noticed the paintings, I'd wanted to ask for more information about them. Were the grim little portraits earlier works, like the more basic collage in the alcove? Now I only hoped Sterling and the guy wouldn't glance my way. I wasn't sure I could keep my anxiety from showing.

Feeling more uneasy by the second, I texted Jimmy. *Where are you? I'm ready to leave.*

I'm in the front room, darling. Near the entry.

I sped past the enormous images of Vespa and Grandma Moses, and into the electric crackle and glare of the TV screen wall. Jimmy stood in the strobing light, hands fluttering as he talked to the wealthy collector with the flamingo strut, the Dogfather's wife.

I gritted my teeth and pushed myself forward. The last thing I wanted to do right now was socialize.

Jimmy saw me coming. "Edie, there's someone I'd love to introduce you to." He motioned to the woman. "This is Elizaveta Volkov . . ."

I heard him continuing the introduction, but I couldn't process what he was saying. The woman being the Elizaveta that Sterling just mentioned on the terrace was barely a shock compared to the connection her surname drew. Elizaveta *Volkov*. Erik Volkov.

I stared at the woman blankly as other connections came together. Anna had said her aunt Evita had offered to buy Erik's townscape. Around that same time a mystery someone had referred to Erik's ability as that of an artistic savant. I had a good idea who that was now. *Elizaveta.* A name too close to Evita to be ignored. A high-profile art collector. I'd been so wrong to simply think of her and her husband as circling vultures. They were much more than the average greedy relatives. Maybe it wasn't the hefty guy in black who'd been talking on the terrace with Sterling. Maybe it was Elizaveta's Dogfather husband or their no-neck son.

Jimmy's touch on my hand brought me from my shock. ". . . Edie has a superb eye for the unique," he finished his introduction.

My throat felt like I'd swallowed a pound of ground glass. Sweat drenched my armpits. I gulped a silent breath, pulled my shoulders back, and extended my hand. I could only hope she mistook my gawking for awe.

"Nice to meet you," I croaked.

She took my hand, gripping it loosely. Her accent was Russian, deep and buttery. "Next time I'm in your area, I'll make a point of visiting your family's shop."

Visit us? My pulse thrashed in my ears. *She was just making conversation,* I told myself. *There was no deeper meaning, hopefully.*

I forced my voice to go light. "That would be wonderful. If you call ahead, I'll make sure I'm there to show you around." My grandpa would have been proud of how convincing I sounded. I looked at Jimmy and lied again. "I should get going or I'll be late for my dinner reservation."

Jimmy hooked his arm with mine. "Well, we don't want that."

Chapter
Twenty-Two

We went up to the gallery entry and out the front door. Low light illuminated the portico, but total darkness now held sway beyond its shelter. Raindrops steadily pinged the ground.

Jimmy stopped walking and turned to face me. "What's going on? And don't give me that bo diddly about dinner reservations."

I stared at him, my thoughts spinning as I searched for a logical excuse. I suspected I was already in over my head, and I didn't need Jimmy to get any more involved than he was already. The less he knew, the less dangerous it was for him.

Jimmy's voice toughened. "Darling, the truth."

I looked down. "I can't tell you right now. I just need to get out of here before I say or do something that makes things worse."

"Not good enough. Do you want me to march back inside and start asking questions to figure out what you've been up to?"

It was smarter to not tell him anything more than he already knew. But it also wasn't fair to act freaked out without any explanation, and I certainly didn't want him asking questions.

There was, however, something I needed from him first. "Who's the guy that sticks close to Sterling—the bulked up middle-aged man, dressed all in black with the beanie."

He rested one hand on a hip. "That's T-Minty."

"Who?" The name sounded young for the man's age.

Jimmy flagged his fingers as if to say the name was so well known that anyone should recognize it. "He's the digital artist responsible for Vespa's NFTs—and an up-and-coming artist in his own right."

T-Minty. I committed the name to memory. It would be easy for Kala to find out more about him.

Jimmy squinted. "You do realize, I'm not letting you leave until you tell me what got your panties in a bunch."

I folded my arms over my chest, unfolded them, took a breath. I still wasn't sure it was a good idea to say anything, but I trusted Jimmy, and I couldn't bear to keep the most over-whelming part of what I'd learned to myself a second longer. I met his unwavering gaze. "I think Vespa is a sham."

He flinched back, shook his head. "What do you mean? An alias?"

"Not exactly. I think Sterling may have created Vespa out of whole cloth—as in she doesn't exist at all." I rubbed my hands down the sides of my dress. "I think there's a strong possibility the outsider artist I've discovered up north made all the Vespa pieces. Sterling's taking—stealing the art from him. He fabricated Vespa as a way to sell the pieces."

Jimmy grinned. "This is wonderful! *Fantastique.*"

I scowled. "I'm glad you think so."

"Don't you get it? If it's true and we can prove it, the news will drive the value of Vespa's artwork through the roof. I already own several and am currently standing in front of a gallery full of others."

A headache began to pound at the back of my skull. I preferred to assume Jimmy's love for outsider art came from the feelings the pieces inspired in him rather than their monetary worth. I hardened my voice. "This is a no-lose situation for you, isn't it?"

"Sure is, sweetie. It's not as if the Vespa pieces will be viewed as any less masterful. It's like when an artist dies." He reached out, resting his hand lightly on my wrist. "I know it's not a nice thing to say, but it's true. An overdose at a society party," he mused. "A drunken car crash in a stolen Maserati. Better yet, an artist dying while handcuffed to a handsome actor's bed. The more scandalous the event, the more the art's value rises."

I closed my eyes for a moment, took a long breath. As much as I disliked what he'd said, I knew down to the depths of my greedy antique-and-art-loving soul that he was right.

"I'll tell you one thing," Jimmy continued. "I want that townscape you found. I told you before, I'd give you a finder's fee. I'll make it more than worth your while."

I nodded. "What I need right now is for you not to ask anyone—or do—anything." I smiled and winked to lighten the mood. "That includes going back inside and making people suspicious by buying up every Vespa piece you can get your hands on."

He pouted. "One more's okay, right? I've already spoken with the gallery manager."

I laughed. "Two's probably fine." I kissed his cheek. "I'll call you once I know more."

"You better—" He stopped midsentence. "Oh, I almost forgot to tell you. I got a phone call yesterday from an old friend of yours."

"Someone from New York?" I asked, confused.

"Not that. They're from your neck of the woods. It was Felix Graham."

"Graham called you?" I couldn't keep the shock out of my voice.

"Don't worry, darling. He's having a private opening for his expanded art gallery. It's the last weekend in August. He wanted to invite me."

"I was at his gallery a few days ago. They were doing a lot of work, but he didn't mention anything about an upcoming event."

"Did you really expect he would? Your family's shop may not be as large as his, but you are competition."

"I guess," I said. It also made sense for Graham to want to avoid reminding his clients of his connection to my mom and her copyist skills.

Jimmy cleared his throat. "Chances are I'll end up going to Graham's soiree—you know, can't resist temptation. While I'm in the area, it would be nice to stop by your place and view a certain townscape."

"Hopefully, that'll happen long before then," I said.

A rumble of thunder sounded overhead. The leaves on a clump of up-lit birch trees shivered and rattled. I glanced at the rain, now coming down harder. "I should get on the road before the storm hits in earnest." I met his gaze. "You take care."

"Don't worry about me. I know how to be discreet," he said.

As Jimmy vanished back inside, I hurried out from under the portico, into the rain and down the walkway, past the urn full of dahlias and silver sedum. I'd probably have to stop on the way home for an extra-large coffee to keep me going, though I did have a couple bottles of iced tea in a travel cooler. At some point, I also needed to call Shane. I'd sworn to tell him what happened, and things certainly had gone crazy enough to justify telling him most everything.

My thoughts went to the worried look in Shane's eyes last night at the pub. *"Promise me you'll be careful,"* he'd said. Had he suspected the very things I'd just discovered? I'd told him that Erik's last name was Volkov, though at the time I hadn't known the significance. If Shane had suspicions about Erik's family, why hadn't he mentioned it?

Lengthening my strides, I stepped off the walkway and into the parking lot. There weren't any people around, only rows of expensive vehicles and glimmering streetlamps, surrounded by darkness and strengthening rain.

I could see the outline of the Volvo in the distance, further away than it had seemed when I arrived. Hugging myself against a chill, I aimed straight for it, dashing along behind a row of parked vehicles.

A thunderclap detonated directly overhead. The sky opened up. Rain deluged down. In an instant, I was soaked to the skin.

Somewhere behind me car tires squealed.

Another squeal. Closer, this time.

I brushed aside my wet hair, glanced over my shoulder—

A car swung out from nowhere, its headlights blinding my eyes as it rocketed straight at me.

Shit!

I bolted into the space between two parked vehicles. The car slid sideways, tires screaming again as it careened down the driveway. I stared after its taillights, receding through the darkness and torrential rain. What kind of idiot drove through a parking lot like that? A drunk? A plain fool? If I'd been a heart-beat slower, they'd have hit me for sure. I could have lain there dying, and no one would have known. There wouldn't have been any witnesses.

As the car flew around the bend in the driveway and passed under the light of a streetlamp, I caught a better look at it. A sedan. It seemed like I recognized it from somewhere—

Sudden panic sent me into motion. It resembled the Mercedes I'd seen at Checkerberry Manor. Bloodred. Newer model. Was it the same car? Could it be . . .?

I rushed out from between the parked vehicles and sprinted for the Volvo. I shoved the key in its lock. The Volvo was older, a true classic. No keyless entry. No panic button to rely on.

In a second, I was inside, doors locked.

My mind went to the other day in the ice-cream-parlor parking lot, me speeding around the corner and the old woman directly in my path. A horrible accident, avoided by mere seconds.

Another accident jolted into my brain. When Tuck and I had first met Anna, she'd told us Erik had suffered his brain injury when he'd come home to Shelburne for a visit and been hit by a car. Had his accident happened like this? Darkness. Isolation.

I replayed my near miss. The car, screaming straight at me. They hadn't even begun to slow. How could they have not seen me in the headlight beams?

A sick feeling built in my gut. Had the driver intended to hit me?

I started the engine and turned on the headlights. Heart in my throat, I winged out of the parking space and sped down the driveway, onto the street. I punched the accelerator and headed northward.

A new wave of fear rolled through me. Whether I was being paranoid or not, home was more than a hundred miles away, hours of driving alone on a desolated country highway. Miles and miles where anything could happen—and the sedan was out there somewhere.

Chapter Twenty-Three

As I drove away from the gallery, through Manchester's busy restaurants and shopping areas, and northward toward the outskirts, my eyes went to the rearview mirror. I half expected to see a dark red Mercedes fly up behind me, its driver readying to finish what they'd started.

Thoughts of the collage at the gallery with the woman sprawled in the alleyway pounded in my head, along with images of the bloody puddle in the townscape.

A real-life event from my recent past crept into my mind. A month ago, my van had been totaled when the masterminds behind the decoy collection theft attempted to put me out of commission. Was a similar scenario about to happen again?

Sweat iced my spine. The steering wheel grew hot under my grip. I passed a speed limit sign: thirty miles per hour. I glanced at the speedometer. I was doing fifty.

I tapped on the brakes. The last thing I needed was to get pulled over for speeding, and the Manchester police station was less than a mile ahead. I'd noticed it when I drove into town.

Thinking about the police reminded me of Shane, and that gave me an idea. Slowing even further, I put on my turn signal.

A Wealth of Deception

I could see the station ahead. A low building, its small parking lot brightly lit. If there was ever a safe spot to stop, this was it. And it made more sense to call Shane now rather than wait.

I pulled into a parking space as far from the police station's front door as possible. Part of me was tempted to walk inside and report that someone had attempted to run me over. I was pretty sure that was what had happened, though not a hundred percent. I hadn't been hurt or seen the driver or even gotten a license plate number. In retrospect, I wasn't even positive the sedan was a Mercedes or dark red. There hadn't been any witnesses, I was sure of that.

I reached down to the floor in front of the passenger seat to get a bottle of iced tea out of the cooler. I hadn't gone any distance, but I was already dying of thirst.

As I retrieved a tea, my eyes flicked over the glovebox. Taz was in there. Kala's Taser.

I shoved the tea in the cup holder, grabbed my phone and texted her. *No questions. How do you use your Taser?*

Instantly she replied. *Safety is orange button on side. Push that up, then point and shoot. There's an extra cartridge stored in the grip of the Taser, but don't take time to reload. Shoot once. Drop the gun and run. What the hell is going on?*

Nothing. Just nervous.

Drop and run is important. You only have seconds to get away. Sure you're fine?

Yes. Got to go. Need to call Shane.

I added, *Don't tell Tuck. I'm just a little paranoid. No need to scare him.*

Please, be careful. Call soon and explain. Okay?

Okay.

I opened the iced tea and took a long sip, then called Shane's number. Taz was fine in the glovebox for now. The "just paranoid" thing was feeling more and more like a strong possibility. Still, I was glad I'd asked how to use the Taser, though I'd pay later for being cryptic.

Shane's phone buzzed twice, three times. It was possible he was working or asleep. I picked at the iced tea's label with my fingernail. He'd probably say I was overreacting.

The phone stopped buzzing as Shane answered. "Edie, glad you called. How did things go? Are you home?"

"I'm just leaving Manchester." I hesitated. "I had the daylights scared out of me. I—it's probably nothing, but I wanted to tell you."

His voice tightened. "What happened?"

"The Vespa show was . . . eye-opening, definitely something strange going on—" I realized I was on the verge of rambling and got to my point. "When I was leaving, someone almost ran me over in the parking lot."

"What! Are you alright?"

"Yeah, fine. It might—it was probably nothing. It was a mid-size sedan—dark red, maybe. I didn't see anything else."

"Where are you now?" he asked.

"In the police station parking lot, but I'm not telling them. I just parked here to call you. Seriously, there was weird stuff going on, and I probably just freaked out. At least that's what I think now." I took another sip of tea. Calling him had been a good idea, and so had asking about the Taser. My pulse was starting to slow. My thoughts seemed clearer.

"What sort of weird stuff?" he said.

"Yesterday you asked me what I knew about Erik and Anna's family. Well, there was an art collector at the gallery named Elizaveta Volkov and—"

He cut me off. "Was her husband there?"

"Yeah," I said, though his blunt interruption gave me pause. He sounded more like Detective Payton now than Shane.

"Was anyone else with them?"

"Their son. Why?"

He hesitated, an extra-long pause as if he were taking a moment to think. "Just curious. What was so eye-opening about the show?"

I set the tea back in the cup holder and reran the last beats of our conversation—him firing questions, me answering, and him avoiding answering. I didn't want to hide anything I'd learned, but he was being evasive with me again, and I didn't like it. "We can talk later. I need to get going."

Another pause. "I'm glad you're okay. Text me when you get home, please."

"Will do."

"I've got a few days off, starting tomorrow evening. I'm planning on not doing anything tomorrow other than catching up on rest. How about we get together Monday?"

"Sounds great. Talk to you later."

"Drive carefully," he said.

I set the phone on the passenger seat—

Tap-tap. Someone rapped on the driver side window.

I wheeled around, wishing even as I did it that I'd taken out the Taser first.

The outline of a large man filled the window, backlit by the station's lights. *The sedan driver,* I thought. Then my brain kicked in. A uniformed police officer stood on the other side of the glass, scowling. He motioned for me to lower the window.

I did as he asked, my face going hot as I instantly shrank from adult to stammering teenager. "Hi, Officer. I—I'm from out of town. I needed to talk to someone on the phone. It's okay to do that here, right?"

His jaw remained tensed. He turned on a flashlight, studied my face under its brightness, then fanned it toward the passenger seat, down onto the floor, as if searching for discarded beer cans or drugs. The light came back to my eyes, and he said, "If you're done, it's time to move along."

"No problem." I hesitated. "Is it okay if I text one more person? I want to tell my uncle I'm on my way home."

The officer nodded. "Sure. Just make it fast."

Chapter
Twenty-Four

I kept my text to Tuck as simple as possible, telling him it had been an eventful visit to the gallery and that I'd be home soon. Hopefully, it would prevent him from worrying if Kala didn't keep her mouth shut.

An hour into my drive, I called Kala and reassured her once again that I was simply being jumpy. She seemed to go along with that, and I promised to tell her everything else as soon as I got home.

By the time I reached the outskirts of Scandal Mountain village, I was feeling a lot more relaxed, enough so that I realized if I didn't go straight home, there was one mystery I could start solving right away. That was, if Pinky was bartending at the Jumping Café tonight.

I cruised past the road to our house, staying straight and turning in when I reached the cafe. The parking lot was full. The throb of country music reverberated from inside. Though Scandal Mountain didn't have a parade or fireworks planned for the Fourth of July weekend, clearly that hadn't dampened the locals' urge to party.

Once inside, I beelined for the pub. Jack was behind the bar, along with an older man I didn't know. I wriggled into a space on Jack's end of the bar.

He came right over. "What can I do you for?"

"Is Pinky working?" I asked.

"What am I, chopped liver?" he said, as if insulted by not being my go-to bartender. Then, he laughed. "She got off at nine, said she was headed to your house."

"My house?" I said, surprised.

I glanced down at the bar, mulling over my new dilemma. If Pinky was at the house, that would make asking her for another favor easier—namely, if she could find out from her cousin Edgar who the elderly woman with the cane was, the woman supposedly named Vespa. But how was I going to convince Pinky to leave after that? I had tons of things I needed to discuss with Tuck and Kala, stuff I didn't want anyone else to hear.

Five minutes later, when I drove up our driveway, I still hadn't figured out a solution to that dilemma. As I got out of the car, the problem only deepened. Pinky's Toyota Camry was parked by the walkway to the house. The back porch light was on, illuminating the path to the door, but the only other light came from the third-floor windows—Kala's bedroom. Back when my mom had hired Kala, she'd given her a choice between the elegant guest bedroom on the second floor or the less refined, but larger and more private third-floor attic. Kala had taken the latter.

I eyed the bright windows. Yeah, if Pinky and Kala were up there in her bedroom, then no way was I going to disturb their privacy.

The last of my energy waned as I scuffed to the back door. Hopefully, Tuck was awake. Telling him what had happened in

Manchester was most important. I'd just have to repeat everything to Kala in the morning.

A rumble of music reached my ear, percussion and brass grumbling from the living room windows, growing louder. A movie soundtrack?

Hurrying my steps, I passed through the pitch-black kitchen, down the hallway to the living room. The room was also darkened, except for the pulse of the TV's light. Kala and Pinky lounged on opposite ends of the sofa. Tuck was stretched out in his recliner. An ice bucket filled with cans of Coke and a bottle of Bacardi sat on the coffee table. Open bags of Doritos and cheese popcorn were strewn nearby. On the TV screen, a gigantic spaceship hovered over the White House.

Kala sprung to her feet as I walked in. "Edie! You're home, finally."

"*Independence Day*?" I guessed at what they were watching; it seemed likely given the general look of the movie and the current holiday weekend.

"You got it." She grabbed the remote, freezing the movie on a close-up of a screaming woman. "Mostly, we've been waiting for you to get home."

Tuck righted the recliner. "How was the drive?"

"Okay. Not a lot of traffic," I said.

Pinky raised her drink in greeting. "I hear you were at some chichi art show."

"Yeah, an opening." I took a Coke from the ice bucket and popped it open. How was I going to ask for her help without letting the entire cat out of the bag? I added, "I went there partly to find out more about that guy at Checkerberry Manor."

"I figured there was more to it than just a party, especially since *someone*"—Pinky pretended to glare at Kala—"refused to spill any details."

Tuck glanced my way. "It might be easier if we let Pinky in on it."

"You can say that again," Kala said.

Pinky folded her arms across her chest. Her rooster-comb hair looked even more razor-edged and unyielding than normal. "Let's put it this way—I want in on whatever's going on, or no more favors from me."

"Uh—I'm not . . ." I bought myself a moment to think by slumping into a chair and taking a sip of Coke. Even back in high school, when Pinky traveled with a rough crowd and I was a college prep kid, she'd always treated me like a friend. She'd declared my mom's forgery charge ridiculous sooner and with even more certainty than I had. She was Scandal Mountain's information central. She wasn't above using mild extortion when it came to getting top prices for homegrown or raising cash for local fundraisers, but no one ever questioned Pinky's loyalty or ability to keep a secret when it came right down to it. In those areas, she was one up on Janet.

"Is Felix Graham involved?" Pinky guessed.

"Not this time," Tuck said.

I locked my gaze on Pinky's. "You can't breathe a word."

"I know the rules," she said.

I glanced toward Tuck then Kala. "This could be even more dangerous than any of us realized."

"Time-to-tell-Shane dangerous?" Tuck asked.

"He knows some of it already." I pitched my voice lower. "I don't want to tell him more until I'm certain I'm not misinterpreting things."

Tuck looked at me steadily. "You don't really believe that, do you?"

I pressed my lips into a slight grimace, shook my head. "Not really. But I think if we bring the police in too soon, innocent people could get hurt, people who are currently being used— Erik, Anna, maybe Vespa—or whoever she is. My chest squeezed as I continued, "It could also be my imagination, but I have a feeling Shane's holding out on me."

"You really think, so?" Kala asked.

I shrugged. "It wouldn't be the first time." Of course, I hadn't always been aboveboard with him either.

Pinky huffed, then dramatically flopped back against the sofa cushions. "Cops holding back, innocent people getting used . . . enough with the cryptic stuff. Tell me what the frick is going on."

"I'll tell you in a second," I said. "First, I need something from you."

Her eyes narrowed. "Figured as much."

I ignored that and kept going, asking the question I'd planned on asking if she'd been at the café. "Can you find out from your cousin if he knows the name of an older woman who rides his bus? She lives at Checkerberry Manor and sometimes uses a cane. Small with wispy, sparse hair. She goes to the same art facilitator as Erik."

"Alrighty," Pinky said, "I'll play along, but you better not hold anything back from me."

As Pinky picked her phone up from the coffee table and began to text—Edgar, I assumed—I turned my attention to Kala. "Tomorrow, I need you to research Vespa. Not just her art. I want to know everything. Set up a whiteboard if that's what it takes, create a time line. When she first appeared on the art scene, right down to the day if possible. Who first mentioned her? What pieces were first shown? And so on."

Kala's eyes glittered with excitement. "What are you expecting to find?"

"I'd like to know that too," Pinky said.

I smiled. "It's more like *not* find."

As the two of them and Tuck scrunched forward and listened intently, I walked them through what I'd discovered at the gallery. I told them that Sterling and Alder had the same last name, that I was assuming they were brother and sister. We needed to find out for certain. I described how Sterling looked surprised to hear my name and how I wondered if Alder had mentioned my visit to the Well-Being Center. For Pinky's benefit, I reiterated the story about the monkey brooch and how it most likely proved the woman introduced as Vespa was the same person who rode her cousin's transport bus.

"Sounds like something hinky's going on to me." Pinky snagged a handful of cheese popcorn and tossed it in her mouth.

"That's not the end of it," I said. "There was an art collector by the name of Elizaveta there, along with her husband and son."

Tuck cocked his head. "You think they have something to do with Vespa and—"

I held up a hand, silencing him. "Wait until I tell you the rest. Jimmy says Elizaveta's husband and son are involved with the NFT art market, double-digit millions, buying and selling."

"Money laundering?" Pinky asked.

"Could well be. The husband looks like a stereotypical Russian mafia godfather." I raised my eyebrows, and asked, "And what do you think their last name is?"

Tuck's eyes went wide. "Don't tell me. Volkov?"

"Exactly. Erik's last name."

"That could be a fluke, just like Alder and Sterling's names could be," Kala said. She enjoyed playing devil's advocate, a job I agreed was important. Still, she didn't sound convinced this time.

"When we searched for information about Erik before, we focused on just his life," I said. "Tomorrow, we need to go wider, find out who he's related to other than Anna. Overlay his life from birth until now with that of his relatives. Search for his accident again but add June 1 to the year. I'm not sure that's the date, but it's worth a try." I took a breath. "Also check into a guy called T-Minty. He's turning Vespa's art into NFTs, and he seems tight with Sterling Meadows." I went on, explaining how I'd overheard someone threaten to "visit" Sterling's sister again, how I'd seen T-Minty near the terrace, with Sterling, before and right after the incident. "It could've been some other guy with a gruff accent, like Elizaveta's husband or son. But T-Minty has a vested interest in Vespa's success."

"T-Minty noted and added to the mental list," Kala said.

I stalled for a second, pouring a jigger of Bacardi into my Coke, then taking a sip. "I also need to tell you about a close call I had in the gallery parking lot. It might be nothing, but . . ." I recounted the near-miss.

Pinky's mouth fell open. "Oh, my God."

"You could have been killed," Tuck said.

I softened my voice, trying to calm him. "I told Shane about it. He agreed it was most likely just some random idiot. There was free champagne at the show. They could have been drunk."

Tuck shook his head. "Normally I'd agree with Shane, but that's an assumption I'm not willing to make."

"Me neither," I murmured.

* * *

It was one o'clock by the time I showered and crawled into bed. The Bacardi and sheer exhaustion numbed my brain enough to let me drop into a deep, dreamless sleep.

But four hours later, I jolted awake with one thought pinned to the forefront of my skull, as clear as if it were written on a laundromat's plate-glass window.

June 1

Attached to that thought was the memory of Shane and me sitting in the booth at the café. He'd looked at photos of the townscape and Erik's unfinished works, as well as the ones Jimmy had taken of Vespa's pieces:

"Pretty similar, huh?" I asked.

He nodded. "Damn creepy too."

"Yeah, hyperrealistic. My mom and Jimmy suggested I look for reoccurring details, symbols . . . I spotted *June 1* in the town-scape on a laundromat window. I think it's significant. Maybe the date of his accident."

Then Shane had switched subjects. "What do you know about Anna's family?"

The smooth nonchalance in his voice made me wonder for a moment if he was hiding something. "She and Erik grew up in Shelburne, Vermont. They're Russian. At least Anna told me her mother was from there, and her father was in the import busi-ness. Why? What are you thinking?"

"Just curious." He'd stopped talking, rubbed a hand over his left forearm—the arm tattooed with a cartoon devil—then switched subjects again, announcing how hungry he was as the waiter arrived.

Why had Shane skimmed past my mention of the date and never gone back to it?

Because the date meant something to Shane, my intuition murmured.

And hadn't Shane more recently used the exact same phrase—*just curious*—to change the subject when we were talking on the phone about who was at the gallery with Elizaveta Volkov?

Just curious. Perhaps a verbal tell I should watch for in the future, especially when it was combined with him rubbing his devil tattoo.

Chapter Twenty-Five

I'm not sure how long I lay in bed, thinking about Shane and his possible tell, before I fell back to sleep. I tossed and turned, sifting through memories of when he had been my probation officer and we'd run into each other at an antique show in the Adirondacks. That weekend, we'd finally given in to our attraction and spent the next three days together in a rented cabin.

On the second day of our retreat, we'd been sitting on a rock at the edge of a pond, pants rolled up, legs dangling in the water like kids. I'd slid my hand down his forearm, stalling as I reached the cartoon angel.

He answered my unspoken question. "I had them done in Daytona on a spring break from college. The other guys were all getting ink. Skulls. Dragons. American flags . . ."

I'd kissed his shoulder, then he'd taken my face in his hands. In a second, the kiss deepened; in another we were making love, and I'd forgotten to question him further about what inspired him to get those specific tattoos. Getting tattooed because the other guys were doing it didn't sound like Shane. He wasn't a rebel, but he also wasn't a follower, and I doubted he'd been one even back in his college years. The tattoos weren't a casual memento to him. They reflected something deeper, like the symbols in an artist's work, though maybe he hadn't realized it at the time. But I realized it now, even more than that day in the Adirondacks.

Cartoon devil on his left forearm. Angel on the right.

They fit Shane as perfectly as his current detective profession. He was good-natured and stalwart. The wise, caring angel who seemingly played by the rules. And the devil, who was probably responsible for us hooking up that weekend and for his continuing interest in me. But now that I'd noticed his tell, the devil tattoo had taken on more meaning, a reminder to watch out for the flip side of Shane, the part that served him well in his law enforcement profession—speak the truth or avoid it, whichever works toward the end you prefer. I supposed, in a way, I lived by a similar rulebook.

* * *

Just before seven in the morning, I woke up for good. Oddly enough, I felt rested and ready to tackle the goals Tuck, Kala, and I had mapped out the night before. Plus, I knew where I wanted to begin. Experience taught me that big jobs were easier to face if you broke them into small bites. For example, when beginning an appraisal of an entire household, choose one cabinet and focus on its contents. There's nothing more energizing than a sense of completing even one stage of a job.

With that in mind, instead of heading downstairs for coffee, I dressed, then went straight to my mom's bedroom. It was at the front of the house, facing east and overlooking the lawn. Everything was as Mom had left it, the sheer curtains pulled across the windows, celadon-green drapes tied back.

I padded across a Persian carpet and past her bed—birdseye maple, early 1800s, a beautiful piece of furniture draped in a pink and white pinwheel quilt. When I reached her secretary-style desk, I pulled the chair aside, then knelt and opened the bottom drawer. Sometimes I'm even surprised by the things I recall from my early childhood. Today, I was driven by the memory of Mom opening that drawer and pulling out scrapbooks she'd made as a teenager, hand-drawn frames around treasured photos and trinkets from various vacation trips, proms, and graduation . . . We'd sat on the soft carpet, five-year-old me listening as she relived her glory days before an impulsive marriage and surprise pregnancy upended her plans.

At any rate, it wasn't just albums Mom kept in the drawer. I took out a stack of yearbooks, checking the dates until I found the one from her and Alder's freshman year. I didn't flip to photos of them, though. I scrunched my toes for luck, then went to the seniors. "M" as in Meadows. If Kala could find out about Erik's past in a yearbook, then maybe it would work for me as well.

And there he was, Alder Meadow's senior brother—Sterling J. Meadows—white-blond hair, chiseled features, even as a young man. Ski team captain. High honors. Prom King, standing next to a poised blonde in a stylish white gown. One photo showed him sitting in a sporty Jeep, along with his freshman sister, Alder.

His favorite quote was: *"Futures don't make themselves; you have to create them."*

I rolled my eyes. It certainly looked like Sterling had lived up to his motto.

Shoving the yearbook under my arm, I headed downstairs and into the kitchen. Tuck was already up, cotton apron protecting his belly as he pulled a batch of muffins from the oven.

I sniffed the air. "Raspberry and white chocolate?"

"Blackberry. I picked them down by the airstrip a little earlier."

"Did you sleep at all?" I asked.

"Required five hours." He nodded at the yearbook. "What's that about."

I opened it to the photos of Sterling and showed them to him. "I'd say we can officially move the possibility of Sterling and Alder being siblings off the 'maybe' pile and onto the 'definitely true' list."

Tuck gave a low whistle. "I'm not shocked, and that certainly lends credence to your other theories as well."

"What pisses me off the most is the thought of a therapist using someone like Erik to get rich."

He raised an eyebrow. "Are you sure you're not being too hard on Alder? You told me yourself she's messed up emotionally. Her ex-husband was a bully. Sterling sounds domineering. She could easily be a victim in this, rather than an instigator."

My anger flared. "That doesn't make it right. She's lying to Erik, telling him creating and letting go of his art will free him from the past. Even if he doesn't care about public recognition as an artist, she's milking him out of a ton of money and not solving his emotional problems."

"I won't argue with you there," Tuck said.

I flung open a cupboard door, grabbed a coffee cup. "I'm not going to let Alder get away with using Erik. Once we've got enough evidence to tell Shane what's going on, and he's got Alder and everyone else involved in custody, then I want to offer to host a show for Erik. No commission. Something to make up for the crap Alder's put him through."

"No commission?" Tuck smiled. "I'd go along with that."

"Well, maybe a trade." I poured coffee into my mug. "I still wouldn't mind owning a piece of his artwork. We could really use the cash selling it would bring in. It would be enough to replace the septic, and then some."

Tuck handed me a warm, buttered muffin. "What do you say we eat on the porch? It's a beautiful morning."

I smiled, anger subsiding. Muffins had a way of doing that to me. Well, actually most good food did. "What would I do without you?"

"Starve to death, probably."

I laughed, and with coffee and muffin in hand I followed him down the hallway and out the front door. Warm morning sunshine illuminated the porch. Robins sang in the gardens and trees. A thrush's call came from the woods.

Looking out over the porch railing, I checked to see if Pinky's Camry was still in the driveway. It was gone. I could only guess she'd left after the movie ended, though maybe she'd stayed longer.

Tuck cleared his throat. "I wasn't kidding about cutting Alder some slack. You said the mystery man on the terrace threatened to "visit her *again*." Sounds like she's in a tight spot."

"Maybe," I relented. "But trust me, Alder's never as innocent as she acts."

Chapter
Twenty-Six

After my second coffee, I went out to the shop, turned on the lights, and put out the "Open" flag. Fourth of July was a family holiday, not a great day for antique or art sales. Still, it made sense to be open while we all were home.

Once I'd put the start-up cash in the register, I settled in behind the counter and began transferring onto the desktop computer the photos I'd taken at Sterling Gallery. The night before, it felt like I hadn't taken very many, but I was grateful to see I'd gotten more shots than I'd realized.

The first photo was of the collage Sterling had been standing in front of when Jimmy introduced me to him, the late-night restaurant scene. In the foreground, two drunk men lurched into a dark sedan. In an alleyway, a woman sprawled beside a dumpster. Blood puddled around her head. A man stood a short distance away, his back turned to the gruesome scene.

The next photo focused in on the physical components that created the restaurant window—paint, gesso, and plastic wrap. My gaze zeroed in on the tiny date on the glass window: *June 1*.

Resting an elbow on the counter, I studied it.

Bing-bong. The shop's door chime sounded.

I looked up to see Kala scuffing toward me, coffee mug gripped tightly in two hands. Her hair was in braids, and she had on an oversized Micky Mouse T-shirt and yoga pants. Her feet were in fuzzy, bedazzled slippers.

She smiled a greeting and said, "Pinky just called."

"Did she hear back from Edgar this time?"

"Yup, sure did. He's stopping by her apartment around one thirty for lunch. She's going to talk to him then. She'll call us after he leaves." Kala walked around the counter and peered over my shoulder at the computer screen.

I went back to the photo that showed the entire collage. "What do you think? This is one of the pieces with the date written on it."

"Creepy cool. It has an Edward Hopper meets *Nightmare on Elm Street* vibe."

"I wish you could've seen it in person. The show was amazing despite all the troubling stuff going on. In fact, I thought about you when I first got there. There was a wall of vintage TV screens displaying the NFTs. One was an animated sandwich hemorrhaging fifty-dollar bills and blood droplets, and another was a weeping woman with a baby."

"Are they exact copies of Vespa pieces?"

I shrugged. "I think so. At least, they're copies from sections of her work. I saw the same sandwich in one of the photos Jimmy sent me."

Kala tapped a finger against her lip. "It's weird, I don't remember coming across any Vespa NFTs in the past, and I keep a close eye on the crypto art auction sites. Must be something new."

"How hard is it to turn physical pieces into NFTs?"

"Depends—animated, not animated. Physical art attached to the NFT or separate. Coded or not coded. They've already got the most important part, the Vespa brand, for a springboard." Her voice lowered. "If they're already stealing Erik's art, hiring someone like T-Minty to create NFTs would be a simple way to double or triple their income."

"Yeah, that's kind of what I've been thinking," I muttered. "The possibilities keep getting more twisted," I went on, telling her about the yearbook confirming a crucial piece of our theory. I was almost finished when I noticed her glancing toward the front window for the umpteenth time in the last few minutes. "Expecting someone? Pinky's calling later, not coming over later, right?"

She looked down, avoiding my eyes. "Speaking of Pinky."

"Yeah?" I prodded for her to go on.

"I'm kind of hoping she doesn't show up today. I like her but . . ."

"Trouble in paradise?" I didn't say it like a joke.

She shrugged. "Pinky's fun. I'm just—I want to keep my options open."

I squinted at her, took a wild guess. "You're interested in someone else?"

"Maybe."

"Maybe like *yes*? Is it someone from town—or someone you knew before you moved here?" I certainly didn't want to dictate Kala's life, and I knew nothing about her past. Still, it would've been nice to know about this potential stumbling block before we let Pinky in on our secrets. I took another guess. "Is this why Pinky didn't stay over? You already told her there's someone else?"

"No way. And I'm not going to say anything right now. I know we need her help." Kala folded her arms across her chest, looked me square in the eyes. "But I'd appreciate it if you didn't get Pinky any more involved in our lives or make any more promises to her."

Embarrassment heated my face. "I'm sorry. I should have asked you first. It was a dumb move."

She gave me a weak smile. "You probably wouldn't have had a choice anyway. We needed Pinky to talk to her cousin, and she got kind of stubborn about that. The worst part is, I do like her. Maybe it'd be more than like if she weren't quite so intense and pushy. Especially the pushy part."

I got up, walked over, and gave Kala a hug. "Pinky may be more understanding than you believe."

Kala snorted. "I'm glad you think so."

Chapter
Twenty-Seven

I figured the older woman with the cane had stayed overnight at Sterling's cottage. I couldn't see her returning to Checkerberry Manor until midafternoon at the earliest, if not later in the weekend. I mean, it wasn't a short drive back, and the gallery event must have stretched into the night. Most likely, everyone involved was taking it easy and moving slow today.

Just before noon, I put on a short-sleeved blouse and nice jeans—formal enough to look businesslike to whoever was on duty at Checkerberry and informal enough to put Erik at ease—then Tuck and I climbed into his Suburban and headed for the facility. It might've been wiser to wait until we had time to finish investigating Erik's family and everything else in more depth, but avoiding being spotted by the woman seemed even more vital. What she didn't see, she couldn't pass on to Alder or Sterling. Besides, talking to Erik might eliminate the need for said research.

Tuck found a parking space not far from Checkerberry's front entrance.

"I'll get the secret weapon." He opened the car's back door and took out a large tray of blossoming African violets.

I smiled to myself. Tuck claimed his hybridizing hobby was intended to supplement his retirement income. So far, I'd only seen him give his plants away for free or use them to butter people up—much like Kala and I had done with Alder and the box of jewelry.

When we reached the entry, I pressed the intercom button and looked at the monitor. "Hi, my name's Edie Brown. We've brought a gift for the residents." I motioned to Tuck and the box of violets.

"They're beautiful!" a familiar voice came from the other end. We'd lucked out. It was Yvette, the woman who'd given us the tour.

The door buzzed, then clicked open. As we went inside, Yvette walked out from behind the reception desk to greet us. "What a thoughtful thing to do."

"The other day, you showed us a houseplant exchange area," I said. "We thought the residents would enjoy these and maybe even start some babies to sell at your Artsy-August event." I nodded at Tuck. "My uncle grew them."

"Really?" She took the box from his arms.

He grinned proudly. "Just a little hobby of mine."

"I'd say it's more like a calling. They're gorgeous."

As planned, I plucked a large deep purple violet out from the center of the box. "Since we missed Erik Volkov the other day, we were hoping to give this one to him in person. Do you know if he's around?"

Her lips pressed together as she hesitated. Just when I feared she was going to send us packing, she glanced at the violets again, then said, "I imagine he's in the cafeteria having lunch right now." She nodded, as if agreeing with herself, perhaps about the best way to handle the situation. "Why don't we go down there together. You can see him, and I'll hand out the rest of these."

"If you'd like," Tuck said, "I'd be happy to come back sometime and demonstrate how to take leaf cuttings and use them to propagate more plants."

Her smile intensified. "That would be wonderful."

We signed the guest registry, then Yvette led the way down a corridor. As we walked, she asked about how to care for the violets and reminded us that Tuck's sister should get on the waiting list as soon as possible if she wanted an apartment. Tuck maintained his previous lie, saying his fictional sister would do just that any day now.

As we neared the cafeteria, the aroma of homemade rolls and minestrone soup made my tastebuds water, but all thought of food vanished when we walked inside and I saw Erik sitting alone at a table near the kitchen door, hunched over a bowl of soup and a sandwich. All the other residents sat in groups, chatting as they ate their meals. It reminded me of high school, the ostracized loner versus the popular kids.

I nudged Tuck with my elbow, then jutted my chin in Erik's direction. "There he is."

"Wonderful." Tuck waved a greeting to Erik as if they were old friends.

Erik stared blankly back at him, but Yvette was too busy handing out violets to notice Erik's lack of recognition.

Leaving her behind, we skirted between tables and over to Erik. I smiled broadly. "I'm not sure if you remember me. We met a few days ago at the Well-Being Center. We talked about your art—out in the garage." I set the violet on the table, gestured at Tuck. "My uncle grows these. We thought you might enjoy one."

Erik's frown deepened. "I remember. It—it's not good to talk to you. Not healthy."

I pulled out the chair next to his and sat down. I softened my voice. "Who told you that? Alder?"

He nodded.

"What about you? Do you want to talk?"

He rubbed a knuckle against his eyebrow, glanced to where Tuck stood at my shoulder, then back to me. "Art's for letting go."

"I understand, but doing that hasn't helped, has it? Your heart still aches."

His eyes went to the half-eaten sandwich in front of him, meat and rusty-brown mustard oozing out from between slices of green lettuce and dark rye bread.

I rested my hands on my knees and bent closer. "I'd like to ask you a couple of questions. Is that okay?"

He answered with another nod.

"June first. What does that date mean to you?" It was the date of his accident. I was almost certain of that, but I needed him to confirm it.

His fingers clenched into fists, tattooed letters standing out like blue veins against the callused skin of his knuckles. "Killed."

Killed? I glanced at Tuck. He frowned and shook his head, telling me he was as confused as I was. It wasn't the date of the accident?

I looked back at Erik. "Who was killed?"

"I loved her." His face became a mask of pain, grief, and frustration reflected in his haunted features.

I wanted to rest a comforting hand on his arm, maybe tell him about the pain of losing my grandparents. How much it still hurt. I wanted to hug him. Instead, I thought about the collages and the details they repeated, then guessed, "In an alleyway?"

His voice grew louder and his accent heavier as he struggled to find the right words. "Nighttime. Blinding headlights." He thumped a fist against his head. "Where? Memories so jumbled. Can't remember. Can't get anything straight . . ."

My mind flashed back to Manchester. The squeal of tires. The car. Blinding headlights, coming at me.

"Who was she?" Tuck softly echoed the question I'd asked earlier.

I held my breath, afraid the slightest movement or sound might distract Erik and prevent him from answering.

BANG! The noise boomed right behind us, pans hitting the kitchen floor.

CRASH, clatter, clang!

Erik rocketed to his feet, face pale, eyes wide. He wrapped his arms across his upper chest. He rocked forward and back, forward and back, and wailed, "Don't know, don't know where, don't know who . . ."

The panic in his voice triggered a memory in my head. I was twelve years old. Grandpa and I were on our way to get creemees when we came across a compact car off the road, front end smashed against a tree. Hood crumpled. Roof caved in. Black smoke, billowing skyward. A pickup truck had stopped, must have been moments before we arrived. Two men were racing toward the car. A woman stood in the road, screaming, "My baby, my baby, I can't get her out . . ."

The police weren't there yet. The fire department wasn't either. Neither was the ambulance.

Grandpa jumped out of our car. I got out too. A baby's wail echoed from inside the smoking car, louder than the woman's screams, louder than the slam of the crowbar against window glass as the men struggled to get into the vehicle.

"My baby." The woman slumped down in the middle of the road. Her face was as white as Erik's was now. She panted for breath like he was doing.

Grandpa got a bottle of water from our car, poured the cold liquid on a towel. He crouched beside her, pressed the cloth against her face. "It's going to be alright. They'll get your baby."

He led her to our car, made her sit while one of the men crawled through the broken window and retrieved the child. A second later, the smoke exploded into flames—

My breath bottled up in my throat as another memory took over. Five years later, my grandparents. The plane. The explosion. My running across the airstrip, unable to save them from the consuming flames.

I shook myself back to the present, turned to Tuck. "Can you get a glass of cold water from the kitchen," I said. Then I went to Erik. Taking his hand, I gave it a squeeze. "You want to go outside, get some air?"

He nodded, then let me slide a steadying arm around his waist. He was much taller than me, an easy hundred pounds heavier, and trembling like crazy. As he and I walked toward the corridor, we passed Yvette. She smiled approvingly. No doubt Erik's panic hadn't taken her by surprise. In fact, with it being the Fourth of July and Checkerberry housing veterans and disabled people, they were probably expecting freak-outs—except from fireworks, not kitchen noises.

Erik and I went out through the common area's sliding glass doors and into the courtyard. I steered him to a picnic table in the shade. He slumped down on one side, and I took the bench opposite his. Tuck slipped in beside me and set three bottles of water on the table.

Erik pressed his hands over his eyes. "I'm so stupid. An idiot. I'm sorry."

"Why? Because a loud noise startled you?" I said, firm but quiet. "Everyone has things that scare them. Storms, snakes, the smell of smoke, fire . . ." I picked up a bottle of water. Its sides were cool. Drips of condensation dampened my fingers as I opened the top and slid the bottle toward him. "Have a sip. It'll make you feel better."

Tuck nodded, agreeing with what I'd said. "That hullabaloo was enough to make anyone jump out of their skin."

Erik held the damp water bottle against the side of his face, then took a sip, his Adam's apple bobbing as he drank. After a moment, his gaze came to me. "Ask me what you want. I—I'll try to answer."

Who was she? That was the question both Tuck and I had asked in the cafeteria. I needed the answer to that, but it was impossible to miss the exhaustion on his face. I had to choose carefully. I might only get one chance. I picked a twofold question I'd failed to ask in the garage. "How do you let go of your art? What happens to it?"

Erik's gaze looked past me, eyes now focusing on some distant point—perhaps the flag I could hear snapping in the wind. The corners of his mouth lifted ever so slightly. "I give them to Alder. I let go. She recycles."

"Recycles?" I failed to keep the surprise from my voice. I had to give Alder credit for taking a modern approach to her swindle. I steadied my voice. "What if you could keep your art? Give it away to whoever you wanted—or sell it if you preferred."

His voice hushed. "Truth?"

I nodded. "I won't tell Alder or anyone."

"I—I'd give them to Anna. She helped Mama. She could sell them. If they're worth anything."

I moved on, eager to learn more while I had the chance. "Do you know the woman with the cane that goes to the Well-Being Center with you? She's small with wispy hair. Do you know her name?"

His mouth tightened as if he'd sucked on a spoiled lemon. "Don't like her."

"Does she do art?"

He folded his arms. "Not her. She's rotten apple. No good. "

Out of the corner of my eye, I saw Yvette coming out through the common room door, walking our way.

I pulled a Scandal Mountain Fine Arts and Antiques business card from my pocket and nudged it toward Erik. You can call Tuck or me anytime for any reason—even if you just want to talk."

His big fingers curled around the card. "Alder's wrong. Talking to you isn't bad."

Chapter
Twenty-Eight

"You don't have proof of what's going on," Tuck reminded me when we got back to the Suburban, away from anyone who might hear.

"Don't tell me that you don't think Alder and Sterling are taking Erik's art and selling it. What else could it be?"

"I agree—and I agree we need to do something. I'm just not sure how much deeper we should get into this. It could turn even more dangerous."

As Tuck started to drive toward the parking lot exit, I glanced in the passenger side mirror, watching Checkerberry's front doors grow distant. I turned toward Tuck. "I'm pretty convinced Anna's hiding secrets of her own, but I think we need to tell her straight-out what we believe is going on with Erik. If nothing else, her reaction might tell us if she knows or suspects anything."

Tuck slid a look my way. "You mean, right now?"

"It's Sunday, the last day of her yard sale. We could stop by, feel out the situation, and talk it over with her if no one else is around."

Tuck pulled the Suburban onto the main road, heading in the direction of Scandal Mountain. "What if she's involved in the scheme?"

I rubbed my hands down my pant legs, thinking for a moment. "Erik doesn't have any hard feelings toward her. You'd think he would if she were involved."

"He's hardly in the right mental space to be the best judge of people."

"I'm not so sure about that. He has mixed feelings toward Alder. He clearly doesn't trust the old woman. But he likes Yvette well enough, and as far as I can see, she has only the residents' best interests at heart."

"All right." Tuck took one hand off the steering wheel, mocking surrender. "We'll go to Anna's. I just wish we knew how her uncle and aunt fit into this. We're talking serious dollars here, and with their interest in NFTs and the money laundering that goes on in that market . . . The connection just doesn't sit right with me."

"That's why I'm calling Kala. I want to hear if she's uncovered anything."

Kala answered on the first ring. "How did it go?" she asked. "Did you talk to Erik?"

I put the phone on speaker so Tuck could hear. "Yeah, we learned some interesting things. We'll be home in a little while. I'll tell you about it then. Did you find out anything new?"

"Loads on the family. Dad's name is Stanislav Volkov. The son is Victor."

Victor. I replayed the name in my head. Another "V." Maybe I'd been trying not to focus too much on the letter, but it was foolish not to give it some weight. *Volkov. Victor.*

Kala's voice sped up, bubbling with eager excitement. "Victor was an amateur boxer at one point. I'm putting it all on a time line, along with when Vespa appeared on the art scene. Then I'm going to move on to searching for the accident again, using June first like you suggested. I haven't had a chance to really dig into T-Minty. If anything, he's so squeaky clean it bothers me."

"Wow. You've uncovered a ton," I said. "Don't skimp when it comes to Victor. Dig deep. But first, there's something I'd like you to try right away."

"Sure. What?"

"When you get to the June first part, add 'woman killed' to the search. Twelve years ago. Vermont. Man injured. Woman killed. Erik would have been in his mid-twenties, going by the year he graduated from high school. The woman was probably a similar age or younger. He's still heartbroken over her death." I double-checked the math in my head, subtracting the year when he graduated from the year when the accident had occurred. Twelve years ago . . . I'd have been fifteen—

Something pinged in the back of my mind. It almost seemed like I did recall a local hit-and-run making headline news, but the recollection was faint and gone from my head as fast as it had come.

"A woman was killed?" Kala asked.

I clarified, as much to convince myself as her. "That doesn't mean murdered."

"I'd vote for assassination," Kala said.

I swallowed hard. "Are you joking?"

"Not really. Rumor has it, the Volkovs are connected to the Russian mafia." I heard what sounded like the rustle of a potato chip bag opening and a brief munching sound before she went on. "Erik might not be on social media, but Elizaveta posts tons of photos. Until the accident, it looks like Erik worked in New York City as a bookkeeper for the Volkov import and export business. At least, he's standing front and center at a company picnic, next to his uncle Stanislav and cousin Victor."

"Keep going," I said. "We'll be home soon."

I rubbed a hand against my upper chest as I thought of Erik sitting across the table from me, struggling to answer my questions. Stanislav and Elizaveta were art collectors. They were also his family. Before the accident, Erik had even worked for them. But it looked like Stanislav and Elizaveta were involved in the Vespa scam—at least the mystery person on the terrace had mentioned her by name.

I shoved my phone back into my pocket. No matter what was going on, Erik needed—*deserved*—to have someone stand up for him, or maybe a whole group of someones.

* * *

It didn't take long to get to Maple Farm Estates. As I'd hoped, Anna's yard-sale sign was still up at the entry to the development. But today the place was bumper-to-bumper traffic. Tuck slowed and stopped as two guys carrying a white recliner lumbered across in front of the Suburban, without looking. A pickup zinged around us and swerved into a vacant space along the curb as if parking there was a life-or-death emergency.

Tuck glanced my way. "Looks like every yard-sale fanatic in the county's here."

"Let's stop anyway," I said. "We can tell Anna we'd like to talk again, that we'll stop by later. When we do, the first thing

I'm going to try to get out of her is whether Stanislav or Eliza-veta where the ones who referred to Erik as an artistic savant—"
My voice died in my throat as I spotted a Mercedes SUV parked crookedly across the entry to Anna's driveway. There was no way to miss the Golden Stag Antiques & Gallery logo on its doors.

"That's Graham's rig, isn't it?" Tuck asked.

I gritted my teeth. "What the hell is he doing here?"

"We could stop and ask him," Tuck suggested.

"Keep going. Graham probably couldn't stand not knowing more about the painting we bought off her. I wish Janet had kept her mouth shut."

"We can't do anything about that now," Tuck said. "Cross your fingers that Anna doesn't mention the townscape to him. Between you ogling it and Elizaveta wanting it on her wall, Anna could be in the market for another opinion."

I groaned. "I hope not."

Tuck drove past, then pulled into the neighbor's driveway to turn around. Anna's house might have been a newer salt box, but the one next door was an ugly, older ranch. A sign staked into the lawn read: "SOLD."

"I bet the new owners will tear that shack down and build something swank," Tuck said as he put the Suburban in reverse.

I looked at the sign. "I imagine that'll make Anna happy." My chest tightened. The ranch wasn't anything much. Still, I couldn't help but think about how we could easily be forced to sell our home. That was, if we didn't get the septic replaced super soon and keep up with the bills. I could almost see our real estate developing neighbor, René St. Marie, counting his dollars as condos and McMansions sprouted up in what once had been our fields and woods.

Tuck finished turning around and headed back past Anna's. Graham now stood in front of the garage, nosing through a box of something.

Just the idea of Anna mentioning the townscape or Erik to him made me as sick to my stomach as the thought of our property being developed. But Tuck was right: there wasn't anything we could do about it at this point. Besides, the townscape might already be in the hands of the circling Russian vultures.

Chapter Twenty-Nine

B y the time we got home, it was nearly one thirty. Kala was in the shop, bent over the front counter, bottom lip clamped between her teeth as she jotted on an eight-foot-long scroll of pack-and-ship paper.

She straightened as we entered. "I didn't expect you back so soon."

"We ran into a snag," I said. "Felix Graham was at Anna's yard sale. We decided it was better not to risk having a confrontation with him in front of her."

"Sounds smart." Kala swept her fingers over the scroll, like an Egyptologist showing off a prized find. "So? What do you think of my time line? I was going to do it on the computer, but this—"

"Reminds you of a murder board?" Tuck suggested.

"Kind of," she said. "I've finished adding what I found out about Erik and Stanislav's family, and some other stuff too."

I studied the time line. She was being modest. There were tons of names and events listed in chronological order and highlighted in various colors. Copies of photos were taped here and there. Footnotes spanned the bottom. "I can't believe you dug

213

up so much information so quickly. This is beyond amazing. Fantastic."

She grinned proudly. "The Anna Gorin part only took a little while—when she sold her home in Shelburne and built in Scandal Mountain, the death dates for her husband and mother—but Erik and the rest of the Volkovs took more time. Some of it's still a work in progress, like the T-Minty part."

"Is Vespa on there?" I asked.

"She sure is." Kala pointed to a series of pink highlights. "Two years before Erik's accident, Vespa allegedly started making collages on a whim. But we suspect Vespa's not real, so that date is probably fake too." She circled it with black and drew an "X" over it.

Tuck moved in closer, resting a hand on the counter. "When did Vespa's art first appear in public?"

"Four years after that. According to *Contemporary Art Magazine*, Sterling held the first Vespa show at his New York gallery—that was eight years ago, less than a year after Alder opened the Well-Being Center."

I glared at the stripes of pink highlight. "Very convenient for her and Sterling, wouldn't you say?"

"Fits perfectly with what we've been thinking," Tuck said.

Kala slid two sheets of computer paper out from under the time line. They were stapled together and turned over, so I could only see their backsides. A sly sparkle glimmered in her eyes. "I saved the best for last. You ready to see it?"

"Yeah, of course," I said. "What is it?"

She began to speed-talk, unbelievably fast. "Once you told me about the dead woman, I couldn't resist looking. And I found it! The accident!"

"Really?" I was shocked. I was elated. "You sure it's the right one?"

"Same date. Twelve years ago. A woman killed. Man hurt." Her voice lowered, as if telling a secret. "You'll never believe where it happened."

I matched her tone. "Where?"

"Here," she said. "In Scandal Mountain."

I gawked at her. "You're kidding."

She picked up the papers and thrust them at me. "See for yourself."

Papers in hand, I dropped down on a stool at the counter. There was a newspaper article printed on the first page, from the *Scandal Mountain Gazetteer*, the same paper where I'd found the obituary for Erik and Anna's mom, the local paper owned by the three generations of Lefebvre men, including Tristan, who I'd been friends with in high school.

Tuck moved in, close behind me. "Read it out loud, please."

I started with the headline: *"Woman Dead, Man in Critical Condition After Hit-and-Run."*

"I can't believe neither of you remember it," Kala said. "In a town as small as Scandal Mountain, everyone must have been talking about it."

Tuck shrugged. "I was living in Pennsylvania back then. I wouldn't have paid attention unless it was someone I knew."

"I vaguely remember something," I said. "Maybe the article will jog my memory."

I cleared my throat, then began to read in earnest:

Scandal Mountain, Vermont—Early Sunday morning, a woman was found deceased, and a man critically injured behind the Scandal Mountain Community Center. Pending further investigation, the local authorities have declined to make any statements as to what happened or who may have been involved. VSP has mobilized its Crime Scene Search Team to recover forensic evidence. Anyone with information is asked to contact the Scandal Mountain Police Department.

"Does it ring any bells?" Kala asked.

"Sort of. I remember everyone being upset because the police wouldn't say who was killed. We figured it was kids that hung out at the community center. I didn't spend time there, but Pinky and a lot of her friends did. It's strange, but I really don't recall anything else."

"The police must've put a lid on it really quick," Kala said.

I went on to the second page. Like the first, there was only a single article printed out on it, published two days later, June third. Front and center was a crime scene photo of a sheet-covered body lying in an alleyway between two dilapidated buildings. Similar settings from the collages flickered in the back of my mind, but I shelved them for the time being and moved on to the article, reading slowly so I wouldn't miss anything:

Vehicle Sought in Connection With Deadly Hit-and-Run
  Scandal Mountain, Vermont—On Sunday morning an employee of C&R Rubbish Removal discovered a woman dead and a man in critical condition behind Scandal Mountain Community Center. Police Chief Roger Ovitt has confirmed that a security camera captured footage of a marooned-colored sedan speeding directly at the woman,

with the injured man rushing forward in a failed attempt to push her out of the vehicle's path.

Twenty-eight-year-old Sable Smith of Colchester was pronounced dead at the scene. The male, whose name has been withheld at the request of his family, suffered significant head trauma and remains in critical condition at the Mary Fletcher Hospital. Anyone with additional information about the vehicle or driver is asked to contact the Scandal Mountain Police Department. Information may also be left on the FBI tip line.

"I wish they'd listed the man's name," I said. "The woman's a little older than I'd thought, but it does sound like the right accident."

Tuck smiled, clearly amused. "I can't get past the name Sable Smith. Sounds like a high-society call girl."

"Maybe a B-movie alias," Kala said. "You know, the nobody actress who dies in the first scene of a horror movie."

I knew they were just trying to lighten the mood, but for heaven's sake there was a photo of a dead woman right in front of us. I wasn't into joking around.

I frowned at them and scanned the counter, hoping Kala had held back another article, one that would reveal all. When I didn't see one, I asked, "Is that it? Wasn't there an article that named the driver? Was it an accident?"

The smile fell from Kala's face. She shook her head. "Like I said, it was hushed up. I couldn't find anything else—in any news outlet. No more pleas for information. No mentions of an arrest. Not even an update on Erik's condition."

"I understand Erik's name being withheld," Tuck said. "His family has clout. He was a witness. But the rest of it is strange."

"How about Sable Smith's obituary? Did you look for that?" I asked.

"Yup, and no can find," Kala said. Her tone brightened. "I could tiptoe into the county medical examiner's records. They'd have information about her there for sure."

As I looked back at the photo of the alleyway and the sheet-covered body, I noticed it was attributed to Tristan Lefebvre. The photo would have been taken the year before Tristan and I briefly became an item, a relationship that fizzled thanks to him wanting more than I was willing to give and to an eager girl he met at a party. After that, Tristan had graduated high school—a year ahead of me—gone away to college, then returned to town to run the *Scandal Mountain Gazetteer* with his father and grandfather.

An idea sparked in the back of my mind. I smiled at Kala. "Hold off on that for now. I think I know how to fill in the blanks without doing anything illegal or traceable."

Tuck slid a look my way. "Really?"

"Well, hopefully."

Chapter Thirty

"You want to go down to the Lefebvres now?" Tuck squinted at me as if the idea was ludicrous. "It's the Fourth of July. They'll be in Burlington covering the celebration."

I handed the papers with the articles on them back to Kala. "It won't cost anything to stop by their place and see."

"Why not just call them?" Kala suggested.

I shrugged. "A message might sit in their voicemail for who knows how long."

"I doubt that," Tuck said. "Didn't you and Tristan have something going on back in high school?"

"More like he had a crush on me, and I hated riding the school bus." I wasn't about to surrender details from my teenage love life and have Tuck and Kala rib me about it from here to eternity.

I smiled at the memory of sixteen-year-old me riding home from school in Tristan's rust-bucket pickup with the "SMG Local News" logo painted on its doors. He always kept a video camara and other equipment behind the seat and an emergency scanner on the dash. And, rumor had it, condoms in his wallet.

One time, I took him to my secret bottle-digging spot, the bramble-covered ravine on René St. Marie's property. Tristan had been more into checking out the decaying junk cars than searching for bottles. I'd gotten mad about that, then we'd made up, and then we'd made out in his truck. It was the first time I ever went very far with a guy—not all the way, but darn close. I never did find out about the condoms, but what we did clearly wasn't a first for him.

Tuck's voice brought me back from my thoughts. "You were smart not to get any more involved with a Lefebvre man than you did," he said. "Nice guys, but there's got to be a reason none of their women stick around for long."

"I think it has more to do with their choice in women than with them," I said.

"Maybe."

* * *

Fifteen minutes later, Tuck and I headed into Scandal Mountain village. Once again, he drove his Suburban, and I rode shotgun. He slowed as we neared the village green, then swung onto a road that ran behind the Congregational Church and the town museum. *Scandal Mountain Gazetteer* was on the left, housed in the old stagecoach inn, a beautiful two-story place built nearly two centuries ago. Their business occupied the front half of the building. The rest of the place served as home for all three Lefebvre men, a generational bachelor pad as it were.

As we neared, I noticed Tristan's now restored pickup parked at the curb. A flash of us making out in that very vehicle sent the heat of embarrassment across my cheeks. Thank goodness trucks couldn't talk.

I turned to Tuck. "Looks like at least Tristan's home."

"That truck is hard to miss," he said. Tuck pulled in and parked behind it.

220

Even before we got out and started up the walkway toward the building, there was no missing the noises coming from beyond its open front door: the blare of TV sets, the clicks and crackles of radio scanners, the whir of box fans.

When we reached the doorway, I peeked inside. The place was neater than I remembered. Instead of out-of-date computers and piles of litter, the desktops now held the latest tech. The file cabinet drawers no longer overflowed like hampers full of dirty laundry.

Tuck knocked on the doorframe. "Anybody home?"

"Be right there!" Tristan's cheerful voice echoed out from a back room. In a flash, he appeared, dressed in a short-sleeved shirt, open black vest, and jeans. His espresso-brown hair was pulled back in a man bun. A thousand-watt smile brightened his face when he saw us. "Edie, hot damn, I haven't seen you in ages."

That heat on my cheeks made a return visit. Tristan had been a bit gawky for my taste as a teenager, but time had done him a lot of favors.

I pulled my gaze off his body, looked at his face, and said, "We weren't sure you'd be here today."

His long strides ate up the distance between us. "I got stuck with desk duty, so to speak." For a second, I thought he was going to hug me, then he let his arms fall to his sides. "I'm sorry about your mom. We tried to keep the reporting aspect to a minimum."

The heat grew even stronger. Not anger at the idea of him reporting on Mom's arrest; more like frustration that this had to be the first thing he mentioned after years of not running into each other. I drummed up a smile. I was so tired of being defined by my mom's behavior. "Her arrest wasn't exactly something you could ignore. You are in the news business."

"We're not convinced she was guilty. A lot of things didn't add up, her attempting to cross the Canadian border with a forgery—" He raised his hands, palms out as if stopping himself. "Sorry again. Promise, not another word. I suspect that's not why you stopped by."

"Don't worry about it," Tuck said. "We wish everyone saw Viki's situation that way."

Eager to move on, I stood up taller and raised my voice. "Speaking of things not adding up. We're trying to find out some details about the hit-and-run that happened twelve years ago, down in the railyard. You took the photo that was published with the article."

He smiled, as if fondly thinking back. "I was sixteen. It was the first time one of my photos made the front page. What do you want to know about it?"

"We'd appreciate anything," I said.

He eyed me. "What are you working on?"

I thought quick. "We're considering buying a piece of outsider art. We think it might depict that accident, but we want to be sure."

"Cool, an art mystery," he said. "Wait here. I'll get copies of the articles for you."

I waved off that idea. "We already looked at those online. What we're wondering is why it was hushed up so fast? Did they ever figure out who was driving the car?"

His eyes narrowed. "You need to know that to research a painting?"

"Was it an accident or something else?" Tuck asked.

Tristan's smile turned sly enough that it reminded me of Kala's. "By 'something else,' do you mean murder?" His gaze went from Tuck to me. "If you buy this painting, I want first dibs on the story behind it, okay?"

"Guaranteed," I said, and I meant it. It was a good deal for us, especially since the chance of us ending up with the townscape or any of Erik's other pieces was rapidly going from slim to none.

Tristan took out his phone. "Let me call my dad. He or Gramps would've written the article. It's better than me taking a guess."

He walked to the door and went out onto the porch, phone to his ear.

Tuck touched my shoulder. He lowered his voice to a whisper, "You think it was smart to tell Tristan this is about a piece of art?"

"It was the best I could think of on the spur of the moment."

Tristan reappeared, big grin on his face. "Dad says the FBI oversaw the investigation. They were insistent it be kept hush-hush."

"The FBI—not the family?" I asked.

"Dad only mentioned the FBI, but it was a long time ago. He said he'll let you know if he remembers anything else." He hesitated, then went on, "Dad's asked Chief Ovitt about the accident over the years. Ovitt's never shared anything other than that it's a closed case."

"Sounds like they never figured out who was driving," I said. Roger Ovitt had been the chief of Scandal Mountain's tiny police force for as long as I could remember. It was puzzling why the FBI had taken charge of the investigation, instead of him or even the state police. Stranger still why the chief remained tight-lipped for so long, unless there was more to the hit-and-run than a tragic accident.

"It's a mystery still waiting to be solved," Tristan said. He grimaced. "Sorry. I can't give you more than that to go on."

I smiled. "Actually, you've helped a lot."

"Good." His gaze met mine, looking deep. "Please, don't be a stranger. We had some good times together."

I shifted uneasily. I had really liked Tristan back in high school. I couldn't deny the physical attraction was still there. But a lot of time had gone by.

Out of the corner of my eye, I spotted Tuck smothering a smile.

Yeah, he'd totally heard what Tristan said.

Chapter Thirty-One

"Don't you dare breathe a word to Kala," I said to Tuck as he pulled away from the curb. "Tristan and I were kids. It wasn't anything then—and nothing's going to happen in the future."

Still smirking, Tuck turned on the car radio and the soft patter of piano music began to play in the background.

"I'm serious," I said, to make sure he understood.

He chuckled. "Don't worry. I won't tell Kala. Anyway, I'm Team Shane all the way."

I glared at him. "Shane and I are off limits, too. No razzing. We're just good friends."

"So you say."

The tone of his voice was more thoughtful than teasing. Still, I had to bite my tongue to keep from arguing the point. I liked Shane. He was up for spending time with me. We had fun, simple as that. Anyway, I had no intention of ruining what Shane and I had by starting something with a guy who'd dumped me because I wouldn't put out.

Tuck stopped at the end of Tristan's street and looked my way. "Before we head home, do you want to pick up anything while we're in town—snacks for Kala? Maybe a latte?"

I was grateful he'd moved on from Tristan, and even happier he'd given me the opening I wanted. "What I'd really like is to go down to the railyard and see if we can find the crime scene. Don't tell me you aren't dying to check it out."

"Never occurred to me," he said with a wink. Then he turned toward the south end of town and the railroad yard. He lowered the radio's volume, the piano music fading into nothing more than a whisper of notes. "You remind me of myself when I was young," he said. "One time, I rented this camp on Cape Cod— it was more like a shack. I brought a date home, expecting to have a fling. But there was another woman already in my bed. You can imagine that didn't go over too well."

My mouth hung open. "I didn't realize you were such a wild one."

"I wasn't really. At the time, I was engaged to the girl I was with. The naked woman was one of your mother's friends, who was using me to make her boyfriend jealous. I found that out later, after he slashed my tires."

Tuck took the road next to Quickie's Quick Stop. The railyard was just ahead, a hodgepodge of dilapidated buildings, barns, and sheds, at the heart of which was the old granary and Fisher's Auction Gallery. Fisher's was in a long and low concrete building, created for function, not beauty. It had once held the county's largest feedstore. After that, it briefly served as Scandal Mountain's community center until the Fisher family bought it along with the rest of the railyard. Today, Fisher's looked deserted, not a single car in front of the celebrated auction house, no one working on the loading docks.

"Where should we start our search?" Tuck asked.

A Wealth of Deception

I closed my eyes and brought to mind the photo Tristan had taken of the sheet-covered body lying in the alley between two buildings. In the quiet of the moment, the background patter of piano music seemed to grow louder. *Narcissus* by Luca Longobardi. The last time I'd heard that music was at the *Immersive Van Gogh* exhibit in Boston. It had been an amazing experience, wandering through two-story-high projections of Vincent Van Gogh's paintings as they transformed and changed along with the music and lights. In his mind's eye, was that how Erik saw his past? Gigantic images, ever-changing, unspooling scraps and bursts of memories, people, and places?

In my mind, I replaced the memory of Van Gogh's surreal landscapes with Tristan's crime scene photo and the noir world of Erik's collages: the townscape's main street, a man standing near a puddle of blood, the family on the beach. The boy with gauze-wrapped hands and the railway station. A woman sprawled by a dumpster . . .

I overlayed those images with that of the briefcase-size collage I'd seen in the alcove at Sterling Gallery: the dilapidated industrial buildings, a single-story warehouse, and a rangy wooden structure. A feedstore. A granary and railroad tracks. Purina Feed's red and white checkerboard.

The details in Erik's collages, I supposed, were like how my mind held onto those moments on the airstrip, and even the hours and days before and afterward. Every detail seemingly unforgettable, yet somehow riddled with chaotic holes and unanswered questions. And unlike Erik, my brain hadn't suffered any physical trauma that day when my grandparents died. Remembering the hit-and-run had to be worse for him, unimaginably difficult.

I took a deep breath, then forced the crime scene photo and images of Erik's work to form a single hazy scene. The woman lay sprawled in an alleyway. On one side of her there was a low, concrete building, on the other side was a dumpster and a tall structure with a red and white checkerboard painted up high. Railroad tracks ran perpendicular to the buildings.

Pinning that image to the front of my mind, I opened my eyes. My throat was dry, my voice tight as I gave Tuck instructions to where we might find that very spot. "Drive out back to Fisher's overflow parking area. The railroad tracks need to be directly behind us. The auction house to our left and the granary tower to our right."

Tuck eased the Suburban forward, down a dirt service road that ran alongside the railroad tracks and into the overflow lot. From that angle there were no alleys to be seen, just a hodge-podge of old structures and a chain-link enclosure that surrounded Fisher's emergency generator.

"Go that way." I pointed toward where the service road exited the far side of the parking area and disappeared into the granary's shadow.

He stepped on the gas, crossing the lot—not rutted and muddy like it was sometimes. Today, it was as smooth as an airstrip.

As we passed the chain-link enclosure, a canyon-like wedge of darkness between two buildings came into sight.

"Stop!" I shrieked.

Tuck stomped on the brakes.

Before the car fully came to a halt, I flung the door open and jumped out. As if trapped in a nightmare, I walked toward the mouth of the canyon, actually a wide alley formed by the auction house's low backwall and the dilapidated granary, zigzagging upward three-plus stories to a ventilated top. It was barely visible, but the remnants of a red-and-white checkerboard colored the top of the granary, nearly wiped away by time and weather.

I swiveled, looking directly behind me. The railroad tracks went north and south, perpendicular to the alley.

"Is that it?" Tuck's voice came from beside me, though I hadn't heard him leave the Suburban and walk over.

"Yeah," I said. "This is where Erik's life changed forever."

My hands trembled as I fumbled for my phone. I brought up a photo of the briefcase-size collage. I held it out to Tuck. "This doesn't show the body and it's not exactly right, but does it look familiar?"

He gave a low whistle. "Sweet Jesus."

I took back the phone and snapped a few photos so we could show Kala when we got home.

"The only thing missing is the 'V,' " I said, "and that has nothing to do with the setting, right?"

"Or Vespa," he added.

"I can't imagine how hard it's been for Erik with all these terrifying bits and pieces locked in his head." I closed my eyes, then pinched the bridge of my nose with my thumb and forefinger, frustrated with myself. "What I don't understand, is why I didn't recognize the location as soon as I saw that collage?"

"Remember, you're not the only one who didn't notice," Tuck said. "I grew up here too, but until I read that newspaper article, it never occurred to me that it happened in Scandal Mountain. I was thinking Burlington, maybe down in Rutland."

I nodded. In truth, I'd occasionally used Fisher's overflow parking when I went to auctions, but I'd never spent time around the back of the buildings.

I hooked my arm with Tuck's and leaned against him. I was lucky to have him in my life, always sane and stable. "I want to take a few more photos. But while we're down here, we should also talk to Pinky. Her apartment is supposed to be somewhere in the railyard. Her cousin Edgar was having lunch at her place around one thirty. It's only a little after four, so he could still be there."

"We could call Kala," Tuck suggested. "She probably knows where it is. We might want to invite her to come with us too."

"Um—maybe not . . ."

As we walked arm and arm into the alleyway, I told him about Kala being interested in someone else as well as Pinky.

"Speaking of missing things, how did I miss that?" he said.

I spotted the outline of a sedan parked in the shadows up close to the granary building. The first newspaper article flashed into my mind:

A security camara captured footage of a maroon-colored sedan speeding directly at the woman . . .

I shivered at the similarity between what had happened here and my close call in Manchester. Yeah, I was starting to not like sedans very much. Still, it was beyond unlikely the maroon sedan that hit Erik and killed Sable Smith was the same car that almost hit me twelve years later. However, it wasn't impossible for it to be the same driver—and a lot of drivers bought similar-sized cars in the same color, over and over again.

My gaze shifted to a vehicle parked next to the sedan, smaller and familiar. I let go of Tuck, gestured at it. "That's Pinky's Camry. C'mon, her apartment must be over there."

"Looks like a kind of seedy place to me," Tuck said.

I laughed. "We're talking about Pinky. Did you expect it to be mainstream?"

I strode ahead of him, trying to not think about the fact that I was walking on the very ground where a woman had died, where Erik had lain on death's door until a rubbish removal man happened across the scene.

Near the Camry, a set of prefab concrete steps went up to a landing. Metal sap buckets filled with marigolds and petunias sat on either side of a door.

The door flew open, and Pinky swaggered out onto the landing. "What the heck are you two doing out there? Sightseeing or setting up surveillance?" She waved for me and Tuck to follow her. "My cousin's here. It's probably about time I introduce you."

We hurried up the steps. As we went inside, I blinked to adjust my eyes to the low light. Clothes and books were strewn everywhere. Cardboard boxes, frog figurines, and vintage lamps covered an antique sideboard. A life-size statue of St. Francis sat in one corner. A repurposed flight of fire escape stairs went up to a loft, partly hidden from view by assorted drapes. The place was very bohemian, though not in the same purposely fashionable way as the apartments of Jimmy's Greenwich Village friends.

Pinky nudged a pregnant golden retriever off a sagging couch "Sit. You want something to drink? Iced tea? Beer?"

"Nothing for me." I gave the dog a stroke as she waddled by, belly and protruding nipples swaying. I didn't want to steal the dog's spot. I just wanted to get past the pleasantries and meet the infamous Edgar—and perhaps find out what Pinky remembered about the hit-and-run while we were here.

Tuck perched on the arm of the couch. "I'm fine too. Have to watch how much I drink, or I spend half the day in the bathroom."

Pinky rolled her eyes. "You two make it hard to be a good hostess." Her lips pressed together, a slight pout. "Kala's not with you?"

"Well, this wasn't exactly a planned visit," I said.

"Okay." She gave her head a slight shake, as if confused by my explanation, then glanced at a door under the loft stairs. "My cousin's trying on some clothes I picked up for him at the Goodwill. He'll be out in a minute."

"I'm glad he's still here," I said.

She frowned. "So, what were you two doing out there? This place isn't exactly a photogenic hotspot."

I licked my lips. "Do you know if something ever happened in the alley?" I was curious to see if, without too much prompting, she remembered more than I did or if the FBI's campaign of silence extended to the community center kids as well as the news.

She smirked. "Lots of things have happened out there. Most of which I'm not going to tell you about."

"I'm being serious," I said.

She settled down on a hassock. "Are you talking about the murder?"

I nodded, then clarified to be sure, "The woman who was hit by the sedan twelve years ago. What was she doing down here? Did they ever find out who was driving?"

"As far as I know, they didn't even find the car. Rumor had it that she and the guy who got hurt were hooking up. Back then, lots of people did that down here—along with buying drugs. But neither of them had drugs in their system."

I did a double take. "How do you know that?"

"My little brother, Bill, swiped bloody dirt from the alley and brought it home so he could run tests on it. You remember Butthead Bill?"

I felt my eyes widen. "Bill? Chipmunk cheeks. Plaid shorts. He really took blood from the crime scene?"

"Sure did. My mom used to keep at-home alcohol and drug test kits to use on us kids. Bill loved messing with those things. He works at the state forensic lab now," she said proudly. "We didn't all end up as lowlifes."

Shocked that a kid had snuck onto the crime scene, I glanced at Tuck. He said, "I bet the FBI just loved Bill."

"I imagine so," I said.

Pinky shrugged. "Bill was big time into that case for a while, but it never went anywhere. As cold as a mackerel, as the saying goes."

The door under the loft stairs opened, and a pudgy middle-aged man with bare feet and a comb-over strutted out, shoulders thrown back, hips swinging, as he showed off dress slacks and a crew-neck sweater.

Pinky smiled. "You look great."

"Darn tooting." He did a spin, then noticed us and flashed a smile. "Pinky's the best fashion consultant ever."

"And the cheapest," she said. She gestured at us. "These are the people who were asking about the old woman at Checkerberry."

I looked down, suddenly embarrassed as I recalled the last time I'd seen Edgar. Namely, at the Well-Being Center when I nearly ran into said old woman. I put on a smile. "She's small with scraggly, thin hair. She uses a cane sometimes and might have recently started wearing a rhinestone monkey brooch."

He looked at me with no hint of recognition, then said, "I know the witch. She's a slippery piece of work."

Thankful he didn't seem to remember me and feeling more confident, I pitched my voice lower, determined to get answers. "Do you know her name?"

"Iris something or other."

"Vesey or Vesper?" Tuck asked, an obvious attempt to see if her last name might just be Vespa—a good move I hadn't thought of.

"Nope. It's more common. Green, Fields . . ."

"Meadows?" I suggested.

"That's it—Iris Meadows."

I sat back. *Meadows.* I could hardly believe it, though it made more sense than any other scenario I'd dreamt up. The woman was related to Alder and Sterling, and this time I wasn't going to second-guess if I was right about the last names being connected.

His lip curled. "You don't want to turn your back on her. I was down there at that Well-Being place with them, and I left my jacket in the bus while I went to get an ice cream. The old bat slipped back onto the bus and stole a brand-new pair of sunglasses outta the pocket." He shook his head. "My girlfriend wasn't happy about that. She'd just bought them for me."

"You got them back, right?" Tuck asked.

"Heck, no. The therapist lady refused to search her. I could see the shape of them even through her shirt."

Pinky got a beer out of the fridge and handed it to him. "That really sucks."

I leaned forward, hands on my knees. "Are you saying Iris Meadows is a thief?" I asked. "Or does she have a mental issue—kleptomania or something?" Either way, I was starting to suspect Kala's monkey brooch might not have been lost so much as freed from her scarf by fast fingers.

"She knows what she's doing all right." He took a sip of his beer, settled into a recliner, and began tugging on a pair of white socks. "Not surprised I didn't get the sunglasses back. Yvette at Checkerberry told me Iris is related to the therapist—her great-aunt. She said the therapist made some deal with the owners of Checkerberry. That old witch gets to live in a fancy upgraded apartment, no extra charge . . ."

He rambled on about Iris's apartment and how she stole and mooched off everyone who rode the transport bus while other clients like Erik never caused trouble.

When he paused to finish his beer, I slid in another question. "How often does Erik go down to the Well-Being Center—twice a week for sessions?" The Vespa pieces first showed up in Sterling's gallery eight years ago. That was quite a few years, but it didn't seem like it would be enough for Erik to create an extensive body of work if he was only doing art two days a week.

Edgar waved that off. "He and that Iris woman are down there four, sometimes five days a week. All day long. If you ask me, that therapist is bilking their insurance companies by adding on unnecessary sessions. No one needs that much head shrinking—not even that thieving old bat." Still talking, he retrieved a pair of shoes from beside the recliner and shoved his feet into them.

Unable to believe my eyes, I gawked at the shoes. They were black slip-ons like the ones I'd seen beside Anna Gorin's front door. Glossy clean. The same or a similar size. *It couldn't be,* I told myself. But Scandal Mountain was a small town. The dating pool wasn't that large.

I blurted, "You don't just know Erik from the bus, do you?"

A rosy hue flushed Edgar's cheeks and washed across his scalp. He glanced at Pinky. "I didn't say nothing about my girlfriend and Erik being related because—"

Pinky laughed. "'Cause you're waiting for your divorce to be final?"

He looked our way. "I gave Anna a ring right after her mother's funeral."

My thoughts flashed back to when we'd first met Anna. She had been wearing a diamond on her ring finger. I'd assumed she wore it out of love for her deceased husband.

"Congratulations," I said. Anna had never been high up on my list of people who might be using Erik, but I had suspected she was hiding something. I'd never have guessed it was a married boyfriend. I scrunched forward another inch, cupped my hands on my knees. This also meant that Edgar might be more useful than we'd assumed. "Have you met Anna's uncle and aunt? Stanislav and Elizaveta?"

He raised his hands, warding off that idea. "Hell no. Erik doesn't even know I'm dating Anna." He flushed again. "I make myself scarce whenever someone visits her. Anna's the best woman I've ever met. It's been hard enough on her with my wife living next door, let alone anyone else finding out about us."

Pinky snorted. "Well, you did a good job keeping it under wraps. I didn't even know half of this."

"Sorry," Edgar said. His eyes met mine. "Anna isn't fond of Stanislav's wife. Once we make things official, she's hoping that side of her family will stop visiting so often."

Yeah, right, I thought. I wasn't so sure the Volkovs were going to be that easy to dissuade.

"Of course, it'll be nice to be open with Erik about our relationship," he added.

Not long after that, the pregnant dog waddled over to Pinky and began to pant heavily.

Pinky looked the dog in the eyes. "What's going on? Are you telling me it's baby time?"

The dog whined, glanced at the couch.

I wasn't sure if Pinky had it right or if the dog was simply demanding her place back. Either way, I used the dog's insistence as an excuse to get up.

"We should take off, anyway," I said. I glanced at the dog, now stretched out in the spot I'd left. "Is she due soon?"

Pinky's expression brightened. "Anytime now. It's her first litter—we're hoping everything goes well."

"You'll have to let us know." I sidestepped toward the door, only slightly slower than Tuck, who already had his hand on the knob.

Pinky grinned. "You can reserve a puppy. Five hundred down. Five later."

"Thanks," I said. "I love dogs, but they're a huge commitment."

"You live in the perfect place to raise one—big yard, off the road.

"I'll think about it. The timing's not so great, though."

Without missing a beat, I waved goodbye and followed Tuck out the door. I'd always wanted a dog, and golden retrievers were the best. But it wouldn't be that many months before Mom got out of prison and came back home—assuming I managed to solve our money issues and our property still belonged to us. Perhaps she'd even be released before the end of the year if her sentence got reduced for good behavior. Once that happened, whether I stayed or went back to my somewhat vagabond life would depend on whether Mom insisted on running the business again or let me remain in charge. Plus, there was the small matter of whether Mom and I could live together without fighting all the time. Definitely not the right time to add a puppy to the mix.

Tuck walked close beside me as we went down the alley toward where he'd left the Suburban. "Unsettling to think someone was killed right here," he said.

Images of a woman lying in the puddle of blood replaced my thoughts of puppies and the future. It was a relief to know Anna's secret, and wonderful that we'd learned Iris Meadow's name and that she was more likely in on the Vespa scam than a victim. Still, Tuck was right: knowing for certain that the darkness in Erik's collages was rooted in a real murder that happened in my hometown did nothing to ease the growing sense of fear inside me.

Chapter
Thirty-Two

B y the time we got home, the shop was closed for the day. However, Kala hadn't given up on her project. The time line was now unrolled across the dining room table.

"Did you find more to add?" I asked.

"Nothing spectacular."

Tuck studied the paper. "Looks to me like you're being modest."

She pulled two chairs out from the table and motioned for us to sit. "I'll tell you everything in a minute. First, did you learn anything new?"

I gave her a rundown on what we'd found out from Tristan and about Tuck and me visiting the crime scene. "While we were there, we stopped in to see Pinky and her cousin. I hope you don't mind we didn't ask if you wanted to join us."

She made a grumbly noise in her throat. I wasn't sure if it was a yes or a no. She squinted at me. "Did Pinky ask where I was?"

I pushed enthusiasm into my voice. We weren't going to move forward until we got past this. "As a matter of fact, she did."

"Good. Absence makes the heart more appreciative," she said with a smile that stayed in place as I told her what we'd discussed with Pinky. It faded when I got to the part about the

239

old woman being Iris Meadows, a general lowlife and a thief. "Are you saying that woman fast-fingered my brooch?"

"Could be. Sounds like she's a real pro," I said sympathetically. Then, before she could start plotting Iris's demise, I moved on to the part about Edgar and Anna.

"Wow. I never would have guessed that one," she said. She patted the time line. "Well, I discovered some interesting stuff myself. You remember the collage with the beach scene?"

"Yeah, the family and the money sandwich that T-Minty made into an NFT."

"Check this out." She pointed to a copy of a photo taped near the beginning of the time line. In the photo a twenty-something Erik stood with a younger version of the no-neck guy I'd seen at Sterling Gallery—his cousin, Victor Volkov. Both were in boxing trunks. Their hands were wrapped in gauze and tape, as if readying for a fight.

I instantly got where Kala was headed. *Wrapped hands.* The beach photo of the mother, father, and two kids. A normal-looking girl and a boy with bloody, gauze-wrapped hands, like a boxer's. "You're thinking that collage is of Erik and Anna with their parents?"

"Erik might not understand the symbolism in his work consciously, but it doesn't take a fancy art therapist to figure that one out," Kala said. "Father eating a bloody money sandwich— blood money, financial crime. Mafia company picnic, not an innocent family outing."

"You'd think that collage would make the Volkovs uncomfortable," Tuck said. "At least once they'd discovered that Erik made it."

Kala scoffed. "Egos. They don't think anyone else will make the connections, especially with Sterling selling the pieces under the Vespa name. If you ask me, I think Stanislav and Elizaveta are the instigators behind the NFTs. They're having them made and buying them too. Laundering money as well as blackmailing Sterling for a piece of the pie. Most likely they're the ones threatening to hurt Alder if Sterling doesn't cooperate. Standard Russian mafia stuff."

I massaged my neck, loosening a knot of tension. Kala's theories were fundamentally assumption mixed with a healthy dose of logic, but I tended to agree with her. At any rate, our digging was unearthing a lot more than just the provenance of the townscape we'd originally set out to find. We were getting in deep; maybe too much so.

As I once more glanced at the photo of Erik and Victor, my subconscious insisted I was overlooking something. Perhaps a vital detail.

Bending close, I studied Erik again. Wrapped hands. Boxer trunks. A glisten of sweat on his brow . . . I moved on to Victor. Red and blue trunks, and a muscle shirt with—

"Oh my gosh," I said. My pulse raced, one beat coming fast after the other. A silver chain hung around Victor's neck. He'd been wearing one at Sterling Gallery too.

"What is it?" Tuck asked.

"Victor's necklace. It's silver, like the links of chain in the collages."

Kala's eyes widened. "I can't believe I missed that. That's where the 'V' signature is always etched, right?'

"Exactly." I took out my phone, brought up the magnifying app. With its aid, one sweep of the necklace told me there wasn't a single 'V' on its links, but suspended from the chain was a silver medal the shape of boxing gloves, engraved into it was an unsurprising word: *Victor.*

The capital "V" was larger than the other letters, bold and broad, almost graffiti-like in style. My excitement dipped.

"Well, what do you think?" Tuck prompted.

"It's a 'V' backed by silver. But I'm not sure. The 'V's' on the collages are perfectly symmetrical. This one isn't. Plus, the medal is shaped like boxing gloves. If Erik's remembering this necklace, then why isn't the 'V' ever etched onto something that shape—and why doesn't Victor's full name ever appear?"

Kala picked up a marker and circled the pendant. "I'm calling it an 'unlikely maybe.'"

"I agree," Tuck said.

I nodded. My subconscious might have nudged me into studying the photo more closely, but now it was telling me we were right to question what I'd found, that it was time to get back to more potentially helpful undertakings. "Okay, we'll put that aside for now. But there are a couple of other things that I don't think we can let slide." I looked at Kala. "Can you try to find out when Elizaveta and Stanislav first started collecting art—especially Vespa pieces? Where that falls on the time line might bring everything together."

"Easy-peasy," Kala said. "I've got some of that already."

I rubbed my hands down the side of my pants, readying to start afresh. "While you're doing that, I'm going to look into Sable Smith a bit more."

She frowned. "I already told you there isn't an obituary, if that's what you're thinking."

"I know. But like you suggested back when we found the article that mentioned her, that name sounds like an alias."

Chapter
Thirty-Three

While I retrieved my laptop from my bedroom and returned, Tuck went to the kitchen and came back with glasses and a pitcher of iced tea for Kala and me.

"How about snacks for dinner?" he suggested.

I blew him a kiss. "You do know you're the best, right?"

"With food, maybe. Not so much with computers."

Kala peered over the rim of her laptop. "Don't forget salty *and* sweet."

"M&Ms or cookies with the healthy junk?" he asked.

"M&Ms, of course. I need all the brain food I can get."

I poured myself a glass of tea, then set to work. Kala was partly right when she'd assumed I was going to search for Sable Smith's obituary. Most often the best techniques are ones that have proven to be winners in the past. In this case, it was the same technique with a twist.

I typed the word *obituary* into the search box. It didn't necessarily mean anything that there wasn't an obituary for Sable online. The family might have asked the funeral home not to publicize her death, given the circumstances. On the other hand, if Sable Smith really was an alias, there could be one under a different name.

Granted, Kala had brought the possibility up as a joke, suggesting Sable Smith sounded like an alias for a B-movie actress. But the outside chance of it being true had stuck in my mind.

I took a sip of tea. Its sweet, lemony flavor refreshed my mouth and soothed my dry throat as I swallowed. I expanded the key words for my search:

Obituary, twenty-eight-year-old woman, died June 1.

I added the year of the accident and *New York City*. Erik was from New York and only visiting in Vermont at the time of Sable's death. It seemed likely the woman he loved might have lived in the city as well.

I hit "Enter."

Pages of obituaries popped up. But strikethroughs crossed out either her age or the date or both.

I tried again, this time using *Vermont* instead of *New York*: *obituary, twenty-eight-year-old woman, died June 1, Vermont.*

"Please, please, please let this work," I prayed. I held my breath and hit "Enter" again.

The first listing read: *Colchester, Vermont. Twenty eight years old. Died unexpectedly. June 1 . . .*

"Gotcha!" I said.

Kala jumped up and raced over. "You found Sable Smith? I can't believe it."

"Hopefully I did." I scanned the obituary, more slowly this time.

Alice J. Moffett, 28, passed away unexpectedly early Sunday morning, June 1.

Alice was much loved by her family and friends. She will be dearly missed.

A celebration of her life will be held at the convenience of her family.

Colchester was where the Well-Being Center was located. Not far from Scandal Mountain or Shelburne, where Anna lived at the time of the hit-and-run. In an obituary, the given location was the person's hometown, but that didn't mean they might not physically live elsewhere, like if they were away at college or overseas in the military.

I glanced at Alice Moffett's photo.

Oval face. Blue eyes. Black hair. Hands steepled in front of her chest. Fingernails, pale peach and neatly manicured—

Peach fingernails?

My thoughts spun. I felt light-headed, unable to believe what I suspected was true.

I studied the photo more closely. Her face was undeniably familiar.

"Oh my God," I said. "I've seen her before."

Kala frowned. "I don't recognize her."

"You should." I scrambled up from my chair and sped from the room, toward the kitchen. With each step, I became more convinced I was right.

As I darted through the kitchen, Tuck called out, "Where are you going?"

"To the shop. I'll be right back."

Not slowing, I ran down the walkway. When I reached the shop door, I punched the security code into the pad and dashed inside. I flew past the checkout counter and up the stairs to the balcony. Ahead, the diminutive oil painting of Madonna and Child hung on the wall.

"There you are, my pretty," I said, taking it down. When I'd first seen the painting, my instinct had insisted it was a somewhat modern rendition of a Russian icon. That assessment hadn't been wrong, though it was possibly even more recent than I'd assumed.

I turned on a side lamp and examined Mary more closely. Oval face. Blue eyes. Black hair. A slightly cleft chin. Hands carefully holding her child. Pale peach, manicured fingernails.

When I'd seen the small Vespa oil paintings at Sterling Gallery, I'd been so focused on the collages that I'd neglected to study them, let alone connect them to the piece we'd acquired from Anna. But now I saw it, the brush strokes, the color choices, the layering . . . This wasn't created by some random artist who specialized in icon-esque paintings.

Clutching the painting closer, I raced back to the house. Both Kala and Tuck were in the kitchen. He was situating a platter of veggies and ranch dip on the table. She was making a fresh pitcher of iced tea.

Since there wasn't room on the table, I hung the painting on the wall, next to the coat hooks. It was hardly the place to show off the piece—squished in next to a mishmash of jackets.

Tuck waggled a finger at the painting. "What's this all about?"

"Anything look familiar?" I stepped back, so he could see.

His face went slack. "Kala just showed me the obituary. That's the same woman."

"You got it. Alice J. Moffett—also known as Sable Smith."

Kala hurried over. "Wow. That's definitely her."

"What's more interesting is that I'm all but certain Erik painted it." A detail I'd overlooked jumped out at me. I dashed to the kitchen junk drawer and snagged the handheld spotlight. Turning it on, I used it to brighten the silver chain that hung around Mary's neck. One link was decorated with a tiny "V." I set the spotlight down on the table, and grinned. "Make that a hundred percent certain."

"Well, now. That's a spot of good news," Tuck said. "Looks like we might be able to get that septic system replaced after all."

For a second my head whirred, and I rested a hand against the wall to steady myself. I'd been so focused on the mystery of Erik and Alice that I hadn't stopped to consider what this discovery meant to us personally. We owned the Madonna and Child painting, a piece with a heck of a backstory, by an outsider artist who—if I had anything to say about it—was going to become even more famous than Vespa. The piece was worth a boatload—and there was no reason we couldn't sell it."

"Do you think Alice had a child in real life? Could that be why Erik painted her holding Baby Jesus?" Kala asked.

I shook my head. "I don't think so. Take a closer look."

Both she and Tuck took another step forward. Kala flinched back, nose wrinkling. "Yikes. Jesus looks like Rocky Balboa. You know, old, like in *Rocky V* when he retires after taking a pounding."

I laughed and so did Tuck. Still smiling, I explained: "Baby Jesus is often depicted as a beardless man rather than an infant in early Russian icons. It was popular in the medieval era, and in other various times and countries as well."

"I'm guessing in reproductions of old pieces too?" she said.

"You got it, like what Erik did when he painted this. I'm willing to bet if it were Alice's real-life child, then Jesus wouldn't look like Rocky."

"That's a relief." She glanced at the painting again and shuddered. "This baby's too creepy to be real."

Tuck's tone turned serious. "Kala, you should tell Edie about the message you got."

"While I was gone?" I asked. I hadn't been out of the house for more than a few minutes.

"I got it around the time you discovered Alice's obituary. But then you took off so fast I didn't have time to tell you." As if to prolong the tension before sharing, Kala plucked a celery stick from the veggie platter, dipped it into ranch dressing and nibbled off a bite. She wiped the corners of her mouth, then continued, "I've officially verified that the rumors about the Volkov family are true. They are connected to the Russian mafia. No ifs, ands, or buts about it. Their import and export business is only one arm of their dealings. Another is their decades-old involvement with art investments."

"Someone you know personally told you this?" I asked.

"More like a friend of mine asked a friend. But, yes, straight from Russia with love. The Volkovs were buying and selling art long before Vespa came onto the scene. Erik and Anna's father was Stanislav's partner before he died."

Tuck gave Kala a sidelong look. "I'm guessing you got this from one of your darknet friends?"

"An acquaintance with *skills*," she corrected him.

I shook my head, amazed as always by Kala's connections and how fast they worked. But this wasn't the time to stand around questioning how she'd met these people or when. I wiped a hand over my face. "I wish I knew where we should go from here."

Tuck cleared his throat. "I think it's time to talk to Shane about this." His voice deepened. "Money laundering. Russian mafia. A murdered woman with an alias. These aren't things to mess around with."

"I'm getting a little nervous myself," Kala said.

I looked back at the Madonna and Child painting, into Mary's blue eyes. It was impossible to look at her and not think of the alleyway, of her body lying there. A real woman from Erik's past, not just a figment of his imagination. A person whose murder remained unsolved.

And there was the close call I'd had in Manchester. What if it wasn't a coincidence? Was I willing to risk something like that happening to someone I loved? To Kala or Tuck?

What more was there for us to gain by staying silent?

"All right," I said. "I'll call Shane."

* * *

Shane's phone rang once, twice . . .

He'd told me that he had some time off starting this evening. He'd planned on catching up on his rest tonight and had suggested we get together tomorrow, but in the end, listening to what I had to say would take priority over his quiet night. He'd also probably lecture me about how I should have told him sooner and a variety of other things.

I took a sip of tea, then swallowed it fast as his voicemail answered.

You've reached my number. Leave a message.

I knew it was Shane, though he didn't use his name.

"Hey, I need to talk to you about something important," I said. "Call back as soon as you can."

I hung up and set the phone on the table next to me, fully expecting it to ring instantly. When it didn't, I shoved the phone into my pocket. Then I fixed myself a fresh iced tea and a plate of snacks, and trailed Tuck and Kala out to the front porch.

My stomach burned and a sick feeling balled in the back of my throat. Calling Shane was the right move—I was becoming more and more sure of that. However, that didn't make doing it any less uncomfortable. Why was it so hard? The fun stuff was easy: skinny-dipping, drinking wine, looking at the stars, sex and more sex.

I flopped onto the wicker loveseat. "What the heck is taking Shane so long?"

"He might have gone for a run," Tuck suggested.

"Maybe," I grumbled.

I sent him a text.

Did you get called into work?

Five minutes passed, then ten . . . Even when Shane was on duty, he normally replied quickly. A voice inside me whispered, *He's ghosting you. That's what guys do when they're ready to move on. That's what Tristan did way back when, right?* I rejected that idea. This wasn't high school. Besides, ghosting someone wasn't Shane's style. Or was it? Was I really that sure?

By quarter to eight, I couldn't stand waiting anymore. It didn't help that the three of us had been talking about the horrific things the Russian mafia were reputed to do to people they deemed enemies or threats—contract killings, car bombs, death by woodchipper . . . hit-and-run *accidents*. I wasn't just scared for us anymore. I was scared for Erik—and for Alder too, though I hated to admit that.

I got up from the loveseat. "Shane probably did laps in the pool and went to bed early. I'm going to drive over to the cabin and wake him up."

Tuck nodded. "Good idea."

"Take the time line with you," Kala said.

*   *   *

It took me barely a half hour to reach Shane's driveway, without even going that much over the speed limit. As I pulled in, I was surprised to find the downstairs lights on, glowing brightly in the deepening twilight. Maybe he'd fallen asleep in front of the TV.

My stomach tensed when I noticed a black Mustang parked beside his Land Rover. He had a visitor? That didn't jive with Shane's plans to rest up tonight.

I shook it off. Sure, I'd never seen two cars in his driveway before. But he drove an unmarked police sedan for work sometimes, a black Dodge Charger. Perhaps he'd just switched his ride.

After snagging the rolled-up time line from the passenger seat, I got out of the Volvo. The gravel walkway crunched under my shoes as I walked toward the front door. Partway there, I glanced in the cabin's front window, hoping to catch a glimpse of Shane laying on the couch with an afghan pulled up to his chin, looking peaceful and handsome—

I stopped, unable to take another step as I spotted Shane.

Not lying down. And not alone.

He stood with his back to the window, talking to a tall, slender woman with long, dark hair pulled back in a ponytail. Tight jeans. Black tank top. She was more fit than I'd ever dreamed of being.

A lead-heavy weight dropped from my chest into my stomach. Shane and I weren't in a committed relationship. We were just friends.

My fingers tightened around the time line, paper crumpling under my grip, like the way the crayons had buckled all those years ago when I scrawled the flames on the memory box.

I wheeled and headed back toward the Volvo, fast strides rapidly covering ground. But when I reached the car, I couldn't make myself open the door. There had to be an innocent reason behind the woman's visit. Besides, my being here wasn't about my relationship with Shane. I was here because of everything we'd discovered. I was here for Tuck and Kala's safety. And for Erik.

Erik deserved a chance to heal from all he'd suffered, to have his story told, to cry, to recover. And to have his art recognized. Erik deserved all that had been denied to him by Alder and Sterling, and most likely by members of his own family as well.

Turning back around, I forced myself up the walkway again, to the steps and Shane's front door.

Chapter
Thirty-Four

S hane answered the door on my first rap, but he only opened it partway. "What a nice surprise. I wasn't expecting to see you."

"I left a voice message, and I texted you." I stepped closer, pushing one foot against the door to keep it open. "I need to talk to you. It's important."

His Adam's apple bobbed. "This isn't—"

"It's fine if you're with someone. I just need a minute." I ducked under his arm and into the cabin. My whole body simmered with a need to talk with him, underlayered with jealous anger I couldn't justify. We both had a right to see other people, and I had a legitimate reason to be here.

My gaze darted to the living room area. The woman rested a hand on her hip and glared at me with cold disdain.

A movement behind her caught my eye.

Under a window, a balding blond man sat on the oversized recliner, the chair I'd been in only a few nights ago when I'd talked to Jimmy about the townscape. I recognized him instantly—then realized I knew the woman as well.

Embarrassment swept heat up my neck and across my face. I'd certainly misinterpreted what I'd seen through the window.

I shoved the time line under my arm, managed a weak smile. "Um . . . Hi?"

The man smiled, as if amused by my pushy entrance. The woman's expression remained stiff and icy.

Shane rested a hand on my shoulder. "You remember Latimore," he said.

I nodded a greeting to the man. Senior Special Agent Latimore of the FBI Art Crime Team. Yeah, he wasn't someone I'd ever forget. When the decoy collection had been stolen from Jean-Claude Bouchard's property, Latimore was the agent who'd interrogated me as a possible suspect after I was found sneaking around in a farmhouse basement. In the end, I had been released. Still, even now, he had an intimidating air about him that made me feel guilty when I hadn't done anything wrong. But that uneasiness was nothing compared to how I felt about the woman. I glanced her way, avoiding her glare by looking at the bridge of her nose. "Officer Medina, right?"

"Agent Medina," she said, point-blank.

"Oh, sorry. I didn't realize." I bit my tongue to keep from apologizing further. There was nothing I could say that would change her low opinion of me. She was the undercover officer I'd sold stolen property to four years ago. It had been unintentional on my part. Well, more a case of me unwisely buying and then selling something when my gut warned against it. On her part, it was an open-and-shut case.

"Medina's with the FBI now," Shane explained. His hand left my shoulder. He walked away from me and into the living room area, then looked back. "Come in. Have a seat."

"Ah—maybe I should come back another time?" Obviously, there was a reason two FBI agents were visiting Shane, and the look on Medina's face told me it wasn't a social call.

"Don't be ridiculous," Shane said. "They stopped by to ask me something. We're done with that." He motioned to my favorite spot, a rustic armchair with plush cushions. "Sit. Relax. I'm guessing it might be good if they heard what's on your mind."

I nodded, though I suspected relaxing in any form wasn't going to happen. I slid the time line out from under my arm and tucked it in beside me as I lowered myself onto the seat cushion.

Latimore moved to a chair close to mine. Shane took up a position on the couch. Medina retreated and stood in front of the fireplace, blending in with the stone backdrop like a sullen chameleon fading into its surroundings.

"I'm not sure where to start," I said.

"Um . . ." Shane's gaze flicked to the time line. I was positive he was going to ask about it. Instead, his hand went to that damn devil tattoo of his, massaging it as if he had a cramped muscle. He was avoiding telling me something. But what?

"Maybe start by telling us what happened at Sterling Gallery," Latimore said.

A sharp pain took root in my chest. I glared at Shane. He'd told his FBI buddies what I'd shared with him in confidence. How else would Latimore know I'd gone to the gallery?

I crossed my legs at the ankles, uncrossed them, then sat up straighter on the edge of the chair seat. I really liked Shane. I respected him. I'd come here because it only made sense to tell law enforcement what we'd discovered. Still, the rules Shane lived by were becoming tiresome. Cop first. Friend second.

"Go on," Latimore said. "Tell us everything."

I took a deep breath, skipped over the gallery, and went straight to the heart of the matter. "Tuck, Kala, and I suspect Alder Meadows is providing her brother Sterling with art that's unwittingly created by one of her clients—Erik Volkov. They're marketing his work under the fake persona of Vespa. But Erik's uncle and his wife are art collectors." I looked at Latimore. "I'm guessing you know that already."

He nodded. "What we'd like to know is, who were the Volkovs interacting with at the gallery?"

"Hmm . . . I didn't really notice. But I did overhear a confrontation between Sterling and some man. It might've been Stanislav or his son, I couldn't really see the second person. It also could've been a guy called T-Minty. He's involved with turning the Vespa art into NFTs." I shifted the time line up onto my lap, gave it a pat. "It would be easier for me to explain if I showed you this. I haven't even gotten into the part about Iris Meadows. She's related to Sterling and Alder, and she's playing the role of Vespa."

I'd been avoiding Shane's gaze, but I looked his way now to catch his reaction to all I was sharing.

He averted his eyes and got to his feet. "You can unroll it on the kitchen island. I'll make a pot of coffee for everyone."

"That would be great," Medina said. "It's been a long day."

We all went into the kitchen. Shane headed for the coffee maker. I set the time line on the island, then continued with my explanation. "Besides the similarity in appearance between the pieces I knew Erik made and the ones being marketed as Vespa's work, it was the overarching presence of the letter 'V' that first made me suspicious. It's generally assumed the letter is Vespa's signature, but my mom suggested we look for other symbols and repeated elements that might distinguish one artist from the other. That's when I noticed a recurring date folded into both artists' works—June first." I unrolled the time line, tapped its midpoint with an index finger. "Twelve years ago. June first. Everything centers on that day—"

In that moment, two things occurred to me simultaneously. Number one, Shane had changed the subject when I'd mentioned the date while we were at the pub. Number two, the hit-and-run investigation had gone silent after local police backed off and the FBI took over. What had made Sable Smith's death so special to them?

I turned toward Latimore, who stood beside me at the end of the island. His hands were behind his back and his legs slightly braced, a stance of professional coolness. But under the brightness of the kitchen's overhead light, a wary spark of curiosity shone in his eyes.

"Go on," he said. His voice was level.

I toughened mine. "Who was Sable Smith? Why was she living under an alias?"

He stiffened. "Who?"

On the other side of him, Medina turned away. She walked toward where Shane was making the coffee and picked up a mug, then mumbled, "Do you have any cream?"

"There's half-and-half in the fridge," he said.

A hiss of steam came from the coffee maker.

Latimore let his arms relax to his sides. He half turned toward Shane and Medina and said, "I'll take mine black."

I clamped my hand on his closest wrist, bringing his attention back to me. "Maybe the name Alice Moffett rings a bell?"

He went rigid. "Where did you hear that name?"

257

I nodded at the time line. "June first. Twelve years ago. Scandal Mountain railyard. Someone driving a maroon-colored sedan hit and killed Alice Moffett." I toughened my voice even further. "Did you know Erik Volkov was in love with her? Her death is depicted in almost all his pieces. A likeness of her face is in at least one."

Shane wheeled to look at me. "Are these things Erik Volkov told you?"

I stood up taller. "He told me that a woman he loved was killed on June first. The rest wasn't hard to put together after that."

"What else did Erik say?" Latimore asked. His voice was still firm, demanding, but his eyes held genuine concern.

I took a guess. "You really don't know how much Erik remembers, do you?"

"We would like to know," Latimore said.

The tension in my chest loosened a bit. "Erik's frustrated. Emotionally, he's in turmoil. He sees bits and pieces, flashes of places and things that he can't make sense of. He puts those recollections into his art. But I'm confident he doesn't clearly remember that part of his life."

Latimore glanced at Shane, voice quieting. "I think we should tell her."

He nodded. "I agree."

"You sure?" Medina asked.

"We can trust Edie," Latimore said. He squared his shoulders, turned to me. "Alice Moffett was with the FBI. A good agent. She was like family."

I blinked at him. I couldn't say what I'd expected, but this wasn't it. "Are you saying she was undercover? She didn't really love Erik?"

He gave a half shrug, I assumed in response to my last question. "Alice was close to getting information we needed to move forward with prosecuting the Volkov family on money-laundering charges. Erik juggled Stanislav's accounting. He'd agreed to turn state's evidence. Alice was there to take him into witness protection."

Shane added, "The railyard was simply a convenient, out-of-the-way place for Erik to leave his car. Authorities would have picked it up and disposed of it later."

"Were they both targeted?" I asked.

Latimore shook his head. "It's been a long time, and we still have very little other than assumptions."

"Stanislav is ruthless, Edie," Shane said. "That's why I told you to stay away from him and his family."

I nodded. Maybe I wasn't all that happy with Shane right now, but I agreed with him about the ruthless part.

Medina took the pot out from under the coffee maker. "How about if I pour our coffees now?"

"Good idea," Latimore said.

I turned my attention back to the time line, walking them through it as we sipped our coffee. By the time I finished, I was drained to the core. Light-headed, in fact, from thinking about the enormity of Alice Moffett's murder, the Vespa scam, and the Russian mafia connection.

"If you don't mind," I said, "I should head home. I'm exhausted. Honestly, I'm a bit worried about Tuck and Kala too."

"Worried you got them in too deep this time?" Shane mumbled.

Latimore shot a hard look at him.

Medina stared into her coffee.

I wanted to think Shane's smartass comment had slipped out because he was as exhausted as I was. But reflexive anger flushed my face, and all I could think about was how he'd already proven how little he cared about my feelings by sharing our private conversations with his work buddies. It was pretty obvious what came first in his book—and for sure it wasn't me or our relationship. In fact, I couldn't help wondering if he'd been using me the way Alice Moffett used Erik.

"I'm out of here," I said. I snagged the time line, folded it haphazardly.

Latimore stood up. "I'll give you a call if I have more questions."

"Whatever." I turned away. I wasn't worried about being polite to him or Medina. I doubted it would hurt their feelings, and I was spent.

Shane closed the distance between us, taking the time line from my hands before I could object. "I'll walk you out," he said.

I scowled at him.

He ignored it, moved ahead of me, and opened the front door when I reached it. He closed it once we were both outdoors.

Night had fallen. Crickets chimed. I could feel the cool dampness of the settling dew on my arms.

Shane held the time line out to me. "I'm sorry about what I said in the kitchen. That was an asshole thing to say."

"You won't get any argument from me," I snapped. My exhaustion and anger took over. "You know, I'm really pissed that you told Latimore everything I said to you in confidence. I bet you told half the state police force too." Now that I'd started,

I couldn't let it go. "Maybe telling them was the right thing to do. But you could've asked me first."

His jaw tightened. "Would you have agreed?"

"I might've. That doesn't matter now. You took that choice away from me. You knew as soon as I mentioned the townscape that you weren't going to keep it to yourself. You avoided telling me the truth, right then and there."

He folded his arms across his chest, lifted his chin. "And who wanted me to think they'd called ahead about meeting Erik at the Well-Being Center? What do you call that—if it wasn't you lying to me?"

The time line crumpled under my tightening grip. "I like being with you, Shane. But I'm starting to think we have very different definitions of friendship."

He grabbed me by the shoulders, a firm grip. "We're more than friends, Edie."

I snorted, twisted free. "Go back inside and talk to your people. Talk about how stupid I am. That's why Latimer and Medina came here tonight, right? You weren't taking the evening off. You were filling them in on everything I'd told you."

"You're wrong. It wasn't that."

"Yeah, sure." I swung away from him, stomped to my car, and left.

Chapter
Thirty-Five

I floored the accelerator, zooming past the speed limit. Outlines of trees brightened, then ghosted into shadows under the fleeting brilliance of the Volvo's headlight beams. No cars behind or ahead of me. Few passed by. The road just went on, a glossy ribbon under a sweep of low fog.

I thought about Stanislav Volkov. As head of his branch of the family and Erik's employer, he was most likely the one Erik was going to testify against. It only made sense that he was the FBI's prime suspect, the man behind the hit-and-run murder of the undercover agent Erik loved. How had Stanislav felt when he saw Erik in the headlights, his own nephew rushing to push an FBI agent out of the way? Had Stanislav set out to kill both of them? Or had he hired someone else to murder Alice, and only later found out that Erik was hurt in the process?

And what about Erik? His life destroyed in a single moment, slowly re-forming after months or maybe years in the hospital, only to be exploited again. An artistic savant. A tool for others to get what they wanted.

Hearts and lives broken, and for what?

Money. Power.

* * *

By the time I got home, it was a little before eleven. I parked the Volvo in front of the shop, then trudged to the kitchen door and went inside. Like the previous night, I found Tuck and Kala in the living room, watching a movie on TV. Tonight, three rock glasses and a bottle of Tuck's prized bourbon sat on the coffee table. The bottle's seal was still intact.

"How did it go?" Kala eyed the crumpled time line. "I'm guessing not so good?"

As I settled down on the couch next to her, Tuck cracked open the bottle, pouring a fingerful in each glass. He held one out to me. "We thought you might need this."

I put the time line on the table, took the glass. "You aren't kidding."

"What happened?" Kala stared at me like a kid waiting for a bedtime story—or in this case, more like a Grimm's fairy tale.

I took a sip, feeling only the bourbon's burn as it went down, without savoring its flavor. "First, I think Shane and I are done."

Tuck squinted. "I find that hard to believe."

"Well, believe it. When I got to his place, Latimore and another FBI agent were there."

"At night?" Kala said. "And on a holiday? What were they doing—state police versus FBI shuffleboard or something?"

Usually, I enjoyed Kala's humor. This time, I was too exhausted to play along. "Shane told them everything I shared with him. I'm willing to bet they were there to discuss the case. Afterall, Latimore isn't just any FBI agent. He's in charge of an Art Crime Team—"

A discordant squeal came from the TV, the screech of a commercial featuring a middle school band and a luxury car. The woman in the driver's seat of the silver Infiniti rolled up the car's window, blocking out the noise. She reclined the seat and peacefully closed her eyes. If only it were that easy to block out the shrieking thoughts in my head—as well as the commercial.

I pressed my fingers against my temples. "Can you turn that thing down, please."

"Sure thing." Kala muted the TV. "Better?"

"Much."

Tuck's brows lowered in thought. "Are you sure that's why Latimore was at Shane's house? Wouldn't they have discussed that when Shane was on duty?"

"I suppose," I said. "But they certainly were eager to question me."

Tuck swirled the liquid in his glass, took another sip. "Years ago, back when I lived in Pennsylvania, I had a friend who did IT work for the state police. Smart guy. Single. Kept his nose clean. The FBI got it in their heads that they wanted to recruit him. They went to see him at work, visited him at home, invited him out for dinner . . . They were like Jehovah's Witnesses, only instead of an offer to save his soul, their spiel was a job offer too good to resist."

I swallowed the rest of my drink in one sip, an attempt to smother the ache pinching in my throat. What Tuck had said was a real possibility. Shane had worked in conjunction with Latimore before. They worked well together. Shane was in his early thirties, plenty of time to take his career in a new direction. He was smart. Devoted to law enforcement. A real up-and-comer. He was single.

"So did you learn anything new?" Kala asked.

264

I let out a breath, grateful to move the conversation in a different direction. I told her and Tuck about Alice being an agent and Erik going into witness protection . . . The one good thing I could say about the trip to Shane's cabin, it had filled in a lot of blanks.

When I was done, I rubbed my hands over my face. "It's getting late," I said. "I'm too tired to think about this anymore. I need to try and get some sleep."

Not waiting for everyone else, I clomped upstairs and into a hot shower. Still thinking too deeply for my own good, I collapsed into bed. A breeze fluttered the curtains in the window. Hazy moonlight bathed the room, transforming it into a surreal landscape as unsettling as one of Erik's collages.

I rolled onto my side. As I drifted toward sleep, the middle school band music from the commercial squawked in my head. The car in the commercial's headlights and grill morphed from an Infiniti into a bloodred Mercedes like the one in Checkerberry Manor's parking lot . . . Perhaps my subconscious was intent on driving me insane.

The nails on a blackboard music faded, and the last words Shane had said to me rose.

"You're wrong. It wasn't that," he'd said when I guessed that Latimore and Medina had come to the cabin to talk about the Volkovs and the Vespa scam.

"Yeah, sure," I'd answered, certain he was lying. But maybe I'd been wrong.

Recruitment. The word drummed in my head. The FBI would be a big step forward for Shane's career. More money. More interesting cases. New friends and travel.

I rolled onto my other side. The FBI training center was in Quantico. That meant Shane would be leaving Vermont, at least for a while. Maybe forever if he was put on a team other than Latimore's.

My heart squeezed. The last time we put our relationship aside, I was the one who'd left Vermont. I'd been gone three years, but I hadn't forgotten Shane. If he left, it would make our breaking up easier. He probably was as angry with me right now as I'd been with him. After all, I'd pretty much told him our fun times were over.

* * *

"Edie! Wake up!" Tuck's shouting jerked me from sleep.

I leaped out of bed, scuffed into my slippers, and flung open the bedroom door. "What's wrong?"

He stood there in his pajamas, rifle slung over his shoulder, phone in hand. "Someone's breaking into the shop. I just got the alarm."

I took the phone. In the live security feed, the shape of a person moved through our moonlit shop, past the display of silver and the front counter. They started up the stairs toward the balcony, carrying something. "Is that a shotgun . . . a crowbar?"

"A bar," Tuck said. "They could do a lot of damage with that. China. Glass. Artwork."

"You're not kidding." I stepped into the hall, one eye still on the phone. "The police were notified, right?"

He nodded. "I'm betting this isn't a robbery. Someone wants to send us a message to back off the Vespa thing."

"Like the Volkovs?" I suggested.

Kala emerged from the third-floor stairwell. Shortie PJs. Hair in braids. "What's going on?"

"We have a break-in." Tuck unshouldered his gun and headed down the stairs.

I wasn't sure I liked the determined look on his face, but Tuck was no crazy man.

I passed the phone to Kala so she could see the security feed. She scowled. "I wish I had Taz."

"It's still in the Volvo," I said.

Tuck glanced over his shoulder. "No one's doing any shooting or tasing."

I frowned. "Says the man carrying a gun?"

"I'm going to fire a few warning shots to flush them out. I want you and Kala to watch from the house. When you see them come out, switch on all the outdoor lights. Brighten them up like it's daytime. See if they're a man or woman. How old they are and how tall. Which way they go—all that jazz."

"Will do." Kala saluted.

When we reached the kitchen, I grabbed the handheld spotlight from where I'd left it on the table. A hundred times better than stationary lights for pinpointing the intruder when they appeared—

My thoughts flashed to when I'd used the spotlight earlier in the day. *Madonna and Child.* A sudden chill raised goose bumps on my arms.

I swiveled to Tuck. "The burglar was headed upstairs. The Madonna and Child painting was displayed up there until I took it down. They could be looking for it. It's one of Erik's pieces. It's of Alice Moffett."

Kala sucked in a breath. "You think they cased the shop?"

"Maybe—or they could've had someone else do it for them," I said. "The real question is, why didn't they just buy the painting? It wasn't that expensive. The Volkovs have plenty of money."

"They probably wanted to send a message as well as get the painting." Tuck eased the back door open.

"Be careful." I followed him out onto the stoop, thumb poised over the spotlight's on/off switch.

Rifle at the ready, Tuck zigzagged through the fog and moonlight, across the lawn, around the flowerbeds, toward the shop. He hunkered down in the shadows behind the Volvo.

Kala stood at my shoulder, just inside the door, with her hand on the outdoor light switches, her eyes trained on Tuck's phone and the security feed. "The burglar looks like a guy. More bulky than tall. He's coming back downstairs."

The phone buzzed. She answered instantly, listened for a second, then whispered, "Yes. An intruder in the antique shop. The police are on their way, right? That's good . . ."

Thank goodness, I thought. We were outside the village, but not too far for a Scandal Mountain cruiser to get here quickly.

Still, the burglar could destroy thousands and thousands of dollars' worth of antiques in seconds if they wanted to—and they were probably angry as hell that the painting wasn't there. We couldn't afford to wait any longer to get them out of the shop.

Sweat dampened my armpits. I looked back at Kala. Her head was down as she whispered into the phone. I glanced toward the Volvo where Tuck was crouched.

Screw it.

Leaving Kala behind, I followed the path Tuck had taken, moving noiselessly except for the swish of my slippers against the night-dampened grass. I couldn't stand back and let Tuck take the brunt of the risk himself.

Thump, clatter-clatter. The muted sound echoed from inside the shop.

I ducked down behind a bed of daylilies, halfway to the Volvo.

Tuck's voice filled the air. "You in there! Come out with your hands up!"

I readied the spotlight. I had a clear view of the shop door from where I was hidden and could easily pinpoint the person when they appeared. In fact, I could now see the door was wide open.

My throat clenched. The security feed had been hazy. What if the person didn't just have a crowbar? What if there was a handgun tucked into their waistband? What if they came running out with it drawn?

BANG! I jumped as the boom of Tuck's rifle rang out. *BANG!*

"Come out or the next shot's going through the window!" Tuck yelled.

The sound of glass breaking came from the rear of the carriage barn. Mom's art studio. The atrium doors that went out into her secret garden.

"Lights!" I shouted to Kala.

Brightness flooded the front yard and parking area. I scrambled forward, leaping over a coil of garden hose and sprinting past the front of the shop, way ahead of Tuck. The intruder wasn't coming out the front door. They'd escaped through the back, into Mom's garden. I was certain of it.

I swung onto a path I'd taken a million times. The path I was on was the only way in and out of the hedge-enclosed garden. If I could intercept the intruder, I'd get a super good look at them.

The scream of police sirens echoed up from somewhere in the valley, moving closer but still a ways off.

The squelch of someone running through mud came from the garden.

"Fucking cesspit," the person grumbled, too low for me to tell if they had an accent. Not mud. The septic overflow.

Switching on the spotlight, I flooded the path in front of me. A man stood frozen ten yards ahead. Black hoodie. Face camouflaged. Wet work boots. Baggy pants.

He bolted off the path into the darkness. I fanned the spotlight, illuminating him as he reached where the lawn gave way to overgrown field and brush. Moderately tall. Husky—

He swung to look at me.

Shit! There was a gun in his hand.

I dropped to the ground, flat in the dirt.

I heard twigs snapping as he took off. I waited a heartbeat, then scrambled to my feet and spotlit the field in time to glimpse him disappearing into the distant woods. I thumped a fist against my thigh. *Damn it.* There were a million places to hide in there and millions of ways out. No way would the police be able to catch up with him now.

Tuck came panting up behind me. "Did you see him?"

"Not well enough."

As we walked back toward the front of the shop, two cruisers flew up the driveway, blue lights strobing, sirens blaring. They skidded to a halt. Doors flung open and an officer jogged toward us. Another strode toward where Kala was coming from the house.

Tuck pointed toward the woods. "It was one person. They went that way. Edie saw them."

I could see now the officer was Chief Ovitt himself, white haired, paunchy, and as alert and eager as an antique picker at a flea market. He eyed Tuck's rifle, then my spotlight. His attention stayed on me. "What did you notice?"

"It was a man for sure. Probably thirties—maybe. Athletic build. He used camouflage paint on his face, like the kind hunters use. He had a handgun. Did you see any trucks or cars down on the road?" I asked. "Or ATVs?"

"Can't say I did," the chief said. He glanced toward the dark field and woods. "Once it's daylight, we'll take a look around out there."

"Why wait?" I protested, though I knew it was a useless cause.

Tuck frowned at me. "Edie, trust the chief. He knows what he's doing."

I huffed out a frustrated breath. "If only I'd been a second earlier . . ."

"You could have gotten yourself shot," Chief Ovitt said. He glanced at Tuck. "Did he take anything?"

"Nothing as far as we know," Tuck said.

"What do you say we go take a closer look." He directed us toward the front of the shop. The door was sprung open, the casing broken, no doubt the work of the crowbar.

Tuck turned on the lights and studied the damage. "That must be what set off the alarm."

The chief scanned the shop, his attention going to a knocked-over table. The Staffordshire spaniel figurine it had held now lay in pieces on the floor. He asked, "How long do you think he was in here?"

"Ten minutes, maybe a little more. It was three fifteen when I got the notification," Tuck said.

I trailed a step behind them as they followed the route the intruder had taken, past the display of silver and the counter where the cash register sat, then up to the balcony. A small Currier and Ives print had been yanked off the wall and tossed aside. Not the artwork they were looking for, I suspected.

I folded my arms over my silky pajama top and clamped my mouth shut. Better to hang back and keep it simple by letting Tuck take the lead. When he thought the time was right, he'd mention the possible Volkov connection and tell the chief to get in touch with Shane or Latimore. Given recent events, the idea of me calmly discussing anything was probably out of the question.

We went back down to the main floor. The door between the shop and Mom's art studio had been kicked in.

Tuck turned on the art studio lights. An easel was toppled over. The atrium doors were shattered, glass everywhere. A metal stool lay on the ground beyond the doors, most likely what had been used to break the glass.

"Are there outdoor lights?" the chief asked.

Tuck nodded, then switched them on. As the two of them went outdoors, a waft of sewer drifted inside.

I called after them, "There might be footprints in the puddle." I could only hope the Chief Ovitt didn't question whether we were dealing with the septic issue or not.

My focus shifted as the hard-soled clip of confident footsteps echoed behind me, striding across the shop floor, headed in my direction. I knew who it was without even looking.

Shane.

Chapter
Thirty-Six

My chest squeezed and my face went hot as my emotions knotted and corkscrewed in a hundred different directions. Shocked that Shane was here. Happy he was here. Mad at myself for feeling so much.

I wheeled around. He stood on the studio threshold, dressed in pressed jeans and a flannel shirt. His badge was displayed at his beltline. He glanced toward where Tuck and Chief Ovitt stood talking in the floodlit garden, then said, "Is everyone okay?"

I hushed my voice, so it wouldn't travel. "What are you doing here?"

"We need to talk," he said. "Let's go to the house."

I gritted my teeth. The last thing I was ready to do right now was talk with him, but a twitch at the corner of his eye told me he was equally as uncomfortable.

"Please." He moved closer, touched my shoulder, a tentative gesture.

"All right," I snapped, not trying to hide my unhappiness from him. It did seem wiser to talk in private, out of Chief Ovitt's earshot at least.

We walked through the shop and out the front door. The other Scandal Mountain officer—a petite younger woman—and Kala were standing by a cruiser talking. Shane nodded a greeting to the officer as we passed. I glanced at Kala and frowned, puzzled by why her conversation with the officer was taking so long. She couldn't have seen much.

Kala slid a sidelong look at the officer and smiled. I wasn't quite sure what she meant by that, and I really didn't care at the moment.

Shane and I went down the walkway and into the kitchen. I dropped onto a chair at the table. He took the chair opposite mine.

He slumped forward, face in his hands. His voice pitched up, as if bordering on panic. "You don't know how terrified I was when I heard you had an intruder."

I swallowed hard. I'd never heard Shane sound so vulnerable, as much like a frightened child as a man. I rested a hand on his, gave a nervous laugh. "You must have driven eighty miles per hour to get here so fast."

He looked up, eyes dark, neck muscles taut. "I was on my way to see you when the call came across the radio."

I frowned. "You were coming here at three in the morning?"

He looked me in the eyes. "Edie, you really don't get it, do you?"

My throat went dry. I lowered my gaze to the tabletop: stray napkins, chicken-shaped salt and pepper shakers, a pile of unpaid bills . . . I didn't trust myself to look at him again, almost as afraid of what I'd feel as the deep emotion I'd seen in his eyes. He'd betrayed my confidence. Lied to me. I'd lied to him. He might've been willing to call it even, but I wasn't sure I could get past it so easily.

His voice lowered. "I need to explain something to you."

Sweat dampened my armpits. *Latimore. Recruitment.* Did he really have the nerve to drive over here at three in the morning to tell me something like that?

I scowled. "I think I know what you want to tell me. I guess now's better than a text on your way to Quantico for training."

He opened his mouth but before he could say a word, more of mine flooded out, tart and hot. "Why weren't you upfront with me about what was going on?"

The worry on Shane's face fell away, replaced by an amused smile. "Are you done yet?"

His smile ticked me off even more. I clenched my teeth. "No, I'm just beginning."

His voice faltered. "Hear me out first." He slid a hand down his arm, the angel this time. "I turned them down."

I gawked at him. "You said *no*?"

His lips curved at the corners, a slight smile. "It was an attractive offer, and not the first I've gotten from Latimore."

"I'm not surprised by that. But I can't believe you didn't take them up on it. Why not?"

His eyes lingered on mine. "Money isn't everything."

I stared at him blankly. No question he was referring to me, or more precisely to us as a couple. But after what we'd said to each other at the cabin, I couldn't fathom where he was going with this.

He wiped a hand over his head. "When the break-in came across the radio, it scared the daylights out of me." He hesitated for a beat. "I can't promise I won't screw up again. Hiding things and occasionally sharing information—even when it's given in confidence—comes with the territory. I'm not saying it's easy. Sometimes I hate that part of my job."

The tightness in my chest loosened a bit. I didn't like what he was saying. But if I thought about it, to a large degree both our jobs were the center of our difficulties. In my case, my involvement with the townscape was why I'd lied to him about being expected at the Well-Being Center.

His voice softened even further. "I care about you, Edie. I want us to start again. But not the way it's been. I don't want an open relationship. I don't want us to be just about sex and good times. I want us to work together through the difficult times as well." He smiled. "You could start by letting me help you with the septic system. I've got a pile of gravel and some drainage pipe leftover from when I ditched my yard. I want you to have them."

My emotions once more jumbled, like junk jewelry tossed into a box: happiness, uncertainty, and even a sense of self-loathing for the way I ached to forgive him. That sort of easy forgiveness was what weak women like Alder and my mom surrendered to.

Only Shane wasn't manipulative or a user like the men they fell for. Gravel and pipe weren't the same as money. Well, they were. But Shane was giving them from his heart, not for any other reason. He was a good guy who just happened to play by a slanted set of rules.

Tears dampened the corners of my eyes. Letting my gaze return to his, I skipped past the relationship stuff. If I didn't, I'd fall apart. "Thank you. That'll help a lot with the cost."

He raised an eyebrow. "I do want you to promise me one thing."

I looked at him skeptically. "What?"

"From now on, I don't want you doing anything involving the Volkovs without me beside you. Don't try and tell me you'll back off. I know that's not going to happen."

"Am I that easy to read?" Inside I felt lighter, buoyant almost, and it burbled into my voice.

"Your tenaciousness, Edie. That's one of the things I like about you."

My face heated, making me feel like a lovestruck fool. Not wanting to cry, I bought myself time to shake it off by getting up from the table. I took the Madonna and Child painting down from the wall, pushed aside the salt and pepper shakers and set the piece on the table facing Shane. "This is Erik's painting of Alice."

He angled the painting until the overhead light illuminated it. "I read up on Alice Moffett last night after Latimore and Medina left. This is her, no question about it."

"This painting proves there was a link between Erik and Alice Moffett, and I think the person who broke into the shop was after it. They walked past lots of valuable items—sterling silver, gold pocket watches—and they didn't even look in the cash register. If they'd just wanted to send a message, they could've smashed a ton of things without going more than a few steps inside the door."

Shane set the painting down, smile fading. "The intruder could have come after you while he was here, broken into the house while you were asleep."

"That's a cheerful thought," I said sarcastically.

"Don't forget about Manchester. They almost succeeded then."

"We aren't sure that was anything."

"Aren't you?" he said.

I looked at the painting, to hide my worry. It was upside down from my perspective. That made me think of my mom's suggestion about studying pieces from different angles.

My eyes went to the perfectly symmetrical "V" on Alice's pendant. Mom might have advised me to not focus on that single detail too much. Still, it was the one thing that was in all of the pieces.

I ran my finger across it. A silver oval with—

My mouth dropped open. Earlier, my subconscious *had* been trying to tell me something. In the advertisement I'd seen on TV, with the car and the middle school band, this exact symbol had decorated the car's grill. A silver oval with an upside-down, symmetrical "V."

Shane's voice seemed far away as he continued to speak. "Here's what I suggest. I'll talk to Chief Ovitt right now, make sure he understands what's going on, and ask him to keep the break-in on the down-low for now. That'll help keep the perpetrator at ease—"

"Uh, Shane?" I said, interrupting him. "I might've just figured out something vital. I gestured at the pendant. "The 'V' isn't an initial. It has nothing to do with jewelry. It's a car logo. Are you familiar with the Infiniti? Luxury Nissan. Not all that common around here, especially twelve years ago."

His eyes went wide. "Oh, my God. You're right."

I picked the painting up, holding it by both sides of the frame. "We have to show Erik a photo of the logo. It might jog his memory."

"I totally agree." He paled. He actually did, there was no mistaking it. "If Stanislav's sent someone here to get the painting, that means he could be starting to run scared. If he's covering his tracks, Erik could be in real danger—like you and anyone else who's been nosing around."

Tuck. Kala. Pinky . . . Fear sent my heart pounding. "We need to warn Jimmy. We were together in Manchester. That alone might have made the Volkovs suspicious."

"I suggest you call him right now," Shane said.

Chapter
Thirty-Seven

As sunrise approached, the trees came alive with birdsong—robins, catbirds, thrushes . . . trilling and squawking with wild enthusiasm. Grandma would have loved to hear them. But right now, their joyful songs felt at odds with the uneasiness pulsing inside me.

Sure, before Chief Ovitt and his officer left, he'd agreed to act as if he didn't know about the likely connection between the break-in and the Volkov family, though he was more than a little excited by the possibility. In turn, Shane promised to keep the chief in the loop. Things were going our way. Still, there was no way I could forget we were walking a razor's edge. One misstep and someone I cared about could end up like Alice Moffett.

With the local police gone, the four of us gathered in the living room with mugs of coffee and a box of donuts Kala mysteriously produced. As much as I wanted to jump in a car and race to see Erik right now, Shane didn't want to take off half-cocked. He insisted we compare notes and come up with a plan in case something went sideways. Yeah, it was probably smart.

Tuck rested his mug on the coffee table. "Once I've got the shop put back in order, I'm buttoning this place up like Fort

Knox. But before I do anything else, I'm stashing that Madonna and Child painting in the safe."

"Not a bad idea," Shane said. "The Volkovs aren't going to walk away as long as they think the painting—or any of you—are a threat to them." He looked at me. "Speaking of threats, you might want to try calling Jimmy again."

"I just did, a few minutes ago. I'm sure he'll call back soon." I took out my phone, double-checked to make sure I hadn't missed a message. Why wasn't he getting back to me? Jimmy always returned calls, day or night.

Tuck surveyed the box of donuts for a second and selected a Boston cream. He eyed Kala. "Where did you find these anyway? I didn't see you leave, and I know we didn't have any in the kitchen."

She bit her bottom lip. "Chrissy had them in her cruiser."

"Chrissy?" Tuck raised his eyebrows. "You mean, Officer Christina Hopkins? You two seem to be hitting it off."

Shane gave a knowing smile. "I've heard good things about her."

Kala bowed her head, focusing on dunking a powdered sugar into her coffee. She sucked off the moistened end and then dunked again with far more vigor than necessary. "Yeah. She's nice."

Puzzled, I looked from Tuck to Shane, to her. "Did I miss something?"

Kala finished taking another suck of donut. "She and I've talked a couple of times at Quickie's Quick Stop—that's it. All right, we had coffee the other day. She's new in town. I'm new."

So, she's the mystery heartthrob, I wanted to say. Instead, I resisted the urge to smile and said, "Makes sense."

"She's nice," Kala repeated emphatically.

Tuck chuckled. "I wonder if she's the cop who pulled Pinky over last month."

Kala threw her hands up and huffed. "Can't a girl shop around without everyone getting in her business?"

"Of course, you can. More power to you," I said.

She scowled at all of us. "If anyone breathes a word to Pinky, I'll know where it came from—and revenge will happen."

Shane zipped his mouth shut with a finger. "I know nothing."

Tuck smiled at him. "You're a wise man, Shane."

I picked up the donut box, held it out to Kala. "They're small. Maybe have two?"

Kala snagged a chocolate one. "Now that that's straightened out. I'm going to go find my laptop and check out the chatter online, see if anyone's talking about the break-in."

"Before you take off," I said, "I want to make sure we're all on the same page." I took a breath, then began in earnest. "Tuck's going to be in the shop for most of the morning. He's got the insurance adjuster coming and people to fix the doors. Shane and I are heading to Checkerberry a little before nine. We're going to show Erik the Infiniti logo to make sure our theory is right and to see if it helps him remember anything else. I'm counting on you to man command central. Okay?"

"No way. I'm going with." Kala tossed back her pouf of hair. "You need someone to keep an eye out for that monkey-thieving Iris Meadows. You don't need her calling Alder and telling her that you're talking to Erik again."

"I'm not sure—" I looked at Shane. "What do you think?"

Kala snorted. "The decision is made. No ifs, ands, or buts about it. I'm going." She swiped a third donut from the box, then made for the hall.

As her footsteps faded, Shane whispered, "She's quite the character."

"Definitely not one to cross," Tuck said. He got up from his chair. "If you two don't need me for anything, I'm going to take a shower. I foresee a long day ahead for all of us."

"I can't disagree with you there," I said.

As Tuck headed upstairs, I set the donut box on the coffee table. I was about to settle down on the couch when the *brrring* of my phone rang out.

"It's Jimmy," I said, glancing at the caller ID. I put it on speaker. "Thanks for calling back."

He immediately started in. "Edie, sweetheart. You won't believe what happened. I'm so irate. Sterling—" His voice pinched, then grew higher, shaking with anger. "After you left, I bought two Vespa collages. Two hundred and fifty thousand dollars in total: *Day in the Park* and *To Whom It May Concern*. They were to be crated and delivered yesterday. And Sterling, that jackass, backed out. Said I hadn't paid for the last piece I purchased from him. That's rubbish."

"You have proof that you paid, right?" I asked.

"Of course, I do. He called me a liar."

I wasn't sure how Sterling making false accusations as an excuse to not sell Vespa pieces to Jimmy fit in, but I suspected it was because he'd been at the show with me.

Shane leaned close to the phone. "Did Sterling or anyone threaten you? By way of emails or on the phone? Has anything else happened, like a break-in?

"Why?" Jimmy paused. "Who is this?"

I spoke up. "It's Shane. This Vespa situation . . . We think the Volkovs are involved with money laundering and the Russian mafia."

"Oh! I'd heard rumors they were connected." Jimmy made a humming noise as if thinking. "Something odd did happen—not so much odd as that it could be related. You remember T-Minty?"

"Yeah. What happened?" I asked.

"He stopped by the funeral home, looking for a donation for a street kids' art program. That's not odd. He's done that before. T-Minty couldn't be involved with the mafia. He wouldn't hurt a fly. A sweetheart—"

I cut him off before he went on forever. "So, what was odd, then?"

"The whole time he was in my office, he kept ogling my Vespas. I thought he might be looking for NFT possibilities, but he never said anything."

I pushed my hair back from my face, hooked it behind an ear as I thought. The main thing that made me suspicious of T-Minty—other than his vested interest in Vespa's success—was that I'd seen him with Sterling near the terrace right before and after I'd overheard the man threaten Sterling. I'd also smelled cigar smoke, though that could've been from either him or Sterling. "Does T-Minty smoke cigars or have a gravelly voice, maybe an accent?"

Jimmy all but twittered. "Darling, I can tell you've never spent any time with him. T-Minty wouldn't dream of smoking or drinking—against his religion. And even the Lord Almighty wouldn't let him sing in the choir. He sounds like SpongeBob, only twangier."

I cringed at that description. T-Minty definitely wasn't the man I'd heard with Sterling. Still, that didn't mean he wasn't involved in some capacity. "It's probably better to steer clear of him. Err on the side of caution."

Shane leaned closer to the phone again. "Whatever you do, don't pressure Sterling about the collages you purchased. Let it be for now."

"That's fine for you to say. I have a reputation to think about. I pay my debts. I'm not a lowlife."

"Listen to him, Jimmy. Things have happened up here too. This isn't just about Vespa and art. An FBI agent was murdered."

"Murdered? When?"

I lowered my voice. "I'll tell you about that later. Right now, promise to play it cool."

He harrumphed. "To think I actually admired Sterling Meadows. I should open my own gallery. Show him who's who."

An idea sparked in the back of my brain. Our gallery was tiny. But with Erik's work, and financial backing and fresh connections like Jimmy had, it could become something again like it had been at the peak of my grandparents' careers.

I took the phone off speaker. "Talk to you later, Jimmy. Hang in there for now. Be careful, please?"

"Sweetheart, anything for you."

* * *

At eight thirty, we took off for Checkerberry Manor in Shane's Land Rover. I was happy he'd offered to drive. Lack of sleep, combined with everything else, had left me shaky. On the other hand, Kala was bouncing on a sugar high.

Lucky for her, her upbeat mood kept me from saying anything when I noticed a Taz-shaped lump at her waistline, hidden by the handkerchief hem of her purple tank top. If Shane noticed, he didn't mention it either. Then again, he was armed as well—one sidearm that I was aware of and most likely a few others. I only hoped their weapons would remain hidden and unneeded. They certainly wouldn't be necessary where Erik was concerned. Seeing the Infiniti logo might cause a fierce reaction, but more likely panic or shock than violence.

The traffic was light, and in no time at all we were walking toward Checkerberry Manor's front entry. Details from Erik's collages flickered in my mind. The "V" in the townscape, the family at the beach with the husband looking away and the sandwich hemorrhaging money and blood, a woman sprawled in an alleyway. June first.

I shivered against a chilling sense of finality, then took up a position in front of Checkerberry's security monitor next to Shane. I pressed the intercom button. "Hi, I'm Edie Brown. We're here to visit Erik Volkov."

"Hi, Edie," Yvette's familiar voice said. "Come on in."

The door buzzed, then clicked open.

Shane rested a hand on the small of my back and whispered, "You seem to have made a good impression."

"I suspect we have Tuck's African violets to thank for that," I said.

"And his fake sister," Kala added.

Yvette sat behind the reception desk. This time she didn't actively come out to greet us. Instead, she stayed put and sipped her coffee as we walked over.

"We tried to phone Erik ahead," I said when we reached the desk. "He didn't answer. We thought he might be in the cafeteria having breakfast."

"Let me check," she said.

As Yvette picked up a phone, I glanced over my shoulder to where Kala was meandering toward the common room. She stopped, looking first toward the doors that lead out into the courtyard, then scanning the corridor that went to the cafeteria. Okay, having an extra pair of eyes was a good idea.

A smell reached my nose. It was faint but unmissable given the clean surroundings. Cigar smoke. Not a cheap cigar. An aromatic, old-world scent like the one I'd detected coming from the terrace at Sterling Gallery. I'd smelled it the first time we'd gone to Anna's house as well. Stanislav? His son, Victor?

My pulse hammered hard against my ribs. The Russian mafia weren't known for sparing family. Were they afraid that Erik was recovering his memory? Had our snooping put them on the defensive? Had they decided to eliminate him?

"Yvette," I said, interrupting her phone call, "was Erik's uncle Stanislav here earlier—or his cousin? Do they smoke cigars?"

She covered the phone with her hand. "I just came on duty a few minutes ago. If they were here, their names would be in the guest registry." She wrinkled her nose. "Victor smokes—awful cigars. I've told him repeatedly it's not allowed here."

I nodded. So, most likely it was Victor—not Stanislav—who'd pressure Sterling on the gallery terrace and threatened to pay Alder another "visit."

I glanced at Shane. He was already striding toward the registry.

Yvette listened to the phone again. She nodded, then looked back toward me. "The staff haven't seen Erik in the cafeteria. He isn't answering his phone. Is something wrong?"

"Let's hope not," I said.

Shane strode back to me. "Victor was here a half hour ago."

I swiveled back to Yvette. "Do you think Erik might have left with Victor?"

"He could have. Let me—" She stopped short. Her gaze winged past me and Shane to something behind us.

I wheeled to see what was happening.

Kala had a small woman cornered against a plastic palm. The woman didn't have Dolly Parton hair or conical breasts, but she wore a hornet-yellow top over black leggings. Iris Meadows, dressed in the same Vespa outfit she'd worn in Manchester, right down to the glittering brooch secured on a dark headband.

"Get your hands off me!" Iris screeched.

"Give it to me." Kala wrenched a phone from the woman's hand.

What the heck? I rushed away from the reception desk. Shane was a step behind.

Iris's eyes went flinty. She snarled at Kala. "Shame on you, stealing from a helpless old woman."

"Not stealing. Confiscating." Kala looked at me. "She was trying to call Alder."

I snatched the phone from Kala, redialed the same number. Alder had been threatened by Victor. If anyone would understand how important it was for Erik not to be alone with him, it would be her. She might even know where they were.

The phone rang. Rang again.

I pinned Iris with a hard look. "Is Alder at the Well-Being Center or at her home?"

She squinted at me. "Why?"

The phone rang again. Sweat slicked my palms. Alder not answering if she suspected I was on the other end was one thing, but this was Iris's phone.

"That's not a good sign," Shane said.

Iris went pale. Her voice cracked. "Alder always answers."

"The Volkovs threatened her, didn't they?" I asked.

She bobbed her head. "That guy—Victor. He gave her a black eye a while ago. Said he'd be back if Sterling didn't pay up."

A thought came to me. I glanced at Shane. "Do you think Victor was responsible for what happened to Erik and Alice, for the hit-and-run?"

He nodded.

The clip of Yvette's footsteps sounded behind us. I silenced and glanced over my shoulder. Not just Yvette headed toward us, but a security guard too.

"I'll take care of that," Shane said, then strode away.

I stepped closer to Iris, even closer than Kala. "Listen to me. We know all about the Vespa scam. But you still have a chance to get out of it without going to prison, and perhaps to save Alder at the same time. Tell me where Erik is." It felt weird to be hard on a tiny old woman. But Kala was right to dislike her, and Pinky's cousin Edgar had warned me about her too. Iris was no baby-kissing, cookie-baking grandma. She was a top-notch con artist, and lives were in danger.

She gave a derisive snort. "You aren't a cop. You can't guarantee nothing."

I pressed on. "You've seen the dead woman in Erik's collages, right?"

"What of it?" she said.

I took her by the shoulders. "That dead woman was an undercover FBI agent. And the Volkovs didn't just blacken her eye. They ran her over with a car. It's time to choose sides. Witness protection or a pine box."

The witness protection part was a total bluff. But even I was taken aback by the resolute strength in my voice, and I felt her shrink under my grip. Her voice croaked out as tight as if my hands were around her neck. "Alder was here before breakfast. Erik left with her. They were going to—" She glared at me. "Promise I'll get protection."

"They went to the Well-Being Center, right? Was Victor with them?"

"Yes—and no. Alder took Erik to the Center to work in the studio. Victor wasn't with them. He was here a little while ago, looking for Erik." Her shoulders hunched as if ashamed. Her gaze went to the floor.

I dropped my voice to a growl. "Did you warn Alder that Victor was coming?"

"Maybe. I—I . . ."

"You didn't call and warn Alder, and you knew Victor had hurt her before?" I couldn't believe it.

"Victor told me to not say anything to anyone, or he'd *visit* me too."

A sour taste crept up from my stomach. Disgusted, I looked away from her toward Kala. "Let's get Shane and get out of here. I'm done with her. Just done."

Kala's eyes narrowed. A dangerous smile lifted the corners of her mouth. "I'll be with you in a minute. I've still got unfinished business." She turned to Iris, stuck out her hand with the palm up. "Hand over the brooch."

Iris scuffed back. She blinked. "What are you talking about?"

"You know damn well. My monkey. I want him." Kala's voice lowered to a dead-cold whisper. "Don't test me, old woman. I know people who make Victor Volkov look like a cream puff."

She huffed. "It's not worth nothing anyway." Reaching up, she unpinned the brooch, as fast as a magician in a Vegas show. She dropped it onto Kala's palm. "Hope you prick yourself."

Kala smiled. "I'll try not to."

Chapter
Thirty-Eight

Shane floored the Land Rover's accelerator, passing a dump truck and then a pickup.

"When we get there, I want both of you to stay in the car," he said.

I shot a sidelong look at him. "Erik knows me. I have to—"

"If Victor's still there, I'll call for backup. You two will stay put. Understood?"

"If he's not?" I asked.

Shane tapped the brake as we entered Colchester Village. "I'll let you know as soon as it's safe to come inside."

Two blocks before our turn, I spotted a sedan parked at the end of a side street. Dark, bloodred. I pointed out the windshield. "Is that a Mercedes? Can you see where its license plate is from?"

"Looks like New York to me," Kala said.

I lowered the window, studying it as we passed. "I think I saw that same car the first time Tuck and I went to Checkerberry Manor."

"Didn't you say the car that almost hit you was a dark red sedan?" Shane asked.

A bead of sweat iced my spine. "Yeah. But it was pouring rain, hard to see."

"What doesn't make sense to me," Shane went on, "is why a man like Victor—who has no problem using physical violence— would choose to use a car for an assassination. Hit-and-run murders usually have to do with the perpetrator being or viewing themselves as physically weaker than their target."

I shuddered. "How about we knock off the speculating," I said. "I'm scared enough."

Shane flipped on the turn signal as we neared the ice-cream-parlor building. Even though it was before noon, the place was bustling, cars coming and going. People everywhere. As Shane pulled in and started toward the rear parking lot, memories of almost hitting the old woman came back to me. "Speaking of hit-and-runs, watch out when you go around the corner. It's impossible to see what's on the other side."

"Yup, for sure," Kala added.

The Land Rover eased up as he braked even further, creeping forward. But there were no people or other cars in the back parking area except for a Subaru pulled up close to the Well-Being Center's front entry. Most likely Alder's car.

Shane claimed the same spot I'd parked in the other day. He unfastened his seatbelt, opened his door, then looked back at Kala and me. "Remember, stay put while I check if Victor's around. If the coast is clear, I'll come back and get you."

"Be careful," I said as he got out.

Sticking close to the edge of the parking lot, he made his way toward the building. When he reached the Subaru, he dashed toward the closest corner of the building and flattened himself against it.

I held my breath as he inched toward a window curtained with dream catchers and half-dead spider plants. Alder's office, most likely.

Shane glanced inside, then hunched down and rushed along under the window. As he neared the front entry, his hand went to his waistline, resting on his handgun.

"I don't like this," Kala said.

A knot tightened in my throat. "I don't either."

He stopped, looked in through the automatic doors, then slipped inside as they slid open, vanishing from sight.

For a long minute, neither Kala nor I made a sound, then Kala lowered her window. "Do you smell smoke?"

I sniffed the air. It wasn't strong, more of a faint background odor, growing stronger. "Is it coming from the Center?"

"I'm not sure."

I opened the car door. "I'm going to find out. Shane might've walked in on more than he was expecting."

Taking my phone out, I readied to call 911 if need be. As I crept toward the building, the pad of footsteps tiptoed up beside me: Kala with her hand on her waistline. Yeah, I was glad she'd brought Taz. And I was glad we'd moved closer. I couldn't see any smoke, but I sure smelled it. A foul stench like burning cloth or plastic.

By the time we reached the Subaru, my stomach ached from nerves. I followed Shane's lead, darting to the corner of the building and then stealing a look through Alder's office window. No one was there. Not Alder. Not Erik or even Shane. No smoke inside—that was a good thing.

For a heartbeat, I held perfectly still, listening for voices or music. Not a sound.

I moved in close to Kala. "It's too quiet, don't you think?"

She nodded and took out Taz.

Hunching, I dashed under the window, slowing as I neared the doorway. Even from there, I could see that the door to where Alder held her group sessions was open, the room bright.

"I'm going in," I whispered to Kala.

She moved even closer to me. "If you are, I am."

I swallowed hard, took a deep breath and a fresh grip on my phone, then stepped forward.

The automatic doors glided open. A wintery air-conditioned chill rushed out. The scent of citrus and lavender. We started inside and—

Shane flew out from the group session room. He halted mid-stride when he saw us, gestured at the room. "Come in here! Alder's hurt. She's bleeding."

I froze, then adrenaline kicked in. "Did you call for help?"

"Yes. It's on the way."

Shoving my phone in a pocket, I raced into the room, on his heels. Alder slumped against the desk, hands over her face. Blood trickled between her fingers and darkened the front of her shirt. She moaned. "He broke my nose."

Kala grabbed a dishcloth from beside the art sink. She wet it, then went and crouched beside Alder. "Lean forward. Put this over your nose. Breathe through your mouth."

Shane knelt beside them. "Did Victor do this to you?"

Her head bobbed, a slight movement. "He told me not to tell, said he'd kill Sterling."

"Where's Erik?" Shane asked.

The blood soaked through the dishcloth. Her shoulders slumped. "I feel sick," she moaned.

I got down right in front of her. "We saw Victor's car down the road. Is he still here? Is he out back with Erik?"

"Where out back?" Shane asked.

"I'll show you," I jumped to my feet. Why delay by waiting for Alder's answer?

I thrust my hand out to Kala. She read my mind and gave me Taz. With Shane beside me, I sprinted to the corridor. I didn't want to give him a chance to tell me to stand down. I wasn't much when it came to backup, but my thoughts were clear, my muscles ready. I was better than nothing—and all he had right now.

"You know how to use a Taser?" he asked as we ran.

"Safety off. Aim. Shoot, drop, and run," I parroted Kala's instructions.

My skin tingled. My heart jackhammered. We passed the room where I'd discovered Erik's partially finished collage. The door was closed, no lights on. I kept going. The rear doors didn't automatically open as we approached. I punched the door latch, and they did as commanded.

I sucked in air, inhaling deeply. The wail of sirens screamed somewhere far away, growing closer. I took another breath—

Smoke! I'd forgotten about it.

I glanced toward the cinderblock garage. Gray smoke seeped out the open side door, low to the ground, hazing the yard. Terror filled me. That day at the airstrip. The plane crash and explosion. My grandparents. Smoke. Flames . . . I shook myself back to the here and now. I screamed, "That's Erik's studio!"

Shane launched forward, sprinting across the deck—

A man flew out from behind the vine-covered lattice, fist cocked.

Thwack-thwack! The fist collided with the side of Shane's head. He stumbled, went down. I rushed forward. Safety off. Aim. Shoot . . .

The Taser darts hit the man in the chest and gut. Center mass. Victor Volkov, I realized as he buckled to the ground, twitching as the volts pulsed through him.

Shane rolled back on his feet, zip cuff in his hand. He yanked Victor's arms behind his back. My gaze went to something else: Victor's shirt was half torn off. His face was covered with blood, one eye partially closed. Victor had been an amateur boxer. So had Erik.

Erik! The garage!

I dropped the Taser and rocketed toward the building. Smoke now boiled out, black mixing with gray. Erik had to still be in there. He hadn't been with Alder. He wasn't in the yard . . .

Erik had been used. Screwed over. He had a gift to share with the world. An artistic savant. An outsider, struggling to survive and make sense of the past.

BANG! Something exploded inside the building. Heat flooded out. The scream of the sirens was louder now. Getting nearer, but not fast enough.

I pulled the collar of my shirt up over my mouth and nose and stepped inside—cinderblocks, no windows, pretty much a kiln.

Squinting against the haze, I spotted crackling flames only yards ahead. Six feet high. Bright and hot. Orange and red. Blocking my way.

My brain engaged. The flames were coming from a box. The box of rags. Leaping and spreading quickly onto nearby stacks of newspaper. The whole building wasn't engulfed. Not yet—

But I couldn't see Erik and I couldn't call out, not with the shirt over my nose and mouth. I remembered a fire extinguisher. I'd seen it before. Near the fridge.

I scrambled forward, into the acrid haze. The fridge hadn't been that far from the door. At least, I didn't think so.

I went a few yards more, then another. Finally, I spotted the refrigerator and grabbed the extinguisher from beside it. Its metal was unexpectedly cool against my hands. I pulled the pin out. Aimed at the fire and squeezed the trigger. The flames hissed. The black smoke turned vaporous. A gray haze clouded the garage and funneled toward the doorway. I swept the spray from the box to the stacks of paper.

The flames flickered, died back. Just smoke and stench. The extinguisher sputtered and died. Pulling the shirt down from my nose and mouth, I shouted, "Erik! Where are you?"

Nothing, only the sirens, very close now.

I tried again. "Erik. Where are you? It's Edie."

A whimper reached my ear. Straight ahead, from somewhere near the makeshift worktable. Deep in the haze.

Hand over my mouth and nose, I set the extinguisher down and moved forward, past the steaming remains of the box. Burnt rags. Burnt paper. I prayed there was nothing explosive still left inside, something still heating, a tin of turpentine, a box of old bullets . . . I'd seen a million different combustibles inside old garages when I'd been hunting for antiques.

"Erik. Where are you?" I called out again.

A scuffing noise came from under the workbench—nothing more than sawhorses and plywood with the collage lying on top.

I spotted his outline, huddled underneath the bench, knees pulled to his chest, face hidden, fisted hands covering his ears as he trembled.

Crouching, I got as close to him as I dared. I wanted to reach out, but I couldn't risk him shifting farther away. "It's all right," I said, forcing my voice to go calm. "It's over. No one's going to hurt you."

Erik rasped, "Victor never tells. Won't ever tell."

I closed my eyes, bringing up tears to soothe them from the caustic smoke. But what could I say to soothe Erik? I had to get him to leave the garage.

I reached out to the universe, to whoever was listening. *Please, please, tell me what to do.*

A chill swept my overheated skin. It prickled the hair on the back of my neck. I'd never been one to believe in ghosts. Well, I talked to my grandparents sometimes, so maybe I did. But in that moment, I knew what to say to Erik—it was the truth, and it didn't come from me.

I slid my hand along the gritty floor, reaching toward him. "Alice"—I corrected myself—"Sable. She loved you. You're a good man, Erik. She knew it."

He lowered his fisted hands. His walnut-size knuckles were split open, bloody and raw. When he spoke, his voice was raw too. "That—that night, I saw headlights. The letter 'V.' I tried to save her. Can't remember where. Can't remember who."

"Your cousin Victor murdered Sable, didn't he?" I asked.

"Victor told me to stop making art." His voice spiraled upward, out of control. "I thought, maybe 'V' is from Victor's necklace, his medal. Why else tell me not to make art? Unless he's worried I remember he was there."

I squeezed Erik's hand. "It's going to be okay. We need to get out of here now. We can talk later."

Under my grip, his hand quaked. "I wanted to kill Victor. I hit him. He hit me back. He'll never tell, never . . . I hid. Victor started fire."

Chapter
Thirty-Nine

As I led Erik out of the garage, the fire trucks screamed into the parking lot. One ambulance was pulling away, and another was arriving. Police lights strobed. But before I handed Erik off to the rescue squad, I had one last thing to do.

I took out my phone, brought up the Infiniti logo, and showed it to Erik. "Does this look like what you remember?"

He went still, utterly motionless. Finally, his mouth opened. "That—that's it. It's not the medal? Not Victor?"

"It's a car logo. But I wouldn't rule Victor out yet. You're right, it doesn't make sense for him to tell you to stop making art." *Something he and his parents were profiting royally from,* I thought, though I wasn't about to tell Erik yet.

"A logo, an emblem on a car," Erik murmured, almost as if to himself.

"That's right. An Infiniti." I spotted a woman in a rescue squad uniform jogging our way. "I'll be right back," I said to Erik. Then I slipped away before the woman could realize I'd been inside the garage as well. I needed to find Shane and Kala.

I rushed across the backyard, sidestepping the Taser. Kala might have preferred if I'd picked Taz up and guarded him with my life, but it seemed smarter to not tamper with evidence.

Hurrying my steps, I went up on the deck and inside. The corridor was empty. No one was in the group session room either, just a bunch of bloody washcloths left behind on the floor. Alder must have been in the ambulance I'd seen leaving.

The front doors automatically glided open as I approached, and I spotted Shane holding Victor with his face flat against the side of the Land Rover.

Victor hawked up a loogie and spat it out. "My dad doesn't know nothing about who killed that FBI whore."

My muscles tensed. For sure, it was Victor's voice I'd heard at the gallery. Same gravelly tone. Russian accent, slightly stronger than Erik's. I also didn't believe a word he was saying. It was more likely Stanislav was right in the middle of it all.

Shane gave Victor's arms a yank. "You think you're so smart. Then tell me, who did it?"

"Screw you."

I marched over to them. Shane's bottom lip was bloody and split. His cheek was red and swollen. I wanted to rush to the ambulance and get an ice pack for him—obviously not the moment for that.

I pinpointed my gaze on Victor. My voice rasped from the smoke I'd breathed in. "It must have freaked you out to see all those 'V's' in the collages, knowing it was only a matter of time before Erik remembered the entire night."

He squinted at me. "What the hell are you talking about? Crazy bitch."

"The night Sable Smith died," I said. I smiled and switched tactics. Cops' rules. Lie or wiggle the truth when it serves your

301

purpose. "That fight you just had with Erik? It didn't go exactly as you planned. He's remembered everything now. The 'V' was the emblem on the car. An Infiniti."

Victor leered, blood-covered teeth showing. "What if it was?"

Shane's firm expression never wavered, but his eyes flicked to me as if he was wondering whether I was telling the truth about Erik. His voice hardened. "It means it's time for you to start talking."

Victor spat again. "Go to hell."

I studied Victor's fisted hands, bloodied and coated with dirt. The cords of his neck strained against the skin. His feet were firmly planted. 'Victor never tells,' Erik had said in the garage. Yeah, lies might work on him, but intimidation wasn't going to. He was far too tough for that.

Letting my expression go flat, I retreated a step. There had to be a way to get him to open up. But how?

It wouldn't get me anywhere to panic like I'd done at Sterling Gallery. Violence, like Erik had tried, wouldn't work . . .

I bit back a smile, channeled my grandfather's empathy, then moved in closer than I'd been before, right up to where Shane now had Victor pinned even tighter against the car. What I needed to do was slicker Victor into turning traitor by calmly suggesting it was up to him to keep himself and the people he cared most about out of even deeper hot water by confessing what he knew.

Inside, my nerves were live wires, my heartbeat fast. My muscles were taut, ready to move if Victor got free from Shane's grip. Outside, I kept my expression and stance relaxed.

I quieted my voice and said, "Shane's a good detective, one of the best. He doesn't need to do this strong-arm act to put you away. With the addition of Erik's testimony, he's going to take you down one way or another."

Victor's brows lowered. He harrumphed. "Sure. Whatever you say."

"I'm serious," I said, still quiet. "I know this situation is difficult for you. Detective Payton and I both know that."

Shane's eyes met mine, a slight smile twitched at the corners of his lips as if he were amused by my playacting and willing to surrender the lead to me. He loosened his grip, not a lot, but enough so Victor could straighten.

I swallowed to relieve the chafing in my throat, then continued, piling the bullshit deeper. "You're a smart man, Victor. I suspect a lot of people underestimate you." I glanced in the general direction of the garage. "You didn't attack Erik in there, did you? He threw the first punch."

Victor's lip curled, a bloody snarl. "Bastard fucking broke my tooth."

"That wouldn't have happened if you were at the top of your game," I said.

He nodded. "Damn right."

"But you're under a lot of stress, aren't you?"

"I guess."

I continued, casual as could be, though every word left a sour taste in my mouth. "If you'd really wanted to, I imagine you could have killed Erik. You could have killed Alder too. But you showed an amazing amount of self-control."

"That kind of restraint isn't easy," Shane added. He let go of Victor's arms, took a step back, but not without resting a hand on his holstered gun.

I softened my voice even further. "You aren't a killer. But you have a problem—that's Erik. He's remembered everything now, thanks to you."

Victor wriggled sideways, facing me fully and studying me closely. "Don't go fooling yourself. Erik don't know nothing about nothing. His brain's fried."

I shook my head. "You're wrong. Erik was going into witness protection that night. You murdered the woman he loved, an FBI agent."

"I didn't kill fucking nobody!" he shouted, blood and spittle flying.

I locked my knees, didn't move an inch, and by some miracle kept my voice steady as I took a guess. "But you were there when Sable was killed—and now Erik remembers, and the police have new evidence . . ." I let my voice trail off, alluding to knowing more rather than creating additional lies. "If someone else was driving, they're sticking it to you good. They've played you. But I know you're too smart to let yourself be used."

"You're screwed," Shane said, equally quiet.

I pulled my shoulders back, standing as tall as I could. "I'm willing to bet that same person told you only traitors tell, right?"

Victor looked down, then snarled, "Dad was going to send Erik away. I told her to let him take care of it. She said Dad was a pussy, chickenshit."

She. His mother? Who else could he mean? Just before we'd turned into the Well-Being Center, Shane had mentioned that the perpetrator might be physically weaker, or subconsciously view themselves as weaker, than their target. It was looking like Shane might've nailed it. An older woman targeting an FBI agent in her prime—not to mention wheedling her son into being an accomplice.

I took a deep breath, then pressed harder than before. I had to get Victor to say the name. We had to be sure. "Your father's more powerful than she'll ever be. He'll protect you. Choose sides, Victor. It's time to save yourself." I paused, waiting a dramatic second. "If you weren't driving, then who was?"

"Elizaveta," he said, barely audible.

I held myself rigid, though I longed to whoop with joy. We had the killer's name. The puzzle behind the horrific images in Erik's work was solved. Now it was up to Shane and his law enforcement friends to do the rest.

Shane opened the Land Rover's back door. "All right, Victor, let's get you out of here. We can finish this conversation someplace more comfortable." Without a word, Victor slumped into the seat. Shane secured him, shut the door, then turned to me and smiled. "You sure you're an antique dealer and not a cop?"

Resting my hands on my hips, I grinned. "I didn't do a bad job for a beginner, huh?"

He bent close, one hand on the small of my back as he whispered, "Amazing. I want to kiss you right here and now."

I punched him playfully in the chest, pushed free. "I'm guessing I should call Tuck for a ride?"

He grimaced. "Sorry. You and Kala will need to give statements too. I'll take care of arranging for that, then give you a call. Don't talk to anyone before then, okay?"

I nodded, and asked, "Speaking of Kala, you don't happen to know where she is?"

"Last I knew she was in the restroom. Washing up."

"I should go find her." I hesitated, looked him in the eyes. "I'll take a raincheck on that kiss."

"I wouldn't have it any other way," he said.

* * *

Reenergized by Victor's confession, I jogged back inside the Well-Being Center and down the corridor to the restrooms. Both doors were shut, but the roar of a hand dryer came from behind one of them.

I knocked. "Kala, you in there?"

The door flew open. "I was about to come looking for you." She wiggled her fingers at the semi-damp spot that covered the front of her shirt. "Had to rinse off nose blood. It was gross." She scanned me. "You okay? What happened?"

"Tons. I'll tell you in a minute. First, I'm dying to know if Alder said anything else."

"When the rescue people were loading her on the stretcher, she started to spill. Mostly she was crying and begging for protection from the Volkovs—and her brother." She squinted at me. "Where's Taz?"

"Uh . . . He kind of met Victor Volkov."

Her eyes bulged. "Ooh! Details, I want details."

"Before that, we need to call Tuck for a ride."

She bit her lip, a bit sheepish. "Pinky's already on her way."

"Pinky? How does she know?"

"I didn't tell her what happened, if that's what you're thinking. Edgar has a scanner. He called her. She called me and said she was coming to help, wouldn't take no for an answer." Kala looked down, studying the damp spot on her shirt again. "I know, I was flirting with Chrissy last night. But I do like Pinky . . ."

As she let her voice trail off, I laughed and hooked my arm with hers. "Don't worry. I'm not going to breathe a word about Officer Hottie."

Chapter Forty

I received a text from Shane five hours later—at 6:34 to be exact.

Things are moving forward. Alder confessed. She claims she and Sterling were unaware of Erik's connection to Stanislav's family, at least until Elizaveta threatened to reveal the Vespa scam if they didn't cut her in on the profits. T-Minty's nothing more than an innocent freelancer Sterling hired to create NFTs.

I dropped onto a wicker porch chair and responded as fast as I could. *Was Stanislav involved or just Victor?*

He got right back. *Appears Stanislav is not involved.*

How could he not know?

There was a pause, then Shane sent another message. *Can't share more. Got to go. I'll stop by later.*

I replied. *Thanks for telling me. I'll keep the lights on for you* ☺

* * *

Tuck poured himself a bourbon and a citrus vodka on the rocks for me. It was just the two of us, relaxing on the front porch as late afternoon drew into evening. Kala had rushed off an hour earlier when Pinky called to announce that her dog had gone into labor. If Pinky had caught on to Kala's wandering eye, she'd certainly figured out in a hurry how to keep Kala from pursuing that interest, at least for now. The promise of impending puppies was hard to resist.

Tuck handed me my drink, sat down in the chair next to mine, stretched out his legs, then eyed me. "So, what do you have in mind?"

I frowned, confused. "What are you talking about?"

"Erik. His artwork. The townscape. You're not going to let them slide. I know you better than that."

I laughed. He was right. I'd been mulling over that exact thing ever since we got home.

The Volkovs, Sterling, and Alder—they were Shane and law enforcement's problem. But Erik and his art were a different story. He was safe but even more on his own now.

Cradling my drink between two hands, I looked down into the liquid, evening light catching on the ice. "I'd like to talk to Erik again—with Anna present—about holding a gala opening for his art here at our shop. Soon, while the whole Vespa story is in the headlines."

"That's a great idea in theory, but it's more than problematic," Tuck said. "For one, how do you plan on rounding up enough pieces to make it worthwhile? You said Erik hasn't kept any. There's a gallery full in Manchester, except it's most likely going to be tied up in a legal mess for God knows how long."

I looked out at the gardens. I'd envisioned clearing out Mom's studio and expanding our gallery into that space for Erik's show. The lighting was perfect. We could put up a tent in the secret garden, have cocktails, hors d'oeuvres, and live music out there. An event like that would put our shop on the map again. Of course, there was the septic system issue. But I'd already decided to solve that by accepting Shane's loan offer along with using his supplies. I'd been foolish not to take it in the first place. He didn't expect anything in return, and I wasn't my mom, I wouldn't neglect to repay him. Worst case, I'd give him the cash in November, after the decoy auction. However, septic aside, were the other things feasible?

I set my drink down, then counted off the artwork I knew was available on my fingers. "We have the Madonna and Child. There's the partially finished piece in the Well-Being Center. There's the collage that was in the garage. Smoke damaged or not, it has quite the story to tell. There's the townscape, assuming Anna still has that."

Tuck shifted forward in his chair. "Your friend Jimmy would probably enjoy showing off the pieces he owns."

"For sure."

A breeze blew up from the valley, arching the lilies and hollyhock spikes. My hair escaped from the ribbon that held it back. I gathered it again, secured it once more. Erik put his heart and pain into his works. Alder and Sterling—along with the Volkovs—had cheated him out of the success he deserved. In my heart, I knew we could pull off a show, and we needed the recognition and commission we'd make by representing Erik's work. But I also wanted to respect Erik by giving him the right to make his own choices, something that had been denied to him so far.

An idea came to me. It was crazy. It would be more difficult to organize. But Erik just might love it. I caught Tuck's gaze. "I'm wondering if Erik would rather have his opening in conjunction with Checkerberry Manor's Artsy-August Craft Show."

Tuck frowned at me as if I'd lost my mind. "Are you feeling alright? Why would anyone hold a high-end art event at an assisted living craft show?"

I took a sip of my drink, wetting my throat. As I began to explain, my enthusiasm grew as fast as a line outside a church bazaar. "Lots of outsider artists hold shows in alternate spaces— train stations, old churches, airports . . . even a freaking stable in the Swiss Alps. Displaying Erik's work at Checkerberry, surrounded by the other residents' arts and crafts, would shine a light on his works' raw reality, enhance its significance. The art world would love it."

Tuck's voice remained skeptical, but a gleam of excitement shone in his eyes. "How do you propose we afford to put this on? There'll be a lot of upfront costs. Are you forgetting our current money shortage?"

I grinned. "It so happens I know someone who'd love to back it financially: Jimmy. He'd like nothing more than to get revenge on Sterling for his nonpayment accusations. Introducing the real artist behind the Vespa scam would do just that."

As the minutes ticked by and a plan for the show came together, both Tuck and I grew more and more electrified by the concept. Of course, it was Erik's work and life. Whether the event happened at all was his choice. There were also Checkerberry Manor's supervisors and owners, whom we'd need to convince. But, as much of a hassle as the flood of strangers through the facility's front doors would be, the potential for them to haul in serious funds—via charging us space rental and various fees— was real. For us, Erik's opening would be the perfect time and place to sell the Madonna and Child painting, not to mention that our involvement in introducing Erik to the art world would boost our business's reputation. This was a no-lose proposition.

Plus, there was an additional bonus. The Artsy-August event traditionally took place on the third weekend in August—exactly one week prior to the fancy gallery opening Felix Graham had scheduled. If collectors flew or drove to Vermont for Erik's show, it was unlikely they'd return the next weekend for Graham's event. It was the same logic Fisher's Auction House had used when they'd decided to delay the decoy auction to November, only this time positioning the events closer would work to our benefit. Take that, Graham. Finally, some payback.

* * *

It was nearly ten o'clock when the headlights of Shane's Land Rover came up the driveway. He parked, jogged over, and all but collapsed into the wicker loveseat.

"Want a beer?" Tuck asked, "or something harder or not so hard?"

"Iced tea would be wonderful." Shane ogled the platter of chicken wings Tuck and I had been snacking on. "Couple of those wouldn't hurt. I'm starving."

I got up, moved the platter onto the loveseat beside him. "Go for it. Have all you want. Tuck and I are done."

As he ate, we told him about our event idea. He was all for it. Finally, I couldn't stand waiting any longer and asked, "So what happened at the police station? Was Latimore there for the rest of Victor's interrogation?"

Shane wiped his mouth with a napkin. "You do realize I shouldn't tell you any of this?"

I drew a finger across my lips, sealing them shut. "Not a word."

He lowered his voice. "When you give your statement, I'd also appreciate it if you kept any discussion of the interrogation

311

at the Well-Being Center to a minimum." He smiled at me. "You really were amazing, but allowing girlfriends to interrogate suspects isn't exactly protocol."

"Don't worry. I totally get that. Now tell us what else happened before I'm forced to use my skills on you."

He took a sip of tea, then began. "There's currently internal bickering about jurisdiction—what with Alice being an FBI agent, and the Vespa scam coming in after the fact." He rested back in the loveseat and grinned as if holding back a particularly good tidbit.

I glared at him. "You better spill, or no more chicken wings for you."

He laughed, then his tone turned somber. "Interpol got the big score. An hour ago, they arrested Elizaveta Volkov at an airstrip near the Russian border."

"Already?" Tuck said. "How did they know she'd be there?"

Shane backtracked for a second. "You asked how Stanislav couldn't have known what was going on. According to Victor, he was aware that Sable Smith was an FBI agent, but he ordered his people not to touch her. He intended to ship Erik off to Venezuela, to put an end to the relationship. When he heard Sable was murdered, Stanislav assumed it was the work of a local gang. As far as Erik went, after that night, Stanislav appeared to have little further concern that he was a danger to the family business."

"He was sure hanging around Anna's a lot for someone who didn't care," I said.

Shane paused, took another sip of tea. "Stanislav's the eldest man in the family. It was his duty to make sure everything was settled properly after her mother's death. Those visits were also Elizaveta's downfall."

"What do you mean?" Tuck asked.

"Assuming Victor was telling the full truth—and I believe he was. Stanislav largely ignored his wife's comings and goings. But she misstepped when she made a fuss over the townscape. Until then, Stanislav was totally put off by the idea of Erik going to therapy and making crafts—not a manly thing to do. But when he saw the townscape, he recognized it as a Vespa, and the images as possible scenes from Sable's murder. For all practical purposes, you and Stanislav were uncovering the truth at almost the same time."

I shook my head. "I'm guessing Stanislav didn't take it well?"

"The final straw was when Victor called him from the police barracks. Stanislav was done with Elizaveta at that point—committing murder against his wishes, using Erik to line her pockets, manipulating his son into doing her dirty work . . ."

"That's one lovely woman," Tuck said.

Shane smiled at that. "One thing is for certain—Stanislav has powerful connections. You didn't hear it from me, but we believe he was busy today, working behind the scenes, making his own deals. He wanted Victor off the hook and his wife taken down for making him look like a fool."

I interrupted. "You don't mean Victor's walking away?"

"Not exactly. He's already been charged with multiple assaults on Alder—and he freely confessed to something else."

"The fire in the garage?" Tuck asked.

"Not that. He confessed to the break-in here. He was after the Madonna and Child painting."

"That's not a surprise, but it is a relief," I said.

Shane picked up another chicken wing, gripping it as he continued, "We don't know what Elizaveta was holding over Victor's head, but he claims everything he did was on her orders."

I looked past Shane and Tuck. Fireflies were coming to life, blinking in the grass and up in the darkness of the trees' canopies. It truly would be wonderful to go to bed without fear of intruders breaking into the shop or worse. It was also nice not to have to be paranoid about vehicles trying to run me over, assuming it was Elizaveta who had almost hit me in Manchester.

I let my gaze go back to Shane. The split lip from where Victor had punched him was crusted over, but a dark purple bruise had blossomed on his cheek. Beard stubble shadowed his chin and jawline.

My mind drifted to Alder. Less than twelve hours ago, slumped against the desk, the blood-soaked dishcloth pressed to her face. A flutter of guilt for my own callous feelings toward her beat in my chest. Whether Alder was a good therapist or not, no one deserved what she'd endured from her ex-husband, from Sterling, and from Victor.

I hugged myself. "What do you think is going to happen to Alder—as far as charges and jail time?"

Shane's smile tightened. "It's hard to say. She confessed to the Vespa scam, even refused a lawyer. She has a lot to offer as a witness, and she's a good deal more believable than her great-aunt Iris."

"Hopefully, her sentence won't be too long," I said, and I meant it.

Chapter
Forty-One

Erik wholeheartedly embraced the idea of combining an opening for his work with the Artsy-August Craft Show. Jimmy jumped into promoting and preparing like a man possessed; so did everyone at Checkerberry Manor. Tristan Lefebvre even joined the scramble, reaching out to his family's media connections across the globe.

The heart of the concept as we pitched it was simple—to show the oft-hidden, brute rawness of physical and emotional suffering in juxtaposition with the naively comfortable and familiar Artsy-August aspects of life. Much the same as how Sterling had contrasted Grandma Moses's quaint folk art to the so-called Vespa pieces. Only there wasn't a lie behind this comparison. It was the grim truth.

But as August drew near, Tuck still feared the concept would fall flat. Okay, I was more than nervous too, especially about the part that involved high-end collectors wanting to mingle at an enhanced living facility.

Then the movers and shakers of the art world began to whisper, and articles about Erik and the show started to trend online:

Erik Volkov is a master artist with a story that has upended the art world. He is a true 21st-century outsider. The narrative of his life and works invites the viewer to step into the darkness all around us—heart, soul, and reality. His latest piece, Angel Rising—which was recently restored and revised after a family member set fire to the artist's workshop—depicts an ash-gray angel, created out of scorched paper and melted plastic, rising above a smoke-stained landscape.

We wait breathlessly to see where Volkov's journey as an artist goes from here. We predict his upcoming opening at an enhanced living facility in Milton, Vermont will be the must-see avant-garde show of the decade."

—Art Enthusiast Magazine

However, as exciting as all the buzz was, it wasn't until the day before the show that I began to fully accept the event was going to succeed.

Kala and Tuck had left the common room to get some lunch in the cafeteria. I'd stayed behind so I could enjoy a moment alone with the results of our efforts. Erik's haunting pieces hung on the walls and rested on easels amid tables piled with the other residents' artwork and crafts: cheerful handknit sweaters, scarves, and mittens, glittering hand-beaded jewelry. Homey quilts and wall hangings. Bird houses. Silk flower arrangements . . .

I folded my arms and smiled, satisfied and proud. Tomorrow was the big day.

"Excuse me, Edie?" Yvette's voice yanked me from my thoughts as she hurried into the common room. "There's a courier outside. He claims to have several pieces of Erik's artwork for you. I didn't think you were expecting any more."

"I wasn't," I said. I glanced at what we'd already hung, seven works in total: the smoke-damaged collage, *Angel Rising*, and the previously half-completed piece from the Well-Being center, now serving as the stars of the opening; three pieces Jimmy had decided to put on consignment; our Madonna and Child painting; and the townscape Anna had thankfully never gifted to Elizaveta.

Yvette shrugged. "The delivery looks legitimate."

I went with her to the front doors. There were actually three couriers—uniformed and armed—waiting outside. Next to them, two narrow, five-foot-square crates sat on moving dollies. A van with a logo on its side was parked in the loading zone. The logo read: "Specialty Transport - Imports & Exports."

An empty feeling dropped into the pit of my stomach. The Volkov family were in the import and export business.

I swallowed back a lump in my throat and went outside while Yvette remained in the lobby.

"Are you Edie Brown?" the tallest man asked. Dark hair. Dark eyes. Formal demeanor. Heavy accent—Russian, perhaps.

I nodded, then asked, "Who are these from?"

The title *Family Outing* was stenciled on one box. That was the title of the collage Jimmy had taken photos of at Sterling's New York City gallery. The parents and children at the beach. The blood-money sandwich.

The tall man held out a phone to me. "The sender requested that you verbally verify the delivery before you sign for them."

I wiped my sweaty hands on the sides of my jeans, then took the phone. "Hello?"

"Edie Brown?" It was an unfamiliar man's voice. Cultured. Accent unquestionably Russian.

"Yes," I said. "Who am I speaking with?"

"Stanislav Volkov. I trust the two crates have arrived undamaged?"

"Yes." I toughened my voice. It was the only way to keep it from shaking. "What is this all about. I'm not sure if Erik would want—"

He interrupted. "Hear me out."

I gritted my teeth. The opening could use more pieces. But for the life of me, I couldn't understand where he got the nerve to think Erik would want something at his opening tainted by its connection to Stanislav's side of the family.

Stanislav cleared his throat. "The pieces are a donation. I do not want or expect anything in return. No money. No recognition. From what I hear, Erik has asked that a percentage of event proceeds go to charity?"

"Yes," I said. "To a rehabilitation center for traumatic brain injury survivors and to a scholarship fund for women pursuing law enforcement careers."

"Good. Sell pieces for whatever you'd like. Split proceeds between charities."

I heard what he said. It sounded wonderful, but I couldn't get past him sending them in the first place. The questions boiled out of me. "How could a man like you not know what your wife was up to? What about the NFTs? Tell me you weren't using them to launder money. If it wasn't you, was it Victor?"

"Are you done?" he asked.

I bit my tongue to stop myself from saying more. The couriers had walked a few yards away, backs turned as if not listening. I lowered my voice. "You're a wealthy man. After that hit-and-run, how could you let Erik end up in this situation? Living in mediocre housing. Going to a half-ass therapist. What are you going to do for him?"

His voice hardened. His accent became stronger. "Ms. Brown, I love Erik. Ever since his father died, I supported him financially, as well as Anna and their mother. Erik chose to live in that facility. He wished to be close to his mother and sister. He asked that I not send him money. I've donated to rehab center that saved Erik's life for over decade now."

"Uh . . ." I wasn't sure what to say.

"As far as the NFTs go, I had no idea Erik was making the original art. I would have taken care of Sterling and his sister years ago if I had known what they were doing." He paused. "If I'm guilty of anything, it's trusting my wife and son—and that's not something you have right to judge."

If I'd been unsure what to say before, I was totally tongue-tied now. He wasn't lying, I could hear that in his voice. Still, I didn't own him an apology either. "I'm glad I spoke with you," I said because it was true. I glanced at the crates. I had no idea when Stanislav had purchased *Family Outing* and the other piece, or how much they had cost him. Somewhere around a quarter million, I guessed. "Thank you for the donation. They'll add greatly to the show."

His tone lightened. "Tell Erik to give me call when he gets chance. He has my number."

"I will," I said. "It was helpful to talk to you."

"Same to you, Edie Brown."

* * *

The next afternoon, when the art world elite poured into Checkerberry Manor to celebrate the opening, the two collages Stanislav had donated hung in places of honor. If I hadn't talked to

Stanislav, I might not have understood why the gift didn't faze Erik in the least. If anything, how Erik was handling the entire event had taken me by surprise.

Sure, sweat glistened on his scarred temples as he waited at the front of the room behind the speaker's dais, next to Anna and Edgar. He unbuttoned and rebuttoned the cuffs of his new silk shirt, and finally just rolled them up. But his slight awkwardness and inelegance only added to his outsider mystique. He looked one hundred percent like the sort of artist collectors could fangirl over.

Jimmy stepped onto the dais. He tapped his finger against the microphone, quieting the crowd. "Good afternoon, everyone. I'm delighted you could join us for this monumental occasion . . ."

As he continued, I set the champagne I'd been sipping down on a serving station and started edging my way toward the dais, past collectors I'd seen at the opening in Manchester and a couple from Paris whom I recognized from my days at Christie's. There were locals in the crowd too, like Pinky and Albert Fisher. I was almost to the dais when I caught a movement out of the side of my eye: Felix Graham headed in my direction.

A touch of uneasiness tightened inside me, but it was quickly vanquished by a ping of devious pleasure. I had a good idea what Graham wanted. He wasn't a person to let things slide.

As he reached me, I pasted on a smile. "Glad you could make it. Nice turnout, huh?"

He moved in closer, so close I could feel his breath on my ear as he whispered, "I'm not going to forget this."

I stepped back. "Whatever do you mean?"

His jaw tightened. "You knew perfectly well when you planned this that my gallery opening was next weekend."

I stage-whispered, "I don't recall getting an invitation."

His voice deepened. "Watch your step, Edie Brown."

As Graham stormed off, I wondered if provoking him on top of stealing the thunder from his show was my brightest move, given his possible connection to my mom's arrest. Still, it was sweet to make him squirm.

Jimmy's voice rose, echoing even louder from the microphone. "Enough from me," he said. "At this time, I'd like to introduce Edie Brown. Her wisdom and sharp eye—along with that of the rest of the Scandal Mountain Fine Arts and Antiques crew—is largely responsible for the discovery of the Vespa scam and for bringing the perpetrators to justice. Without Edie, none of us would be having the pleasure of meeting Erik tonight and getting to know the true story behind his monumental work."

As the crowd applauded, I went up onto the dais to the microphone. "Thank you, Jimmy. And thank you to my uncle Angus Tuckerman and Kala Acosta"—I glanced toward where they stood near Erik—"for being with me every step of the way, not to mention thanks to everyone else who lent a hand. Erik's talent is truly unique, and I am grateful we were able to play a part in bringing him and his work into the light so it can receive the attention it richly deserves."

Applause rose. I waited for it to die down, then turned the mic back over to Jimmy. As he welcomed Erik onto the dais, I headed back into the crowd. I'd only gone a few steps when I spotted Shane hanging out by the courtyard doors.

"Glad you could make it," I said when I reached him.

"Sorry I'm late," he whispered. "How're you holding up?"

"Fine. The crowd is more than I could have wished for." I wasn't about to tell him how I might have slipped up with Graham. Not right now, at least. Today was about celebrating.

The entire room hushed as Erik began to speak. "Art is freedom," he said. "Freedom from nightmares. It is not forgetting. It's discovery. Strength. Acceptance . . ."

I turned away from watching him for a moment, and looked at the townscape that hung nearby, trying to hide the dampness rising in my eyes. The piece was as magnificent as I'd first thought, even more moving now that I knew the meaning behind its details. It was surreal the things people could do to each other, out of lack of empathy, greed, and . . . Well, in this case, mostly out of greed.

". . . Thank you all. Enjoy your afternoon," Erik said, smoothly releasing the crowd to go back to their champagne and finger food.

Music drifted in from the other room.

The clink of glasses and the murmur of chatter rose.

"Want to get some fresh air?" Shane suggested.

"Definitely."

We started toward the courtyard doors but only got as far as the easel that held Madonna and Child before Erik, Tuck, and Anna caught up with us. Edgar was now nowhere to be seen.

Erik shook his head. "This is crazy. Everything."

Anna smiled. "A man from Texas told Jimmy he'd like to buy *Angel Rising*. When he heard Erik was donating half the proceeds to charity, he offered to pay double the price."

Erik looked down, shoulders and head bowed. "Kind of sad. Letting them go."

My heart squeezed and those tears began to rise again. All I could think of was Alder taking Erik's works away in the name of therapy. It was his choice this time. But did it really feel that way to him?

A Wealth of Deception

My gaze went to Madonna and Child, sitting on the easel so close to us. The woman Erik loved and the child they'd never have—or a miniature Rocky Balboa, I supposed. A piece Tuck and I had put up for sale, a painting that along with the various commissions we were earning, could net us what we needed to repay the loan Shane had given us for the septic, as well as buy fresh inventory for the shop.

I glanced at Tuck. Catching his eye, I nodded toward the piece and raised an eyebrow, silently asking permission to do what was in my heart. Tuck nodded his approval.

"Hey, Erik," I said. "Would you like to have the Madonna and Child piece? To keep. For yourself."

"Really?" His eyes seemed to take on a distant look, as if staring into a hazy past. He smiled. "Sable smelled like dried roses and wild violets. Mama would've liked her. I don't want to forget."

Love and loss. Death and grief.
There comes a time to open the box, to remember the past, and bring the truth to light.

—Edie Brown

Acknowledgments

To Casey Griffin and Jaye Robin Brown for your friendship, encouragement, and wise critiques. You both deserve giant gold stars. Marlene Stringer, you deserve a whole sky full of stars for your wisdom and support. To Toni Kirkpatrick, so much gratitude for the faith you have in me and for allowing me a free rein. And to James Bock for your wise thoughts that challenge me to work harder and dig deeper. Madeline, Melissa, Dulce, Rebecca, and the entire Crooked Lane team, thank you for all you did and continue to do to bring the Scandal Mountain Antiques Mystery series to life—you are the best! Special thanks to Alan Ayers for yet another gorgeous cover.

Last, but certainly not least, a huge thank-you to readers who have purchased my novels, requested them at libraries, reviewed them, and recommended them to friends and family. You are the stars that brighten my sky and keep my imagination lit.